DANGEROUS DEVIANCE
A Dark Mafia Romance

The Adler Brothers

Audrey Rush

Dangerous Deviance: A Dark Mafia Romance by Audrey Rush

Independently Published

Copyright © 2021 Audrey Rush

All rights reserved. No portion of this book may be reproduced in any form without permission from the publisher, except as permitted by U.S. copyright law. For permissions contact: audreyrushbooks@gmail.com

Cover Photography from DepositPhotos.com
Cover Design by Kai

Paperback ISBN: 9798595602266

This is a work of fiction. Names, characters, places, and incidents either are the product of the author's imagination or are used fictitiously. Any persons appearing on the cover image of this book are models and do not have any connection to the contents of this book.

*For my Lady Alphas,
Rhonda and Michelle*

I bow down before your brilliance.

Dangerous Deviance

CHAPTER 1

Wil

Everything, including the man in front of me, had its own unique attributes. The coward wasn't a friend, but business. A spineless rat. Target practice.

"I thought we were friends," the man said. "We are *friends*, right, bro?"

Friends. The word almost made me laugh. I'm good at making people think that we're friends. As the networker for my family's business, I've put a lot of time into honing my image, making myself the important connection and face of the family's crime syndicate.

But that doesn't mean I'm anyone's friend. The man, Brad, flicked his tongue over his lips as he tried to think up an excuse. We had known each other for years, but still, he bailed on me when it came time to pay. After we had taken his two fingers, I had almost expected it, which would make the finality of this interaction all the more satisfying. What a birthday present.

This is what it meant to be an Adler. Conquer. Annihilate. Rule. Birthday or not, everything was in the name of family. And if you didn't have Adler blood? I would cut you in half. And if you hurt my family? Everyone you loved wouldn't stand a chance.

No one messes with an Adler.

Brad bit his fingers, the ones that were left anyway, the nail beds bloody and torn. He shivered and looked down at his hands again, as if a gun could magically appear in his palms. But he didn't need magic: Don't want to die for your bad decisions? Don't spend money you don't have.

Sometimes, I thought of myself as a god. I dealt in chance in the gambling hall, helping men thrive or wash away their lives, and back here, dealing with business matters, I chose between their lives and their deaths. Their fate was up to me.

"Look, man," Brad mumbled, "I told you, I have the money, I just need time. I was going to get it for you. Just not here. I've got an uncle—"

"Word has it that your step-daddy cut you out of the family business," I said. Brad cowered. "So tell me. Why were you in my gambling hall?"

"Look, man. I know I can get back into the business."

"I talked to your family. You've been cut off. They're not willing to help you pay."

Tears welled in his eyes. The poor asshole. But debts were debts, and if he didn't have the cash or the capital, then he had to pay in one way or another. We had already taken two of his fingers. It was time to move on.

"Can't we work this out?" His fishbowl eyes pleaded up at me. "Can't you take one of my cousins instead? We've been friends for a long ass time, man. You're like a brother to me."

Brad reached over and slapped my arm, two of his fingers missing. I glared at the touch, then removed his hand as if it were dirty. Axe, my *actual* brother, was leaning against the door frame, the only exit out of the room. His eyes were blank, staring forward. He had delivered Brad. Now it was up to me to finish the job.

He knew I liked it too. Playing god. I knew it was a birthday present from him.

"You're right," I said to Brad, my voice low. "We were friends. And if we were in a different line of work, maybe I would let a friend slide." I shook my head, pretending to be sad. "But you know that what we do here is different. And if I let you slide, then everyone will expect a free pass." I tossed a hand to the side. "And I can't let that happen."

"I'll do anything, Wil. Anything."

I took my pistol from the desk and pulled the hammer back. Brad's eyes widened. Power surged within me.

"Shit, man," he stuttered. "Take my hand. Break my knees. Not a fucking gun."

I aimed at his forehead and he lifted his hands like the flesh and bones of those eight fingers could defend him from a bullet.

"Please, Wil, I—"

The bullet went straight through his forehead, clean and efficient. His body fell back against the chair in a thud.

Axe adjusted against the wall, then nodded at me.

"Where'd you find him again?" I asked.

"In the line for TSA."

The bastard had almost gotten away. "What'd you tell him?" I asked. Axe had a reputation for getting his point across quickly. I could picture him whispering a thousand nightmares in a few words.

"That I knew where his wife lived."

I whistled. That would get a man to move. At least his wife wouldn't be held back by him anymore.

"You'll take care of him for me?" I asked.

Axe nodded, then slipped out through the back hallway, presumably to get his supplies to dismantle the body. While Axe was the main enforcer, the family's gambling hall was mine. It was a place to network. I was supposed to be an enforcer too, but I had wanted my own branch of the business.

I went out the door to the main banquet hall of Jimmy's. The atmosphere was full of smoke and wood and alcohol being poured like rain from the sky. Dark-paneled walls surrounded us, without a window in sight. It didn't matter what time of day it was; it was always night when it came to Jimmy's. You could get lost in there, and I often did.

There was a restaurant in the front, but this 'banquet room' was hidden in the back. There was a bar along the back wall, and the rest of the space was set with various tables: poker, craps, blackjack, roulette, and in the back, another door that led to a luxury theater with plenty of sporting events on display.

An older gentleman smacked my back. He was a regular here who liked to spend his hard-earned retirement funds. Who was I to stop him?

"I hear it's your big day," he said. "Congratulations on making it to the big three-oh, my good friend. Wait until you join me in the over-sixty hall of fame."

I shook his hand. "You're telling me you're not fifty?" The dude was well into his seventies, but I knew how to butter him up. He cackled at the joke.

"I bet you're making your dad proud," he said.

"Yeah! Happy Birthday, Wil!" another man said.

I flicked my finger at the bartender, and she started pouring us a round of shots.

"What shall we do to celebrate?" I asked.

"Did you want Sarah?" he asked. He winked, then nodded towards a young woman with her legs tucked underneath her to the side of the room, a slim metal collar on her neck. Hearing her name, she sat up, her gaze pegged on me. "She's been eyeing you for a while now." The gleam in his eyes was like a lantern in the night. He must have wanted to watch us fuck. Perhaps he couldn't please her like that anymore? I wasn't sure. "She's come prepared. I had her practice last night."

With dark hair and eyes to match, Sarah was gorgeous, and decades younger than her husband. That old man had bought her outright, mail-order-bride shit, but Sarah didn't care because she would live off of his money until the day she died. The idea of sampling her was a pleasant one, but unlike him, I wasn't one to share. If a woman was mine, she was mine. And Sarah was far from that.

"I want one for myself," I winked. The man slapped my back.

"I can get you the number for Sarah's house," he said. "I got her from Brackston."

Brackston was another big city a few hours away, controlled by the Midnight Miles Corporation, one of our biggest rivals, turned ally and connection. At least, that's the way we had hoped to push it. The way my father, Gerard, wanted to.

For a moment, I let the idea roll around in my mind; if I could buy a woman who was mine to take care of, mine to control, mine to play with when I wanted, why not? It made it simple.

But I wanted a woman who would fight me too. Taking control was only satisfying if you could feel the woman relinquishing it. If she gave it freely, like Sarah, then what did it matter? Most of the women from Sarah's house would probably be obedient to the core.

But again, it was my birthday. Why the hell not?

"Sure, give me the number," I said. "Now, are you going to take a shot with me, or are you too old for that now?"

"Do you know who you're talking to?"

A cocktail waitress in black booty shorts and a corset brought us the round from the bar. I eyed her round ass, and she winked at me. That was an ass I could use and forget about. The only problem was they always wanted more. I needed someone who I could keep at a distance, someone to keep for myself.

"Get a shot for yourself," I said to her. She thanked me and slinked away.

"To your big day," the older man said.

"To thirty more," another regular said.

"Cheers," I said, lifting my shot. We clinked glasses, then threw back the alcohol, the liquid numbing my throat. Another day on the job, another shot guzzled down. It was my kind of career. I went to the side of the room, taking my place at my favorite felt-lined table, one with a view where I could watch everything from afar. The gambling. The dealers selling our products. The women strutting around.

Derek appeared at my side. He was older than me and Axe; he was in his mid-thirties and kept his dark hair styled. His dark brown eyes judged the room, always watching everyone, always ready to fight at a moment's notice. The man didn't know how to have a good time; it was business, business, business with him. That's why I was in charge of the gambling hall, and he wasn't. Leave him to the leadership crap; give me the pleasure of crime.

Derek nodded to the different groups, acknowledging the fact that Jimmy's was in full swing.

"Are they celebrating your birthday?" he asked.

I shook my head, then shuffled a deck of cards. "Just another day in paradise," I winked. Derek smirked, then slid into the seat across from me. He hit the table, and I dealt: one card face down and a seven for me, and a king and an eight for him. I peeked at my card, then nodded at him.

"You've done good with the place," Derek said. The truth was that he was supposed to take over Jimmy's, as well as the rest of the family business, with Axe and I as leading enforcers, but I hadn't wanted that for myself. I didn't mind killing; in fact, I enjoyed it. But when it came to the gambling hall, I wanted a piece of the pie for myself. Besides, I was Uncle Jimmy's namesake. Wilhelm James Adler. What a name.

I didn't respond to Derek's comment. He was leading to something. He tapped the table and I dealt another card. A king, an eight, and now, a two. There wasn't much of a chance of getting better than that.

I hit as well, then flipped over my second card. A seven and a nine and a face-down mystery. If he was smart, he'd stand.

"You hear anything from Muro's men?" he asked. He put a hand over his cards. Good man. I showed him my final card: a five. The house won again. I always did.

"You were close that time," I said. He shook his head, smiling. "And about the Muro's men, they weren't giving their share."

We had negotiated with Miles Muro of Midnight Miles Corporation a decent, but low cutback, since we had delayed delivering a man who had stolen a rather large diamond from him. Our response, to keep things civil, was to agree to terms in which Muro could spread his drug trade in our region without dealing with a large percentage cut. We each specialized in different substances, so it made sense to work together, and our cut was reasonable, as an apology for the lacking delivery. We were supposed to deliver the diamond stealer *and* his daughter. But my half-brother had fallen for the woman and ran off with her. So her father was delivered *eventually*. But not her.

We needed to smooth things out with Miles Muro. That was part of my job.

"They didn't pay?" Derek asked. "What'd you do?"

I nodded towards the back doors. "Let them out." I shrugged. Gerard, our mob boss and my father, insisted that we kept things civil. The Adler family had networked with other syndicates for ages; we had to keep that reputation. "Didn't kill them. Just told them to get their shit and leave."

"Have you talked to Muro about it?"

I shook my head. "I was waiting for you."

I was good with networking and making connections, but Derek was still the next-in-line for the throne, which meant everything had to go through him. I could respect that. He had proven, repeatedly, that that's what he had been raised to do. But it was boring bureaucratic shit if you asked me. I'd rather deal with the connections and numbers behind the scenes, with the drug fiends and the gambling addicts without a home to keep them in line.

"You want to set up a meeting then?" I asked. Derek nodded. "I'll make the call."

"Good," he said. He nodded towards the exit. "We got you a present, by the way." Then he shook his head, smiling to himself. "*Axe* got you a present," he corrected.

"It better not be—"

He smirked. "Not this time," he said. He tilted his head. "Let's go."

I shrugged. What did I have to lose?

After I left a few of my men in charge, we drove back to my place in a high-rise in the middle of Sage City. My home was on the thirty-sixth floor, a penthouse with the rooftop patio all to myself. Axe stood up from the kitchen island, his clothes as clean as ever. Had he already taken care of Brad, or was the body still in his car downstairs?

"I hear you got me a present," I said.

He gestured towards the guest bedroom door. "She's inside."

"*She?*" I asked. He nodded. "Who is she?"

"Don't know," Derek said. "She could barely utter a sentence."

"Doesn't remember where she came from," Axe said.

"It's perfect," Derek said. "You're always talking about wanting to play god, right? This is it. This is playing god."

"I never—"

But then I thought about it. Really thought about it. If she didn't remember where she came from, and therefore, didn't have a past, then who was I, but a god, to her? To mold and change and shape her life. To make her fit to serve me.

And if not, I would move on. She would be killed. Like any angry god would do.

Intrigued, I opened the door. On the bed, sitting on the edge of the bed, was a woman with light brown hair. Full pink lips. A toned, muscular body, but softness there too. Her breasts hanging and bare.

"Found her naked in the woods," Axe said.

Her back was uneven, marked with patches of pink and white, like a rash or a scar that had healed over repeatedly. Glazing over, my eyes focused on the blush of her cheeks, the scratches of red across her stomach. She must have been running from something. From someone. But Axe had caught her.

And now? She was mine.

I stepped into the bedroom, closing the door behind me, coming towards her. She stiffened. As soon as I was close enough to touch her, she grabbed my shoulders, pulling me down with a hard crack, bringing a knee to my chest. Hard. I grunted.

A literal fighter, huh?

I grinned, then grabbed her leg and pulled through until she crumpled onto her back. I pulled out my gun, aiming it at her head. She didn't move, her face stoic. She stared into the barrel, then shifted her eyes to me. Those blue gems pierced through me and saw to that spark within.

I could kill her right then, and it wouldn't make a difference.

Or I could let her live, and explore that passion within her.

I took a step back, then headed to the door. I closed it behind me.

"Did you have to lift a hand when you were in the woods?" I asked.

Axe shook his head. "She came willingly."

"Well, I had to lay her flat just now," I said, smirking.

Derek laughed. "She's perfect for you then."

The passion of a caged lioness with blue eyes and light brown hair, and no expectations beyond being mine, was, in fact, perfect. She was simply a gift.

Yeah, birthdays didn't get much better than this.

CHAPTER 2

Ellie

You aren't safe here.

I blinked. That voice sounded familiar. Male. With the authority of a father figure, but not quite family. I couldn't place it. A dim light came from the windows. Steel-gray clouds covered the sky, the sun shining behind them, reflecting across their backs. The cityscape stretched far and wide to the coastline in the distance. The echo of a lighthouse. Traffic lights. Mist hovering over the woods near the coast.

Here? I thought. Where are we?

You aren't safe here. You need to be careful, Ellie. They're watching you.

Ellie?

Where are we?

We?

I looked around, but there was no one there. It was a voice inside of my mind, like a detached part of me, always there, always filling in the blanks. What was going on? I touched my face, as if I could find the voice there. But my skin was cold. It felt strange, like I was touching myself for the first time. My head was filled with fog, like I had awoken from a deep, deep sleep. I closed my eyes tight, until tears started forming in the crevices, then opened them wide, staring out. Four posts at the corners of the bed. A large window. A closet to the side. A full-length mirror. An attached bathroom.

I looked down; the blankets and comforters in shades of gray layered underneath me. So soft it almost hurt.

A bedroom. I was in someone's bedroom.

You need to be careful, Ellie. They're watching you, the voice said. A male voice. A familiar one. Like a father. Like a friend I trusted. Someone I knew.

That's right. That was my name. Ellie.

The bedroom door opened; a tall man with dark hair entered the room, his eyes shadowed. A navy blue suit jacket fit his arms, a red tie in the middle like a stripe of blood. His jaw was angular and tight, his muscles stretching the suit's sleeves. His brown eyes lingered over my breasts, my waist, my hips, between my thighs. I touched my face again, suddenly hot, wanting to make sure that I was awake. That this wasn't a dream. As the man's eyes met mine, his face darkened, and it was as if I could feel his thoughts. What he wanted to do to me. What he *would* do, if I wasn't careful. A shudder ran through me.

Who was he?

The man came closer, and it took everything I had to hold still, to let him think that I wasn't ready.

Kill him, the voice said. *Kill him now!*

Not yet. Not until he was closer.

As soon as he lifted a hand to touch me, I grabbed his shoulders, pulling him down until I kneed his stomach, but then he grabbed my leg and threw me back onto the bed, immediately pointing a gun at my forehead.

So that hadn't worked.

I waited for him to shoot.

But he backed away, closing the door behind him, and I was left alone once again.

I sat up, pressing my thighs together. A red and gold sash, tied into a bow, lay on the bed. I remembered it: a man had given that to me, asked me to wear it. *For my brother*, the man had said. *He'll take care of you.*

But he won't take care of you, the voice argued. *He won't take care of anyone. You need to get out, Ellie. Figure out where you are. Then find her.*

Find her.

Who was she?

And who was that voice?

Sliding off of the bed, my bare feet clicked on the wooden floors. I went to the window and stared out. From the height alone, I could tell we were in a tall building, possibly near the top. Only one building off in the distance looked as if it might be taller, a round disk high in the sky, futuristic in its design. I knew that building. It was a landmark. I had been there before. Back when I was younger. Still a kid. When we were kids.

We. Who were we?

The door opened again, the airflow brushing against my bare skin. I looked down. I was naked, with my bare ass to whoever had just opened the door. I covered my breasts, crossing my arms in the front, and turned around. *Act helpless*, the voice said. *The less they know about your capabilities, the better your chances are.*

It was the man from before, the one who had put me on my back. His eyes landed on me, his gaze hot.

He sat on the bed as if it were his place. His lair.

"Let's not fight this time, " he said. "Come sit." He patted the bed, waiting for me to come, like his pet.

No way. I didn't obey anyone like that.

Do it, the voice urged, *You might not like it, but you need to play. Play his game. Figure out his motive. Then get out.*

It was the only conscience inside of me, so I listened to the voice, *not* the man in front of me. I sat on the bed, beside him, keeping my eyes cast off, not wanting to meet his gaze when I didn't know where either of us stood. What was I doing here? Why was I obviously in his home? What did he want with me?

"I'm Wil," he said, his voice smooth and deep. "Let's start with your name."

Don't tell him. Don't tell him anything.

I shook my head. "I- I-" I stammered, "I don't—" I shook my head frantically, the voice getting louder in my mind: *Don't tell him. You can't trust him. You can't trust anyone.*

"My brothers said you don't remember much. Do you remember your name?" he asked.

A sheen of sweat broke out over my body. Chills ran through me, my body shaking uncontrollably. He reached over to hold my hand. I froze at the touch.

"It's okay," he said, "We can figure this out together." His words were kind but I pulled away. Then the voice grew louder: *It's a lie. You can't trust him. You can't trust anyone. You need to get out. Find her.* He put a hand on my thigh.

"Let me go," I whispered. He didn't hear me. He nodded at the door frame. A woman with dark red hair emerged. "Let me go!" I said louder, pulling my leg out of his grip. I bared my teeth, shifting back onto my haunches, ready to strike.

He cocked his chin at me, as if he was amused.

"You were on our property," Wil said slowly. "I hate to break it to you, princess, but we're not letting you go. Not until we find out how you got there. What you were sent to do. You're lucky it's my birthday." He smirked. "Think of me as your god. You're going to abide by my rules until we figure out what to do with you."

Lucky? What was he going to do with me?

A god? What an arrogant sonofa—

They'll kill you, the voice said, *just like they would kill her.*

I balled my fists.

"I'm not—"

His hand curled around my fingers, crushing my knuckles, twisting them in pain, and he leaned in close to me. The smell of smoke and old leather surrounded me. Like he spent his days between walls with men who had far too much power, far too much money, and if I closed my eyes too much, I would fall deep within the rabbit hole, until I couldn't see the sky anymore.

"If it were up to my brother, you'd be in a cage right now. But you're not," he said in a low voice. "You were gifted to me. Like an offering to a god," he said. The man was obsessed, idealized himself in a way that made me sick. "Don't forget, I *want* to be nice to you." His eyes stared deep into my soul, and it felt like his fingers were wrapping around my heart, squeezing it until the muscle palpitated in my chest, making my breath catch in my throat. *He wants to be nice to you because he's filled with cruelty*, the voice said. *He wants what he can't have. You can't fight him, not yet. It will end badly for you.*

Unless I played by his rules. Let him play god.

"Don't make me the bad guy, princess."

The bad guy? Princess?

He is the bad guy, the voice said. *He captured you. And he would do the same thing to her.*

He tilted his head back, glancing behind us, and the woman with mahogany hair came forward again. "This is Maddie. She's going to take care of you for a while."

"Take care of me?" I asked.

"All right. Out of here. My turn," Maddie said. Wil got off of the bed and whispered in her ear. "Of course," she said. Then she sat on the bed next to me, placing a plastic grocery bag full of clothes on the comforter. She leafed through it. "Tell me your size and I'll bring you better stuff tomorrow. These will do for now. They'll either be too big for you or just about right," she said. She glanced at my body, then turned back to the bag. "I think my hips are bigger. Do you work out?"

Work out? Why was she asking me about exercising when I had been ripped from my life and dropped into this one? A life where I didn't even know where I was. All I had was my name.

I couldn't figure out what to say. I could hardly remember anything, and that was terrifying.

I was a walking joke.

"Hey," Maddie said, stroking my arm. I stilled, waiting to see what she did, trying to calculate how far away the nearest weapon was. A pen on the desk. A letter opener. A pair of scissors. I could break a glass and use the shards to stun her. Run away as fast as I could. "It's okay," she whispered. "You're okay. You're *alive*." Because death was my only other option. She stared at me, her eyes softening, realizing how deep the fear ran inside of me. "What's your name?"

Don't think for a second that you can trust her. You can't trust anyone.

But I wanted to. I needed to hold onto something to pull myself out. And she hadn't tried to hurt me yet.

Maybe she would know how to help me.

"Ellie," I whispered.

"Ellie," Maddie said. "That's a pretty name. Is it short for anything?"

No. Don't tell her. It's too much. Too much.

She put a hand on my arm and I froze again. "My name is Maddie. I'm here to help you."

"Who are you?" I asked.

"The housemaid," she smiled. I glanced her over; jeans were tight over her thick thighs, a loose purple top on her busty chest. Makeup decorated her face, subtle but complimenting her. She didn't look like a housemaid to me. "Wil hired me, but I work with all of them. Mostly just Wil and Derek though. Axe on occasion." She shrugged. "Their parents once or twice too."

Too many names. Wil? Derek? Axe? Who the hell were they?

Ask her, the voice said. *Ask her who they are. She knows more than she's letting on.*

"Who are they?" I asked.

"They're brothers," she said, nodding at the door, where I assumed they were waiting on the other side. "They're here to help you. Wil is, anyway. I think Axe and Derek would have had other plans for you, but Wil's got a soft spot for women like you."

"Women like me?" I asked. What was that supposed to mean?

It means he thinks you're weak. You're helpless. And he'll prey on you like he preyed on her.

"Vulnerable," Maddie said. "And feisty," she laughed. "I can't believe you attacked him."

It's not like I had gotten that far. But the way she spoke about him made me stop; she was fond of him. They must have been close.

"Are you married to him?" I asked.

"God, no," she cackled. "Don't get me wrong. They're all gorgeous. But Wil? He's like a brother to me. I've been his cleaner for a long time now. Become a friend of family lately."

"They're a family?"

"Brothers," she said.

Your sister. Where is she? the voice asked.

"My sister," I whispered. "Where is she?"

It was weird to hear a voice, then repeat what it said, letting it control me. But it was all I had in a world of emptiness. And with those words, I knew. I was looking for my sister.

"Where's who?" Maddie furrowed her brows. "Your sister? I—"

"I will cut anyone who hurts my sister."

Maddie and I stared at each other, each of us waiting for the other to speak.

"Did you hurt my sister?" I asked.

"Slow down, tiger," Maddie said, raising her hands, putting them up. "No one is hurting anyone."

"Did you hurt my sister?"

She shook her head, her eyes cast down. I exhaled, letting my shoulders relax.

"Do you know where your sister is?" she asked.

"No." My heart burned in my chest. Longing swept through me; I had been looking for her for a very, very long time. And now, I knew I was close, but I was far away too. I needed a glimmer of light to help me see through the tunnel.

"No one is going to hurt your sister," Maddie said. "We're here to help you. I am. Wil is. But you have to be smart about it." She narrowed her eyes at me. "To think in terms like Wil, you need to play your cards right. If you act too quickly, they'll kill you. Because at the end of the day, you were trespassing. If it weren't Wil's birthday, you probably would be dead by now."

"Wil's birthday?"

"You were a gift to him," she said, nodding. "Wil's birthday present."

"How can a person be a birthday present?" I asked.

Because the birthday man doesn't have a soul.

"When you're the youngest son in a crime family, your birthday gifts get a little more elaborate each year." She shrugged, her lips flat.

"Trust me; you're lucky."

There was no way that being a man's gift made me lucky.

"I'm telling you the truth, Ellie. They *will* kill you if you're not careful."

She's right, the voice said. *Play the game. Figure out the players. She's not your friend, but she's not your enemy either. He is. He knows where she is.*

Your sister.

Footsteps passed in front of the room, going down the hallway, casting shadows from the crack underneath the door. Their presence seemed larger than life.

Like a god.

"Who are they?" I whispered again.

"Think of them as a family. It's easier that way," she said. She forced a smile. "Close brothers. Best friends." She pushed the bag towards me, offering the extra clothes. She nodded in the brothers' direction. "They'll help you, but you have to give to them too, especially Wil."

Listen to her. Play the game, the voice said. *You always knew you would be subjected to this.*

I nodded. "Okay."

CHAPTER 3

Wil

Maddie was talking to the nameless woman who could barely speak, while the three of us sat in the study. Half of me wondered if I should have felt guilty about what we were doing. The other half didn't care. She was on our property without any rights to be; she should have been dead.

Instead, she was mine.

My brothers were talking about a business matter while I zoned out, trying to figure out how best to control the situation. Playing a woman's god was an interesting situation; you chose the outcome, but you had to get her to bow down of her own volition. Otherwise, any completed acts weren't truly given. True loyalty resulted from rule. And what I wanted, through every fiber of her being, was loyalty.

"Dead?" Derek asked. My world came into focus with that word.

Axe nodded slowly, then said: "Chopped to pieces."

"Butchered?" Again, Axe nodded. Derek shook his head. "And you're sure it was Lance?"

"I picked apart the pieces myself."

I lifted a brow. Lance, one of the security members we had working on our father's property for the last decade, was dead?

"The hell is happening now?" I asked.

"I found Lance butchered to death," Axe said. "Sliced up, like someone had used a cleaver on him. Slit his throat, then chopped him up."

"Where?"

"In the woods."

Our parents lived in one of the oldest neighborhoods in Sage City, resting against a vast forest. The property had been in our family for generations, the eldest son always moving in, taking over the leadership role of our family business, our mafia. We owned the acres surrounding the house, including most of the woods in the back, and had many guards placed throughout to monitor the property. When he wasn't enforcing, Axe was one of them. He had his workroom camouflaged in the woods as well.

"So you found a naked woman and one of our guards dead on the same day?" Derek asked. "Shouldn't we put two and two together and make the assumption?"

That woman? Nope. Didn't make any sense.

"Can that woman even talk?" I argued.

Axe shook his head. "I checked her for marks. There was nothing. No signs of distress. No signs of fighting." I tightened my fist, thinking of Axe checking her body, but then I released it. He knew, even then, that she was mine. He hadn't looked at her in that way. "But I take it that whoever put her there, might have had something to do with Lance."

"Or maybe it's bad luck," Derek said. He shrugged. "Stranger things have happened."

"Who the hell knows," I said. "I'll watch her now."

"You still got your gun?"

I nodded. I kept a pistol with me at all times and had several hidden in the penthouse. You never knew what would happen in our family, and you had to be prepared. "It's not going to come to that."

"What are you going to do then?" Derek asked.

It was always the same when it came to any person. Whether you were dealing cards or cocaine, people usually had one desire. All you had to do was figure out what it was that they wanted and dangle it in front of them. Keeping the hope alive, and the light flickering. A little reward and a little surrender, and she'd be mine. *My offering.*

"Same thing I always do," I smirked, "Deal her a hand, watch how she plays. She'll see who's in charge."

As the words came out of my mouth, the door to the bedroom opened. Maddie's deep red hair cascaded down her back. A curvy woman with large hips she flaunted, I had thought about her once, but good help was hard to find, and I had backed off once I realized how hard of a worker she was. She had been working for our family for over a year now.

"She's all yours," Maddie said. Derek watched her turn towards the door, and though his eyes followed her, he said nothing. My chest tightened at those words: *all yours.* She was all mine. All I had to do was make her see that.

"How'd she do?" I asked.

"She's frightened," Maddie said, "Understandably so." She shrugged. "But I think she'll come around."

"Good," I said. I trusted Maddie's instinct. "Her name?"

She paused, her hand lingering at her side as she clutched it to her jeans. "Her name is Ellie."

"Ellie," I said. "Short for?"

"She didn't say."

Those words floated in the air, a mystery about them. We said our goodbyes, and Axe and Derek walked Maddie down to the floor.

Once they were gone, I opened the door, finding Ellie standing at the window, gazing out, wearing a loose sweater and jeans that were tight around her ass and loose at her calves. She had a muscular body with thick arms, but a delicate throat, like a swan's. A ponytail held up her light brown hair, revealing a tattoo on her neck: four rounded hills crushed together, in red ink.

I hadn't seen any other art on her body. The tattoo must have been important to her.

"Do you like the view?" I asked. I stood beside her, watching as her eyes flickered across the horizon. To the ocean. To the woods. To the streets that were alive with people and cars and everyday life. Ellie didn't say anything. "Where are you from?"

She opened her mouth, her lips soft and inviting. The smell of moss and decay filtered to my nose. How long had she been in the woods? Had she seen Lance's body after he had been murdered? Or had she never crossed his path?

She faced me, her eyes fluttering about, unable to find a place to stop. "I don't know," she said quietly. "I don't remember. I can't—" she shook her head, "I can't remember anything."

I grabbed her chin, lifting it until her blue eyes met mine. Hard like sapphires, and deep like the ocean. Was her memory loss a lie? What was she hiding inside of there?

"Your name is Ellie," I said. "That's a good place to start."

A small breath escaped her lips.

"My name is Wil," I said again. She nodded her head. "I want to take care of you." Because Ellie, you will learn that you're mine. "But you have to work with me." She nodded carefully.

People never change, and most of them were awful, but at least with family, you had blood that linked you forever, and that loyalty was never forgotten. My brothers and parents were the only ones I trusted. Everyone else, including Ellie, could turn on you in a second.

But that didn't mean I couldn't mold Ellie so that she was close to that level of loyalty. Because this was my chance to be different. To create a new set of rules specific to us. To show her how to surrender to me. To teach me how to be her god.

"My brother found you in the woods," I said. "Do you remember any of that?"

Her eyes scanned the ground, searching for that memory. "No," she muttered. "No. No, I don't."

"He found you naked in the woods," I said. "You weren't able to speak. Do you remember who brought you there? Left you in the woods?"

She closed her eyes, squeezing them shut. Her lips moved as if she was trying to think something through, but then she opened her eyes wide.

"No," she said, her tone flat. Stronger than I had expected. Almost defiant.

I clenched my teeth, my heart rate increasing at the urge to discipline her. To teach her a lesson.

"What do you need, Ellie?" I asked.

"I need to find my sister," she said, her voice resolute, assured. She might not have been sure about many things in her life, nor about how she came to be here. But this? Her sister? She was sure of that.

"Where is she?" I asked.

"I don't know."

"What's her name?"

She touched her cheek hesitantly, a vein in her neck throbbing, making her whole face twitch. "I don't know." She wiped her palms on her sweater to get rid of the perspiration. "But I know she's in trouble. And I have to find her. Please. You've got to help me." She stared up at me, her eyes filling with tears.

Growing up in the mafia, you learned to see past the tears to the true, depraved soul underneath. It made death easier, knowing that everyone had their faults and that there was nothing different about one person from the next. I knew, without a doubt, that Ellie was just like anyone. Hiding wicked intentions. A devious past that would cut her down to size. Those tears? They might have been real. But I didn't trust her.

She would do well not to trust me either.

But using her desire to make her bend the knee? That was exactly what I needed.

"I'll help you find your sister," I said. And in some ways, it was the truth.

"Really?" her voice perked up.

"But you have to agree to my rules."

She lifted her chin, looking me in the eye. I put a hand around her neck, touching her there, feeling the movement of breath going in and out of her throat. She hesitated, but she wasn't afraid. She stared at me, unmoved, and my cock swelled with heat. This was why I wasn't a man who could have a normal life, a normal love interest; I wanted this. Control. Domination. A toy that I could use however I wanted. A strong woman I could destroy.

I dropped my hand.

"Your rules?" she asked.

"You have free rein of my property. I own this entire floor and the rooftop, but you may not leave unless I'm with you."

"I can't leave?"

I shook my head. "When we do leave together, you won't speak to another man. My brothers and father? They're the only exception. Anyone else—" I let a gleam fill my eyes. "Not a single word."

"Why?"

"Because you're mine, Ellie. If you want to live, you'll obey me."

Her eyes fell to her feet. I put an arm around her back and pulled her closer to me, the scent of decay and her musk heavy. I wanted to bathe her, to wash her from head to toe, bury my head between her legs and devour her completely. But first, she needed to fear me. To realize that I might have been a playful, mischievous god, but I was still a violent deity.

"If I want you, then you will offer yourself to me," I said. She bit her lip. "If I say 'kneel,' you kneel. If I say open your mouth, then you open your mouth. And if I say to spread your ass for me, you will pull apart your cheeks. And if I say to eat my come, you better lick every last fucking drop off until my cock, the floor, until *everything* is clean."

She sucked in a breath, her chest expanding. Her nipples hardened, forming points through her sweater. I licked my lips.

"And in exchange, I'll help you find your sister. And you'll be treated like a queen." I grinned. "I don't take any offering lightly, Ellie. Think of me as your god." I flicked a finger across my chin. "You can choose to disobey me. You can choose to resist me. But I'll be watching, and punishment will be delivered swiftly." I dragged a hand along the curve of her spine, the knit fabric pressed against her warm skin. The bumpy, scarred skin, weathered, hiding a story there. "You may not like your punishment, but I will."

She shivered, understanding what I meant. She tucked her arms around herself. I had never had a woman here overnight before. I always dismissed them or met them in the back of Jimmy's. On occasion, I met them in hotels where I could leave as soon as it was over. I had almost let my ex stay here once, but right before I made that call, I had found her 'gathering information' for one of our rivals. That ended our relationship.

Ellie would be the first woman to sleep in my home. This forced us to move quickly.

"And if I say no?" she asked.

"Of course you can choose to say no," I said calmly. "That is your choice. But if you do, that means you will go back to living with my brother. And trust me when I say that I'm a fair man," I said, narrowing my eyes. "I'm willing to give you a chance to prove your loyalty to me. My brother? He'll see you as taking up too much space."

She nodded, her eyes flicking down, then back up to me. "But you'll help me find my sister?" she repeated.

"If you agree to be mine," I said, "with every rule obeyed."

After a moment, she whispered, "I'll do it then." She looked up at me, her blue eyes vibrant. "I'm yours."

"Then take off your clothes," I said. She flinched. I motioned towards the bed, then turned my gaze toward the window, giving her a moment to follow my command. The world continued outside, shifting and working and twisting, making bets, taking chances. That's what Ellie was. A chance. A new hand. "I want to see what's mine," I said. I turned my chin to the side so that she could hear me better, but I didn't look in her direction. "Set your clothes to the side, then sit on the bed and wait for me."

A moment of silence passed. Then the rustle of her clothing against her skin told me that she was obeying. Good.

Once the shuffling stopped, I turned slowly around. She was leaning against the bed, her bare ass on the comforter. A few freckles spotted her chest, right above her breasts, like a constellation written in her skin. Her chest was different from her back; it was blank, unmarked, as if whatever had happened had always been focused on her back. Her breasts were small in comparison with her firm body. Athletic, not slim, and muscular to the core. Still, the softness of her pink nipples matched her lips. Those electrifying blue eyes saw me, saw past the bullshit, and still wanted to fight me, but were holding back for now, surrendering to her god.

I gestured behind her. "Lay on the bed."

She shifted her weight, her back on the comforter, grimacing at the contact. I pressed on her thighs until her legs were spread before me. Her folds were covered in stubble, a small black line near her opening, her beaded clit and her pussy lips slick with moisture.

My cock twitched. So Ellie liked being ordered around? That was promising.

With my hands, I spread her lips, looking at her in detail. That black line spread, a scar dashed across her skin, healed, but dark, marking her forever. Another on the inside of her lips too. And her ass? A pink scar on her hole, as if she had a cut there once too, but had healed over. Perhaps she had surgery. Or perhaps, it was far more sinister.

I rubbed my cock through my pants, rubbing the head as I stared at her folds. Scarred as she might have been, her cunt was decadent and showed how much she had been through. With her eyes up at the ceiling, I stepped back. There would be time to take Ellie, but not yet.

"Get some rest," I said. "It's been a long day for you."

She opened her mouth, but I shut the door behind me.

Tomorrow would be different.

CHAPTER 4

Ellie

The night gave me fitful rest, but when I finally fell asleep, I dreamed of my sister. We were little, then, playing on the shores of a rocky river, our mother and father sitting at a nearby park bench, watching us from afar. A castle of mud and rubble was constructed before us, lumpy and leaning to one side, covered in soggy leaves. We removed a snail from the bushes and put it on top, named our shelly friend the queen's knight. My sister was a few years younger than me, but when we were together, we always had fun. Life was bliss.

But then everything changed in that dream. The clouds covered the sky, and when I looked up at the park bench, it was empty, and my sister was gone. The rain dissolved our castle into muddy remains, covering me in its dirt. The water choppy, crashing into the shore.

I woke up with a startle, expecting to be met with thunder and lightning. Instead, the sun blinded me through the window and beat down onto the lands below it.

There was no sign of him. And there was that silence. Terrible, complete silence.

Where was that voice?

My stomach churned, gurgling in annoyance. I slid off of the bed, and a swampy funk came from my pits. I needed to eat and shower. I remembered one of his rules; I had free rein of the entire floor and the rooftop.

Large stones covered the walls of the attached bathroom, and a giant rain shower head was in the middle of the stall. I stayed in there until the steam made it hard to breathe, trying to see if the warmth would stir any memories. But nothing came.

I picked through the bag of clothes Maddie had left behind and settled on a pair of leggings and an oversized shirt. In the kitchen, a note was placed on the counter: *Help yourself.* —*W*

My stomach grumbled in response, but helping myself to *his* food seemed like an admission. I could stomach a shower, but food too? That was giving in. And before I did that, I needed to figure out where I was.

I roamed the penthouse. There were five bedrooms, one of which had been converted into an office, and two of which were dual masters. I assumed Wil had slept in one master, letting me sleep in the other. But there was no sign of him anywhere, except for the note in the kitchen. It was like walking onto a stage set, not exploring a real home.

In the other master bedroom, I went to the window, staring out. It was a different angle of the city, but still, I didn't see anything I recognized. I slid the curtain to the side, but the fabric caught on something hard and metal. I pulled it back, revealing a set of metal cuffs anchored to the wall. Another set for the ankles. My stomach dropped, but I sucked in a breath. It's not like I hadn't expected it, the way he had acted, touching my throat, demanding that I was his. But still, seeing the restraints right there, hidden behind the curtain as if they were just a blemish in the paint, was alarming. What did Wil want from me?

Sometimes, we have to do things we don't like, the voice said, sending chills down my spine. There it was. I wanted more. What did it mean? Did I want to know?

He thinks you're weak, the voice said, calm and cathartic, stroking my bruised conscience. *That you're helpless. And he'll prey on you like he preyed on her. Unless you stop him.*

Stop him from *what*? Where was my sister? If he hurt her, I wouldn't need a voice to tell me what to do. I would kill him.

In the office, one wall was covered in books, while the other had a large wooden desk taking up most of the space. In the middle, there was a small round table with an empty vase. I sat behind the computer, tapped the device awake. If I searched my name, maybe I would be able to find more information. But the device was locked. I slammed my fists into the desk, staring up at the ceiling. Then I noticed something: in the corner of the room was a small, black camera, almost like a button. I checked the other rooms too, and sure enough, Wil had every corner covered. Wil might not have been around, but there was a chance he was watching right now, wherever he was. I passed through each room, glancing up at the corners, trying to determine what kind of person would be like that. What exactly did he do that would require that much surveillance?

He's your enemy, the voice said. *A man that needs to be eliminated.*

I understood that, but why?

There was a black and white picture on the office wall. It was a family portrait, with three sons fully grown, one of which I recognized as Wil, the other two looked related. But the father made me stop. Black hair with flakes of white. Dark eyes. He seemed familiar, like I had met him before, but I couldn't quite remember why. Maybe he just had one of those faces. Or maybe I saw Wil in him. The same eyes. The same lips.

Where is he? the voice started. *Find out where he is. He's the key.*

"The key to what?" I said aloud, frustrated with the voice. I was met with silence. I groaned. "The key to *what?*"

I closed my eyes, expecting the voice to fill me again, but nothing changed. It was like having a guardian angel who only spoke when he wanted to, and not when I desperately needed him.

In the back of the hall was another door that led to a separate staircase. The walls were concrete, and the staircase wrapped around to the rooftop. An enclosed fire roared in the wall, and the patio furniture was arranged so that it looked like a courtyard. A long sofa was near the edges of the roof, and I took a seat, looking down at the ground, letting the fresh air and smog whip against my face. The cars looked like thumbprints from this height, the people like specks of dust. All it would take was one leap over the edge and I could be done with this. This voice. This lack of memory. The lack of purpose.

No. I *did* have a purpose. It was her. My sister.

But he knows, the voice said. *He knows where she is. Your sister. Find her. Save her.*

I blinked away the voice and raced down the staircase, threw open the door to the penthouse, and turned through the hallway until I found the front door, but it was already open; Maddie adjusted the bags on her wrist, a plastic bag with styrofoam containers, and a reusable one with pink flamingos on it.

"Going somewhere?" Maddie asked, laughing. "Good. You're awake. I was hoping to catch you this afternoon."

This afternoon? "What time is it?" I asked.

"Noon. A little past, maybe," she shrugged. "Why? You got somewhere to be?"

There was a smirk on her face, showing that she knew my predicament. "I—" I started, then stared past her, seeing the lobby with the elevator doors. "What floor are we on?"

"The thirty-sixth." She motioned to the dining table with her free hand. "Have you eaten yet?"

I touched my stomach, the hunger pangs instantly attacking me at full force. "No."

"Good. I brought some lunch." She motioned towards the kitchen. "Let's eat."

She set the bags on a dark wooden table, off to the side of the kitchen. It seemed like a dining table, but one that wasn't used that often. Maddie brought plates that looked like stone slabs from the cupboards, easily finding them. How often did she clean this house? How much did she know about Wil?

"Little bakery place down the way. Does half sandwich, half soup or salad deals. So I got one with soup and one with salad. What do you want?"

Besides the circular container of soup, everything was tucked into rectangular boxes, making it all look the same. *Don't trust her*, the voice said. *She knows more than she's letting on. Eat the food, but then figure a way out. You don't have much time.*

But I needed to eat. Escaping on an empty stomach wouldn't leave me at my best, and if Maddie saw where I was going, then I needed her to think I was obeying the rules.

"I guess the one with soup."

She pushed forward one of the boxes and the soup container.

"So tell me about your night," she said, stuffing a forkful of salad into her mouth.

"What about it?"

"How was Wil?"

"I don't know." I shrugged, slurping a spoonful of potato and cheddar. *He sent her. Don't tell her anything*, the voice said. But what was there to tell? "We talked about his rules, then he left."

Maddie pressed her lips together, then nodded. "And the rules?" She ate another piece of lettuce.

"I'm his," I looked down at the food, rolling my eyes, "Whenever he wants."

Maddie whistled, then ate another crunchy bite of lettuce. "You okay with that?" I lifted a brow. Was she seriously asking me that? As if I had a choice. She laughed, reading my reaction. "You're right. Fair enough. I shouldn't have asked," she said. "But he's really not that bad. Of the three of them, he's the most fun, to be honest."

"The most fun?" Because I always wanted a date to the carnival.

"Out of the brothers, yeah. He's always ready to enjoy himself. I guess that's why he runs Jimmy's."

What's Jimmy's? the voice asked. *It's a clue. It has to be.*

"What's Jimmy's?"

"The restaurant with a gambling hall in—" she stopped mid-sentence, then gawked at me. She leaned forward. "Are you even from Sage City?"

Sage City?

Where is that? The more you know, the better off you'll be to find her.

"Sage City?"

Maddie's lips pressed together. "I guess not. Where are you from, then?" She shifted her weight, leaning back in the seat. "Do you remember?"

I closed my eyes, trying to reach as far back as I could, but there was nothing. Just the dream of my sister, the ghosts of my parents, all four of us on that river shore. I went there in my mind, trying to see more, and after a few seconds, I saw it: flashes of dome buildings, rounded with glass walls, safety washing over me. Then a ringing started, shattering the image.

Look forward, the voice said. *Help your sister.*

The dome buildings with endless lines of people. Nameless, faceless, all of us—

Ask her, the voice interrupted. Then the ringing grew, dissolving the image, a pain growing behind my eyes. *She knows more than she's telling you.*

I shook my head, getting rid of the sound. "What can you tell me?" I asked. "About Wil. About this place. And Sage City?"

"Sage City is the capital of the state. And the family? They have their hands in a *lot* of it." She shrugged and ate a few more bites. "You can spit in any direction and hit something they control."

"The police?"

She nodded. "Everyone bows to the family."

"And Wil?"

"He runs the gambling hall. Runs a lot of the drug deals too." She smiled to herself. "Has more money than any sane person knows what to do with."

I raised a brow. She seemed a little too eager to compliment him. "I thought you saw him as a brother?"

She laughed. "I'm just saying, is it really that bad?" She gestured around us. "It could be so much worse. But you get this all to yourself. And all you have to do is be his toy."

The word 'toy' put a bad taste in my mouth. He might not have been the worst of the brothers, but that didn't mean he was good, simply because he wasn't bad. At the end of the day, he had still forced me into a sexual relationship. And no one deserved that.

Maddie bolted upright, her eyes lighting up with an idea. "You know what you should do?" She nodded like it was the best idea she had come up with all year. "Get him to fall in love with you. Then you can do whatever you want!"

I furrowed my brows. "Love isn't real."

"Really?" She cocked her chin. "What makes you so sure?"

Because family was the only kind of love that didn't leave you. And I refused to believe that my sister had left me. She had been taken. I needed to find her.

I didn't have time to make a man fall in love with me, just so that I could get a promotion from sex toy, to wife. I needed to find my sister. Now.

Perhaps she has a point, the voice said. I shook my head, squeezing my eyes shut. Go away, I thought. Stupid voice. Stop trying to tell me what to do. But it continued anyway: *Love is a dangerous drug. If he's under your spell, you can control him. Just like he wants to control you.*

And then you can use him to find her.

I didn't want anyone's help. Especially not his. And Wil didn't seem like someone who cared either way. Live or die, all he wanted was a toy.

But he had said that he would help me find her, if only I agreed. And I had agreed.

Where was my sister?

When I opened my eyes, Maddie was staring at me, her eyebrow raised.

"What?" I asked.

"Look," she said flatly, "All I'm saying is that if he falls in love with you, you can do whatever you want. You'd be one of the queens of the family empire," she laughed and shrugged. "It's just an idea. And you're not really in a predicament to be choosy."

I couldn't argue with that, given the circumstances. Which was why I had to get the hell out.

"Sure," I said.

After we ate, Maddie cleaned the kitchen, then went on to dust the bedrooms. I needed her to leave. I couldn't do anything while she was here. The antique clock hanging in the kitchen ticked away the time, the mechanical motions making me anxious, each tick shaving another sliver off of my brain.

Finally, after an hour, she zipped up that big flamingo bag and headed towards the door.

"All right, I'll be back in a few days to check on you," she said.

Finally, the voice said. *Once she's gone, you can leave.*

"Okay," I said. "I'll see you then."

"But Ellie?"

I looked around frantically, waiting for her to leave, but she didn't move. She wasn't going anywhere. She had something else to say.

"Ellie?" she asked again. I gave a slight nod. "You're searching for your sister, right?"

"Yes?"

"You'd do anything for her?"

Where was she going with this? "Yes," I said. Obviously. Who wouldn't?

"Then sometimes you have to be cautious to get ahead." She looked down at the ground, then her eyes found mine again. "I wouldn't go anywhere if I were you." She tilted her head, gesturing behind her with it. "If Wil finds out you escaped, he'll kill you. It won't be one of his brothers." She shrugged. "You know too much about the family now, you know?" Her voice was light and sympathetic, not to me, but to them. She trusted them, more than she trusted me. It made me sick. "But once you earn his trust, you'll be able to do whatever you want. But you *have* to be cautious. Make him believe you."

I wasn't sure what to say. Maddie seemed kind; she had brought me lunch, knowing that I needed it, and given me conversation when all I had in this world was the voice in my head and the desperate need to find my sister. My only family.

There is more than one way to be cautious, the voice said. *Once he's asleep, you can make your move. That's how you can be careful.*

I nodded, and Maddie smiled back.

"I never care for cleaning up blood," she said. "It's a bit of a hassle." She winked, then turned away, locking the door behind her.

No matter how many times I wandered the rooms and opening drawers, there was nothing to uncover: no secrets, no hidden messages, nothing that gave any clue as to what was going on. His office was more for show than it was practical, and that was the same as the extra bedrooms. My being in there must have been more action than his place had gotten in months.

The voice fell silent too, as if the owner was watching me pace the house. Trusting me to know what I was doing. And I was trusting Maddie to be right. For all I knew, the threat of death was a cover.

But if he was sleeping, I could kill him, or, I could leave. The front door hadn't made any noise when Maddie had opened it. I could make a silent exit.

The night was my best choice.

I stayed on the rooftop until night came. The couch cushion was gentle on my legs, and I stared out at the cityscape, until one by one, every item seemed to melt into a blurry, dull light, becoming an image I didn't understand. Because nothing made sense.

A chilly breeze made me hug myself tighter. Darkness came, slowly covering the rooftop and the penthouse windows until it was soaked in it.

Wait until he's asleep, the voice said.

Was Wil as bad as the voice said? Was he worse, or maybe better? Was Maddie on the right train of thought? His selfish desire is what kept me alive, but still, I was alive. And he could have just used me for his cravings, but instead, he had offered to help me find my sister.

Where was she? That question was the only thing that kept me going.

My footsteps were soft through the silent house. The darkness crowded each window, making the once bright interiors shifting with shadows. Every time I turned, another silhouette, tall and wiry, seemed to grow, casting its presence in longer stretches, making the hair on the back of my neck stand. I might have been alone, but there was someone always there, always watching me.

He's always watching, the voice said. *You need to be careful, Ellie.*

Maybe it was the voice that was watching me. But was it watching out for me, or sending me into a trap too?

Just then, a sharp pang shot through my skull, making me grab my head. But then it dissipated into nothing, like it had never happened. I straightened, returning to my thoughts. I would be careful until Wil was asleep. This was his home; the man had to sleep at some point.

As I turned down the hallway, passing one of the bedrooms, a shadow appeared in my peripherals. I shook my head. I was seeing things now. But as I walked faster, footsteps joined mine. And when I turned, I saw him.

A hood slammed over my head, and the scent of smoke and leather filled my nostrils. Putting me in a headlock, the canvas threads of the hood seemed too tight, rubbing against my face, taking away my air. I stepped back as hard as I could, shoving my foot into his, but he kept his grip on me tight. Dragging me back. I pulled at his arms, but he had too much power over me.

Don't give in, the voice said. *Fight back! Fight him!*

He turned a corner and I used that half of a second to wedge my mouth over his arm and bit down as hard as I could. He groaned, but tightened his grasp until the world darkened, blood filling my head in red bursts, ringing filled my ears until nothingness swallowed me whole.

When I woke, he had me pinned on the bed, his warm body weight resting on my chest. My wrists were behind my back, and I pulled at them, but the sharp edges of a metal restraint dug into me. I pulled anyway, trying hard to let my wrists pull through the cuffs, but nothing moved.

He pulled off the hood. I blinked rapidly, trying to get the world to focus. Wil looked down at me, his cock hard and bulging in his pants. He sneered, his teeth gleaming.

"Time to play," he whispered. "Play the victim, princess."

He leaned down, pressing his mouth to my neck, his breath hot and heavy, giving me chills. His lips dragged down my skin, as if barely there, then his teeth sunk into my shoulder, as if he could bite straight to the bone, giving me his sweet revenge. I whimpered, trying hard not to let it get to me. To not enjoy the way it made me helpless.

He might think that you're weak. That you're helpless. But the less they know about your capabilities, the better your chances are. Besides, this is what he wants, the voice said, *You have to fight it.*

But how could I fight when I couldn't control my hands?

My ankles were spread apart, each one restrained in a similar manner. I couldn't have been out for that long, and still, he had managed to restrain me completely. What the hell was I going to do? I shook my head, not daring to look into his dark eyes, to search for the hint of light shining in them, and fail.

This was what Wil wanted. To use me however he saw fit.

I had to be cautious, to be smart. Like Maddie had said. If only to find my sister.

The swift click of a pocket knife snapping into place made every hair on my body stand straight. A knife? No—it couldn't be. Maybe it was a ruse to get me to stay still so that he could fuck me and kill me because that's what he got him off. The sick fuck. To get me to comply when all he wanted to do, was to destroy me.

The sharp end of a knife dug into my throat, and his dark eyes bore into me. I closed my eyes, a flash of an image settling inside of me. A body cut up. Blood pooled underneath, soaking into the grass, mixing with the dirt. Caked against her body.

He breathed on my neck.

"You're going to do exactly as I say, aren't you?" he asked.

No. Not a knife.

He pressed the blade underneath my chin, making me lift my face. He was so close that the air from his nostrils crashed into me. I couldn't bear to look at him, but this was too much. *He* was too much.

Her frayed neck. Her glassy yellow eyes. The purple bruising. The chopped remains of her body, thrown into a pile, to decay in the shade of a tree. Blood dripping from her mouth, from her neck. From every exposed part of her.

But she couldn't be dead. It was a nightmare. Only a nightmare. A way to process the fact that I couldn't remember anything about her, and it was my fault, wasn't it? Because I needed to do something to change this. To find her.

Wil's cock pressed into my leg, and a tear slipped down my cheek. I couldn't close my eyes without seeing my sister's body like that. Hacked to pieces.

Wil's eyes met mine, and he stopped, giving me a moment to breathe. I let it all out, exploding into hyperventilation. He scrutinized me, his eyes narrowed.

CHAPTER 5

Wil

Twigs crunched under my brothers' and my feet. The farther you got into the woods, the thicker the trees and brush were, making it darker. The moisture was heavy in the air. My throat was tight. Derek whistled at the humidity, and Axe grunted in response. It wasn't often that Axe dragged us into the woods, but whenever he asked, Derek and I knew it was important.

"Over here," Axe said, pointing past an old tree that had been knocked down, lying on its side. Just past it, a man with a slit across his throat, his eyes wide and stuck in pursuit. His body had been cut in half, the limbs broken into pieces, left in a pile together. I didn't know him by name, but I recognized him. He was one of the newer guards, having worked here for two years or less.

Whoever had done this, had killed the man, then *chosen* to chop him up into pieces. I would have guessed it was for transport, but he was left behind as if they had wanted us to find him.

"A warning?" I asked.

Axe shrugged.

"A dropped attempt?" Derek asked.

Axe motioned with his hand for us to follow him. There was more? That wasn't good.

A few yards away, through a clearing of ivy, a naked woman lay on her side, her hands covering her stomach. Axe pushed his boot over her arm, and her hands jerked away, revealing a deep cavity. A bullet wound.

"You think he shot her?" I asked.

"How?" Derek asked. "His throat was slit."

"Enough adrenaline and you can pull the trigger," Axe said. I believed him. He knew how to get the adrenaline going in the most resistant victims.

"So, he shot her and thought she was dead. Or maybe he was still hunting her," I pieced together, trying to get the story straight in my head. "But then she snuck up from behind and cut his throat?"

None of us said a word. Sage City had been in our family's territory for generations, and while we had the occasional dispute with our rivals, nothing like this had happened before. Our feuds were usually dealt with by gun on the streets or out of sight. But we had never had an enemy hunting our guards, especially not so close to our family's house.

"The woman was found here too, right?" Derek asked.

He meant Ellie. She had been found naked too, though Axe had said she was untouched, too frantic to be a threat. The only scrape on her chest had been from a twig she had brushed against when he saw her trying to run away.

But anyone could act. That included Ellie. She could have been hiding anything.

"We should stay here for a while," I said, gesturing in the direction of the Adler House, where our parents lived. We had a rotating group of men surveilling the woods, but I wanted someone inside of the house too. "We can take shifts," I continued, "Guarding the house. At least until we've got this figured out."

"You've got that woman to deal with," Derek said, shaking his head.

"She has a name," I muttered. "I can keep Ellie in the workroom." I turned to Axe. "You've got room, right?"

Derek shook his head again. "Forget about that. Axe and I will stay here. But that woman, Ellie, she's connected to this. Can you get information out of her?"

What he was asking was whether I was willing to use creative methods to see what she knew. Methods like Axe often used. I didn't like the idea of torturing her just to get information, but if I did it simply because I wanted to fuck her, somehow, that was better.

Two birds, one stone. You did what had to be done when it came to family. Someone was clearly trying to go after Gerard. It was up to us to protect our family's legacy.

I nodded. "Got it."

I checked the security system on my phone. Ellie was in the shower, sitting on the stone floor, her knees bent in front of her, her arms wrapped around her legs. I clicked the rewind button and saw that she had been in there for over an hour, sitting and waiting. Her lips moved as if she wasn't alone, but when I turned up the volume, no words came out. The hairs on my neck stood up.

Last night, once I brought out the knife, something had changed inside of her. Her eyes went from violent and vengeful, to terrified. Beads of sweat gathered above her lip, and a single tear ran down her cheek. I could have fucked her right then. Could have established that power dynamic and made her see that I would always take what I wanted, whenever I wanted. That I didn't care if she was crying.

But I couldn't do that. If I had made her cry, then hell yes, I'd fuck her. But her fear was focused on the knife. I had to figure out why she had that fear before I could move on.

I might not have understood where she was coming from, but I knew, without a doubt, that there was another layer to the mystery. One I intended to decipher.

By the time I got back to the penthouse and had changed back into a suit, she was dressed, sitting on the rooftop, looking out at the horizon. A loose tank top hung on her chest, her light brown hair whipping past her shoulders. It was always colder up there; I'd have to send Maddie to get Ellie more clothes.

Ellie looked at me, her eyes blank.

"Let's go," I said, gesturing for her to follow me.

We were silent on the way to Jimmy's, but what was there to talk about? I wasn't going to keep her in the penthouse, not when we had found three people dead in the woods, and she was the only one who had lived.

"I've got work for a few hours," I said in her ear quietly. I gestured at the room, the tables all occupied, the bartender busy making cocktails. "Get whatever you want. The bartender can order from the restaurant too."

Without a word, Ellie nodded and slipped through the tables, exploring the space. I watched her scan the room, taking in the perimeter. She was muscular, and while strong didn't mean aggressive, I started to wonder if Derek was onto something, if Ellie was a threat. I could see her killing *for* her sister, but for pleasure? That didn't seem likely.

The scent of whiskey entered my nose as a warm, bulbous hand landed on my back. "Who's the babe?" the regular said, a man in his fifties. "Is she your new pet?"

I waved a dismissive hand. "She's something," I said. I wasn't sure how to explain it, especially to a stranger. Ellie was supposed to be a gift, but she was turning out to be more of a hassle than a gift should have been worth.

Still, I could control her circumstances; I just had to figure out how to make her tick.

"Do you like her?" the regular asked, a hint of dull amusement in his voice. But ever since my ex, I hadn't wanted to get close to anyone. She had never understood why I ended things with her, as if the enemy with his dick balls deep inside of her wasn't enough of a clue. She had claimed it was all part of her extraction process; she used her cunt to get information. Hah. If only I could use my ex to extract information from Ellie the fun way. Her methods would be a lot more forgiving than mine.

"I don't like anyone," I said to the regular. I knew better now. Emotions were what made you weak, what made you forget about where loyalty truly lied. No one was loyal, not even the people you trusted. My ex was proof. The only thing you could count on was family.

Which was why a gift like Ellie was better than a relationship. I could keep Ellie exactly at the distance I needed.

I got the attention of one of the dealers. "Midnight Miles show up yet?" I asked.

The dealer shook her head. "Not that I've seen."

The door swung open, and a few men came in, none of which were the Midnight Miles men. I had a feeling our deal was falling through, but if this was what our father wanted, to treat the situation with civility, then we'd have to go forward with that.

But hell, all three of us brothers hated it. You didn't rule by being nice.

Maddie entered the hall too. I nodded towards her. "You get anywhere yesterday?" I asked. I tilted my head in the direction of Ellie.

She shook her head. "Nothing."

"Tight-lipped, isn't she?" I said.

Maddie leaned an elbow on the table. "It's not that. She truly doesn't remember anything."

I raised a brow. Maybe Maddie was right, but that didn't mean that I trusted Ellie.

"I see you let her out of the cage," she said.

I shrugged. "It happens."

She patted my arm. "All she wants is her sister," Maddie said. I followed her gaze over to Ellie, sitting on a stool, her legs crossed, her entire body aimed towards one of the other regulars we had here. Sullivan. A gruff-looking man with gray in his beard, his skin tanned like leather. His eyes were locked on Ellie, looking down at her breasts.

She spoke, and Sullivan opened his mouth in response, his posture stiff.

Her nipples pressed through the thin fabric. I should have made her change her clothes before we came here. I clenched my fists and headed toward them. Maddie put a hand on my arm, holding me back.

"As a friend," she said, "Do you really want to start a fight over her?"

It wasn't just about her. It was about respect. Ellie knew my rules. And Sullivan had seen me come in with her; he knew she was mine.

And if he didn't? He'd know now.

"As a friend," I said sharply, "I'd appreciate it if you took your hand off of me."

Maddie immediately removed her hand and I strode towards the two of them. Sullivan's fingers, blunt and grimy, ran down her arm. She looked at his hand and pulled away slightly.

Now he was touching her?

I stood between them, getting in front of Ellie, blocking his view of her with my body.

"What are you doing?" she asked.

"Sullivan," I said calmly. "I see you've met Ellie."

"Dude," Sullivan narrowed his eyes, bleary with booze. "We're just talking."

"Just talking?" I laughed.

I grabbed his hand and pulled him off of the barstool, shoving his head and chest into the table to the side of us, twisting his arm around his back. He kicked his legs, throwing his free arm wildly, but it was useless. He whimpered, and I held his arm tighter. I leaned into his ear.

"If you ever talk to her again, I'll cut out your tongue," I sneered. "And if you touch her again, I'll cut off your hands." I wrenched his arm again. "Got it?"

I let him go, and the asshole fell into the table, groaning. The entire hall had turned towards us, most of them gawking at Sullivan in pain, or looking from me, to Ellie, wondering who the hell she was.

It didn't matter who Ellie was. What mattered was that Ellie was mine. And no man was going to talk to or touch her, except for me.

I turned towards her slowly.

"You," I said, narrowing my eyes at her. Her deep blue eyes were wide, her mouth hanging out, her pink lips pliable. "You knew better," I growled.

"I—" she started, but I grabbed her waist, flipping her around and pushing her forward.

"Not here," I said in a low voice so that only she could hear. "I told you I had only a few rules." The muscles in her back clenched, and my dick pulsed, thinking of what was to come. "I'll show you what happens when you break them."

CHAPTER 6

Ellie

I held my breath, waiting for Wil to speak. But he was silent, sliding into the car beside me and nodding at the driver as if nothing had happened. The driver wouldn't look me in the eye. He knew, better than the other guy, about what Wil expected from the men around him, especially when it came to me.

He doesn't want anyone talking to you because he doesn't want you to find out what he's hiding, the voice said. *And he's hiding everything. Including her.*

If Wil knew where my sister was, I would find out.

By the time we were in the penthouse, my stomach was twisted in knots. It's one thing to put up a facade like you're a badass, but it's another to deal with a man who threatens to chop off another person's hands. A man who openly tells you he'll kill you. I knew he wouldn't stop there. Not many people mean it when they said they were willing to kill for someone, but with the way Wil had handled the guy from the bar? It wasn't a bluff.

But I wasn't bluffing either. I could kill too. I just needed the right moment.

In the office, he made me wait for a few minutes, while he did something in another room. *He's preparing for your funeral*, the voice said. *He'll kill you. Just like you knew he would. Just like he killed her.*

But she's not dead, I tried to scream back in my head to get the voice to stop. But it wouldn't stop repeating those lines: *He'll kill you. Just like he killed her.* So instead of blocking out the voice, I tried to dull it by concentrating on what I *could* do. I stood in the middle of the room, glancing around at the bookshelves and at the one frame that decorated the walls. The picture of what I assumed was his family. It was hard for me to imagine a family with a father and brothers who were worse than Wil. They had gifted me to him as a present, as a nice gesture. What would they do when you were their enemy?

You know what they do, the voice said. *They'll kill you. Like they killed her.*

Stop it, I thought. Leave me alone.

Once Wil returned, he took a seat behind the wooden desk, then gestured for me to sit in front of it. My chair was lower than his, making it so that I had to look up at him. His eyes were dark, unwelcoming, filled with rage and passion swirling into one. Though his facial expressions on the surface seemed blank, the lack of emotion was eerie. He had been filled with smiles, reassuring touches, promising words that he could give me what I wanted. That he could give me my sister. He had even backed off when I resisted the knife the night before.

Now? It was different. I was no longer on that same footing as before. I grit my teeth.

"We have a few differences to discuss," he said, putting his fingers together as if he was sizing up his opponent.

"Yes?"

"Why were you talking to Sullivan?"

I hadn't gotten as far as getting his name when Wil interrupted us. The man, I guess his name was Sullivan, was one of the few that was willing to talk to me. So despite the voice trying to stop me, to warn me that Sullivan was the enemy too, I word-vomited at Sullivan. Let it all out. I couldn't trust anyone, but at least this man wasn't holding me hostage. At least he might be willing to help me.

"I was asking him about my sister," I said, crossing my arms in front of me. There might have been a rule against speaking to other men, but there wasn't a rule against asking about my sister.

"And what did he say?" Wil asked.

I thought back for a moment. My immediate memory was fine, but the fact that I couldn't remember certain months, maybe even a year of my life, left me second-guessing myself. What had Sullivan said? There had been a twinkle in his eye when I asked him about her, a glimmer that had immediately told me that he knew nothing about her. It wasn't about helping me, but preying on me, and her. *I'll help you find your sister*, he had said, touching my arm in a way that made me cringe, as if he was a vulture and I was a carcass. *Does she look like you?*

And what would have happened if I had followed him? Would he have taken me to my sister, or would he have hurt me in worse ways than Wil? Sullivan seemed like the kind of man who would want a favor in return. The kind of man who would lie to get what he wanted.

And yet Wil was upfront with his demands, with our arrangement. I knew exactly what he expected of me.

And I had disobeyed him.

"He said he'd help me find her," I said.

"And you believe a gambling addict stuck at the bar midday can help you more than I can?"

That stoic expression screamed thousands of words in that one question. As if I should have known better. The smug asshole. I wanted to spit in Wil's face. To prove him wrong about everything. That he might have been right about that man, but that he had underestimated me.

Wait until the right moment, the voice said. *It'll come to you. Then you'll make your move.*

"I don't even know who you are," I said, finding courage within me. "How am I supposed to know what you're capable of?"

"He wouldn't be the first person I've killed, but it would be for a far lesser reason than the rest," he said, his voice so calm that it made my skin crawl. I scoffed, and Wil laced his fingers together, as if this were simple a business matter we were dealing with.

"This will be the last time I give you this warning, Ellie," he said. "You will speak to no other man, besides my brothers, my father, and me. You can save a lot of lives by following my rules."

I gulped down a dry swallow, then looked away, trying hard to stay strong. I couldn't remember anything since my sister had disappeared, and even the circumstances surrounding that were hazy. I concentrated, trying to think back. She was about to start her first year—no, her second year of college. She wanted to be on her own, and I had let her. Finally, I let her.

But she had gone too far.

That was more than I had unlocked before.

"Next matter," Wil said, interrupting the foggy memory. He shifted his weight in the seat, then leaned to the side, looking down on me. "Why are you afraid of knives?"

Flashes of those images of my sisters' butchered body glimmered before my eyes. My whole body shook, trying to get them away.

If you tell him, he will know, the voice said. *He will know where you came from.*

I wanted to scream: Know *what*? Where did I come from? I didn't know a damn thing, so how the hell would Wil know anything?

"I know there's something going on in that mind of yours," he said. "Spit it out."

The voice got louder, booming at me: *He will know. If you tell him, he'll know exactly who you are. Where you came from.* But I had to do something. Had to reach. Had to trust my instincts. Had to trust myself.

I had to hope that what I was doing was going to be okay. That it was the right thing to do to save my sister.

"I've had this nightmare," I stammered, my voice suddenly frantic, "Not really a nightmare. More like a waking-dream. A vision." I closed my eyes, letting the images of her corpse wash over me. The blood a vivid red at times, a dull burgundy at others. Had she just been murdered, or was I looking at her decomposing body? It always changed. I could never get the images to make sense.

"And in this nightmare?" he asked.

"My sister is dead," I said. "In pieces. Her body sliced into dozens of chunks. Like a puzzle. I can hardly tell if it's all her." I opened my eyes immediately, not wanting to see her like that anymore. "Like a murder you've never seen before."

Wil studied me like he was pulling back the skin of a fruit. I sucked in a breath.

"I've seen a lot of things," he said.

I shrank back. I twisted my wrists back and forth, trying to pull my focus away from those images, and back to the present. It was like experiencing her death over and over again, seeing her body splayed out, the life draining from her eyes.

"Do you need help sleeping?" Wil asked.

I raised a brow, coming back to the room. It was such a strange question, coming from him. "Help sleeping?" I asked.

"For the nightmares," he said. "I can get some pills for you."

My heart sank. It was a kind gesture, one that was hard to believe. The man who kept insisting that he was my god, wanted me to be able to sleep? To relax? And yes, sleep sounded good, so damn good, when I couldn't stand the silence at night, waiting to hear the click of the lock on my door. It would almost be better to sleep, to wait for his demands that way.

He wants to drug you, the voice said. *Don't accept it.*

And I knew the voice was right that time. Even if I wanted to sleep, I wasn't going to let drugs change my ability to think. Not when everything was so screwed up to begin with.

"No," I said, "but thank you."

I turned to the side, staring at the room I had wandered in countless times already, wondering what the hell I was supposed to do. If Maddie was right, if Wil was willing to kill me just for leaving, then I had to stay put. Had to get him on my side. Had to actually accept his help. If his help was even real.

And I knew, now, that Maddie was right. Wil might have been the kindest of the three brothers, but that didn't mean he was 'nice.' Nice enough to offer me sleeping pills. Cruel enough to kill a man for speaking to me.

"Do you remember anything else?" Wil asked.

I paused, then nodded. "She was supposed to start her second year of college."

"That's a start."

A few minutes of silence passed. Neither of us moved. All my life, from what I remembered of it anyway, I had listened to that voice or things like it, telling me what to do. First, it was my parents. Then it was society, telling me how to protect my sister. Then it was the voice. But doing what they said had landed me here, putting my life into a criminal's hands, hoping that he had the answers to what I needed, in a position where he told me what to do.

And what was I supposed to do? Playing his game was my best option for survival, but I needed more. I needed to find my sister.

"For a woman that's been taken from the woods, who has lost so much, you're awfully quiet," he said. "Subdued. As if you're always looking out a window, never in the action yourself."

Don't do it, the voice said. *Play by his rules. Fall in line. He'll reveal the truth sooner or later. But if you speak up, if you tell him, he will find out where you came from.*

But I couldn't stop myself. I was tired of him underestimating me.

"Just because someone is quiet doesn't mean they're not planning your death," I said, my eyes locked on his. The tension was thick, making it hard to breathe. A glimmer of a smile passed over his lips.

"Are you threatening me?" he asked, amusement in his tone.

"I'm stating the truth," I said, my voice strong even though all of that confidence leaked out, deflating me.

He looked pleased with that response. "Funny, isn't it?" he asked.

There wasn't anything funny about the situation. "What?"

"Two of our men wind up dead, chopped up. And then you have these dreams about your sister being chopped up too." He went around the desk and pulled me up by the arm, gripping me like I was a child. I glared at him. He leaned in, his breath on my lips. "Perhaps you're responsible, Ellie. Perhaps you can't remember what happened to your sister because you killed her. Is that it? You killed her, then you killed our men. Why shouldn't I kill you?"

I blinked back the tears. I couldn't say for sure what had happened, but I knew that if his men had died by my hands, then I had done what needed to be done.

But my sister? No. That was impossible. I would die before I let anything happen to her.

He pulled me towards the door, but I stumbled, doing my best to resist.

"Let go of me," I snarled. I wasn't going to let him throw me around easily. I may have been under his control, but that didn't mean I had to bow before him.

He whipped me around, making me face him. That smirk danced across his face like I had done exactly what he wanted. He pressed his body into mine and he seemed taller then, towering over me. As if he could make me smaller. Smoke seemed to pour out of him, surrounding me, swallowing us both in an atmosphere where you could lose yourself and never find your soul again.

He grabbed my hand, putting it down his pocket. This was a sexual act, made clear by the venomous lust in his eyes. I didn't flinch until I skimmed the cold metal with my fingertips.

A knife.

"Do you really want to tell me no, right now, Ellie?" he whispered. I shook my head, biting my lip again. "Good."

He gripped my arm, yanking me into another room, and this time, I trotted behind him, keeping up. There were things I was willing to mess with; a knife wasn't one of them. Once we were in his room, he put a blindfold over my eyes. I clenched my fingers shut, keeping my posture open, ready to fight.

"Let go of those fists," he said in a low voice, "Or I will drag you down to the bed and cut your throat."

I pinched my teeth shut, then slowly relaxed my fingers. This was supposed to be fun. Not to me, but to Wil. A sexual fantasy explored, another game played. But a weight settled inside of me, filling me with dread. I hated him. He might have been good-looking. Might have been merciful in a messed-up way. Might have had a nice moment or two. But he was using my fears against me and using my sister as bait to keep me pliant.

And still, I had no choice but to do what he said.

He pushed the tank top over my shoulders, letting it fall to the ground, then unhooked my bra, leaving me topless and naked. Then he placed something on my shoulders, a heavy weight. Not a chain, but something abrasive and coarse. A necklace, or something like it, loose around my throat. Then my pants and underwear were pulled down, and it was clear that he wanted me to step out of them. Once I did, he held my wrists behind my back in a firm grip.

"Keep your wrists together like this," he said. "Or I'll get the restraints." I rolled my eyes, grateful that the blindfold covered them, but I did as I was told. That was a command that I could follow if it meant keeping my hands free. I thought about what Maddie had said, *Is it really that bad?* It was almost as if she was here too, arguing with the voice inside of me, going to war with me. Of course he wasn't all bad, but did that excuse him from what he did? *All you have to do is be his toy*, she had said.

A man with his toy.

He cupped my breasts, squeezing my flesh. I bit my tongue, focusing on the sharp bite of pain, ignoring the tenderness of his hands. I was his toy, all right. But I didn't have to like it. His fingertips skimmed my collarbones, skipped over the harness on my shoulders, or whatever the hell it was, and he tickled my neck, and I couldn't stop myself from enjoying it. Electricity surged to those points as if he was lighting my whole body on fire. He was supposed to hurt me. Not please me. What was I supposed to do with this? Then I realized that he was using my own desire against me. He was playing with me, molding me to his grip. He moved his leg between my thighs, using it to move them apart.

"Spread your legs," he said. I moved then, the bare minimum I could without being an obedient, sick little pet. Then with one hand on my nipple, pinching it tightly, and the other hand between my legs, Wil explored me. His finger skimmed my slit. A shiver ran through my body, but I only shook once, trying to suppress it. He wasn't supposed to tease me. Wasn't supposed to make me feel good. What the hell was he doing?

I lifted my head, as if I could look down on him, not giving in to the way he made my body clench.

"Too good for everyone," he said, a chuckle in his voice. "But your body doesn't lie, Ellie." He pressed a finger between my folds, and the ease at which he dipped inside of me made me shudder. His finger was thick, pushing against my walls, breaking me down, one touch at a time. "You want this more than you'll admit."

And I knew it was the truth. But *why* did I want this? Sex was an invasion, the destruction of my private body, and I had thought I had no desire for it—and yet, I couldn't help but like it. My chest tingled and my cheeks flushed with heat as he rubbed his thumb over my clit. Wil was a smug bastard, and yet the voice had gone silent, letting Wil take me away, almost as if my body couldn't fight it anymore. As if my mind knew what it wanted. Whoever controlled that part of my brain, the one with the man's voice, that never trusted anyone, couldn't resist Wil's touch. I wanted to kick Wil's face so hard that it left a permanent dent, but I also wanted him to possess every inch of me. Because it was easier to give in to what he wanted, easier to give in, than it was to resist.

Because it was what I wanted too.

After shuffling around, his presence lowered, and a piece of furniture creaked. He must have been sitting on a chair. He guided my hips on top of him, his cock sliding into me, long and full, threatening to break me in two. I bared my teeth at the pain, threatening to bite him, but he laughed and pulled off the blindfold.

The darkness surrounded us as I blinked, getting used to the room. It was darker than I had expected. Had the blinds been shut? Or was it night already?

Then I realized it wasn't a necklace or a harness resting on my shoulders, but a noose. A hangman's knot tied with the rope around my neck.

My eyes widened. "What the hell, Wil?"

"Let's play a game, shall we?" he asked. Without missing a beat, he lifted my hips up and down, making me fuck him. My pussy tingled as if there was nothing wrong. "Your hands and your legs are free. But if you move in any direction," he pointed up, "You know what will happen."

My stomach dropped as I looked up; the rope was tied to a bar on the ceiling.

"I-I can take it off," I tried, "I can remove it."

"No, you can't," he said, that smile evident on his lips. "It's a special knot, one that will get tighter the more you mess with it." His jaw was harsh, pointed at me, daring me to try it out for myself. "Or you can fuck me how I like." He let go of my hips. "And I'll untie it for you."

He scooted the chair backward, and the rope pulled tighter around my throat.

"You're moving!" I yelled.

"Fuck me, Ellie, and I won't move," he said. I was stunned, stuck in place, but as he flinched to move backward again, I moved my knees, bouncing up and down, trying to appease him. "You have to trust me. You have to believe that I'm here to help you. That I'm only doing what's best for you." He smacked my ass, the sound ricocheting across the room, then he palmed my cheeks, cupping my curves. Heat ran all the way up to my forehead, from knowing that he wanted me. More than I understood. That he was willing to show me how my life laid in his hands, to force me to accept the fact that I did like this, this way he consumed me. "You want your sister and I want your body. It's a fair exchange. But you have to trust that I'll give you what you want, if only you give me what I want."

His cocky attitude was a mix of contradictions; he knew that I had no choice but to obey, but he also knew that I would enjoy this. That fucking him while my life and death were literally in his hands, put my body's defenses on alert, making it easier for me to accept.

But it wasn't just that. It was that he wanted me. He reached up, teasing my nipples, rolling them between his fingers, his mouth open as he watched for my reactions. I pressed my lips together, kept fucking him, trying so hard not to like it. But I did, because in Wil's eyes, this was about me. Making me feel fear and pleasure. He wanted me so badly that he hurt another man for talking to me. That simply entering the building with him meant that I was his, and his alone. That I had to bow down to his demands, even if I didn't want to.

"Let's go over the rules again, shall we?" he said. I bounced up and down, my thighs burning, slick with sweat, my mouth open in need. A smirk danced across his lips. "If you leave the house, I'll kill you." His fingers dug into the flesh of my hips, and I was almost sure that he was making me bleed, his fingernails were so damn sharp. "If you talk to another man, I'll kill you both." He snapped his teeth tight, and his cock pulsed inside of me. He grabbed my hair, tightening his grip, pulling my head back. "You want your sister? You'll do as I say, Ellie. It'll only be as hard as you make it. Make this the lesson that you learn today." He threw back his head. "You're mine, Ellie. Your words. Your touch. Your body. All fucking mine."

And though I knew it was wrong, I nodded my head. Thrust myself against him, squeezed my muscles, tried harder to make him come. The voice was silent now. It was me. Just me as I fucked the man who held my life in his hands, his rope around my neck. I could give him what he wanted. And he would help me find my sister.

But I knew that I might lose myself in the process.

I couldn't let that happen.

CHAPTER 7

Wil

The drive to Brackston was about four hours, three if I was driving. But Derek preferred to drive, and either way, I didn't care; we were going to get there one way or another. A few of my men were taking care of the deals at the gambling hall, and Derek had a team running his tasks for the day. Being on the road gave us a chance to talk things through before meeting with Miles Muro himself.

I had spoken to Muro on the phone a few times, to smooth out what should have been a done deal. But it wasn't, thanks to my half-brother, Ethan. The whole stolen captive situation eventually blew over, but because we were his competition, Muro thought we had done it on purpose, to screw him over.

Understandably, our working relationship hadn't been great before, and now, it was even more tenuous. Ethan had caused plenty of damage, and now, we were left to pick up the pieces. Funny how love could mess up your vision entirely.

Glancing over at Derek, his elbow leaning against the car door, eyes fixed on the road, it made more sense now than it ever had, that love wasn't trustworthy. Ethan had lost himself to some sweet pussy, but me? I was smarter than that. I understood that family was all that mattered. I wasn't going to choose a chick over the family just because she made my dick twitch. Better to keep them at a distance. Then everyone knew where they stood.

My dick pulsed at the thought. I had taught Ellie that lesson and had enjoyed it far too much. Which was why I needed to remember it myself. Distance was a necessity in this business.

The building for the Midnight Miles Corporation was at the center of Brackston. It stretched tall, as if it looked down on all of the buildings around it. Inside, the furniture and walls were white, and a long, low table in the middle of the lobby held a single red orchid, the only splash of color in the entire room. The guard adjusted the collar of his white shirt, then let us up to the top floor.

A woman in white opened the door and let us into the office. Muro sat up from behind his glass desk.

"So kind of you two to join me," he said. He hit something under his desk and smiled down. A thin woman crawled out from underneath it. Once she was standing, she gave a subtle nod to Muro, then left the room. Muro watched her leave, then turned to me. "You must be Wilhelm. We finally meet in person."

"You can call me 'Wil,'" I said, shaking his hand.

"Ah, Wil," Muro said, his voice raspy. "And it's good to see you again, Derek."

They shook hands. "Likewise."

Muro motioned to the side, and a huge man in a white outfit, more of a boulder than a person, began pouring shots. Personal assistant, or bodyguard, or both? The shots were served, and the three of us lifted the glasses. Muro tossed his low ponytail behind his back.

"Cheers," he said.

We drank, and as we washed it down, I studied Muro. He had a lightning bolt tattoo to the side of his eyes, tendrils curling from the edges, almost like the underside of a leaf. He was shorter than I had expected, but sitting behind his desk, you couldn't tell. Regardless, the man had balls. No one had attempted to infiltrate Sage City in decades. Muro was the first one to try.

Gerard wanted this to be a peaceful alliance, though. Not a blood-soaked dispute. Derek and I had to remember that.

"Now, what brings me the honor of your presence?" Muro asked, a flash of light shining in his eyes. The honor? What a condescending prick.

"When I spoke to you over the phone, we had agreed that your men could sell in our territories, with our protection, in exchange for a cut of the profits," I said.

Muro nodded. "We agreed to that, yes."

"But your men haven't been showing up," Derek said.

"And when they do, they refuse to share the proceeds," I said.

"We want to give you a chance to adjust your directions," Derek said. "We want to honor our agreement."

"Well, you ruined that chance, didn't you?" Muro sneered at us. Then he threw back his head, and belly-laughed. "Kidding, kidding." He hit the desk with his fist. "Sometimes, my people have a mind of their own, but mostly, I like finding yes-sir kind of workers, don't you agree?" He sat up, leaning forward on the clear desk. "Makes it easier that way. Obedient pawns. Tell them exactly what to do. What to think."

I raised a brow. "You train them well, then?"

"For the most part, yes." Muro nodded deeply. "Down to their very core."

There was something off about Muro. I knew our business ties would be stiff, but it was worse than before.

"I propose a new deal," he said. He laced his fingers together. "We send you the products directly. You sell them as is."

"So we would be paying you," Derek said dryly.

"Precisely." He bared his teeth in a smile, but he looked more like a hyena than a human. "My men won't have to be in your territory. They would simply deliver. It would be your men, free to work with the product however they wanted."

I looked at Derek, but he didn't move, staring straight at Muro, judging him. I didn't trust the proposal and tried to communicate that with my glance, but Derek didn't look at me. He nodded at Muro.

"We'll have a trial period," he said. "To show that you're working in good faith."

"Excellent," Muro reached forward and shook his hand. "I knew you had a good head on your shoulders."

In the corner of the room, a woman was waiting. A white dress lay flat against her body, but her head was turned down, staring at the floor. Not as if she were bored, but as if she were being ordered to never make eye contact. Did Muro control her down to her eyes?

And was I any better, if I controlled exactly where Ellie went, what she wore, and who she spoke to?

Did I care?

Perhaps I did. Perhaps I didn't. I wasn't sure.

"You like what you see?" Muro asked.

I turned to him. "Excuse me?"

"You like women, don't you, Wilhelm? Wait, it was Wil, right? *Wil*." Muro smirked, then rubbed his chin between his fingers. "Do you like them weak or feisty?"

"Why?"

"Curious," Muro said. "You seem rather interested in mine. Let me guess." His eyes washed over me. "You like taking the feisty ones and ruining their spirit, knocking them down until they've got no choice but to take what you give them."

I thought of the woman that had crawled out from under his desk, how he had hit the back of her head to tell her to stop sucking him off. And there was the woman in the corner, waiting for his command. She was no better off.

Was that how I was treating Ellie?

No. It couldn't be. Ellie might have been restricted with who she could talk to, but she was able to roam my property freely.

But she wasn't allowed to leave.

That was the way things had to be. With my family, I didn't have much choice.

"I keep them at a distance," I said. "Locked up. Ready to use."

Muro smiled, a genuine one at that. "Good. That's how it should be."

My skin crawled at those words. I wanted to punch that smile off of his face, though I couldn't explain why. We all shook hands, standing to signal the end of the meeting.

"I'll have my men deliver the first shipment soon," Muro said.

"Looking forward to it," Derek said.

In the car, I stretched out, angling the seat backward, trying to relax before we discussed the meeting, but I couldn't get comfortable. I clicked a button, and the seat adjusted to a sitting position. I stared out of the window at the hills rolling beside us. The whole ordeal put me on edge. There was something off about Muro, and I knew that Derek could sense it too.

"Muro is bad news," I finally said. I angled my elbow onto the door. "Might as well start a war. That bastard isn't out for an alliance."

Derek kept his eyes focused on the road. The mossy green hills grew, shadowing us.

"Gerard wants us to form a bond," he said. Not our father again. He was phoning it in, leaving all the hard parts for us to figure out. Dreaming of retirement. Derek had to know that.

"Gerard hasn't met Muro yet," I said.

"Gerard has been doing this for a lot longer than either of us have," Derek said, his face turning towards me for a few seconds. "We need to respect his wishes."

"He never had to deal with infiltrations," I said. "Sage City has been sitting quiet for years. It's been too easy on us, and you know it."

"It's been easy because of the foundation our family has laid."

"You know Muro isn't going to play fair."

"Then we let him make the first move," Derek said. His hands gripped the steering wheel, the leather crunching in his hands. "In the meantime, we protect our family." I scowled and looked out the window, watching the green landscape turn to a dull brown as we passed through more terrain. Might as well open our gates. Invite the enemy in, and say, Take what we've got! We don't care!"

"Look," Derek said, interrupting my internal rant, "I agree. Muro has never been trustworthy. But we've got to know what he's up to before we do anything that might affect the family." He tilted his head. "Because I'm not going to let anything happen to our family." He straightened. "We'll send Ethan to spy."

Ethan? Our half-brother who skipped out on us for a woman?

"You're kidding me," I said.

Derek shrugged. "He's been good to us. He'll do the job."

I sighed. A few minutes passed. Though Sage City and Brackston were the two biggest cities in our state, there was a two-lane highway between them. The car's engine hummed, filling the silence. This deep into the state, you couldn't see or smell the coast, and it didn't drizzle with rain. It was just dry.

"Anything new with Ellie?" Derek asked.

I shook my head. "Still doesn't remember anything."

"You put any thought into contacting Kiley?"

Kiley was a genealogist back in Las Vegas. At least, that's what her business card said. In reality, she was somewhat of a personal detective and a hacker, and so skilled at it that her name often came up in business discussions. She could find anything about anyone; she only needed a thread or two to get started. We knew her through our contacts in the area, and though she was one of the best at her job, she wasn't the easiest person to be around. This is coming from me, a man who can smooth talk with almost anyone... Except Muro.

I couldn't shake that feeling of distrust with Muro, which meant I had a hard time faking the charm.

And Kiley. She wasn't my favorite person to contact either.

"You think that's a good idea?" I asked.

"You said it yourself. She's the best." Derek shrugged. "If anyone can do it, she can."

I sighed and dialed her number right then. Screw it. Why not, right? I had promised to help Ellie, and Kiley was my best shot at keeping that promise.

"Yo, asshole," Kiley said.

I shook my head. "Look," I said, "I've got an issue I need help dealing with—"

"I don't get a 'hi, how are you?' No excuse, like, 'I'm awful at keeping in touch but I never stopped writing you letters, Kiley?'"

I held back a sigh. She could be difficult, and this wasn't even Kiley in her prime.

"What's up, Kiley?"

"Thanks, asshole," she said. "Now, that wasn't so hard, was it?"

"Anyway," I said, pausing, waiting for her to interrupt me, but when she didn't, I continued: "I've got a situation. A woman was gifted to me and she has a pretty bad memory." And by that, I meant almost nothing. "Doesn't remember where she came from. She just knows she's looking for her sister. Can't remember where her sister went though."

"Huh. Amnesia. Haven't dealt with one of those in a while," Kiley snickered. "What's her name?"

"Ellie."

"Is that her nickname or her first name?"

I thought it over. Had Ellie mentioned that? "Not sure," I finally said.

"You got a last name?"

"No."

"Then figure it out. Bonus if you get the sister's name too."

"I thought that's what you do," I said. "*You* figure it out. That's your superpower."

"Cut the crap, Wil. It's not like I'm asking for much," she argued. "I need her name."

"Or?"

"It's either that, or I come there myself and interview her personally." She shifted the phone, the speaker cracking as she moved. "I need a spark. I can work with a spark, but you've got to give me that, or I can't do anything."

I sighed. "All right," I said. "I'll find out."

"Thanks. I'll send you the invoice after I deliver."

She hung up. Derek smirked when I looked at him.

"What?" I asked.

"Better you than me," he chuckled.

Once I got back to the penthouse, I went straight to the rooftop. The sun was setting, casting a purple glow over the horizon. The ocean was choppy then, the breeze erratic. And like I had come to expect, Ellie was sitting on one of the patio couches, staring out at the water.

She stared at that view every single day. Sometimes, on the surveillance footage, I caught her lips moving, her eyes flickering back and forth, but I could never hear or see anything.

So what did she see?

I lifted a blanket towards her. She smiled and gave me a subtle nod.

I could have taken her on that rooftop. I had thought about it often, fucking her across the couch, stripping her bare, exposing her pussy for my pleasure. But seeing the way it pained her to look out at the world and get nothing back, leaving her alone, made guilt settle in my stomach. I hadn't kept up my end of the bargain, and I should have.

But now, I could start.

"What's your name?" I asked. She gazed toward me with a question in her eyes, then waited for me to finish. "Your real name," I explained. "Your sister's."

She closed her eyes, pressing her eyelids together tight. Tears built in the crevices, her skin growing blotchy, almost as if it was painful for her to think. It must have been hard to not remember your past, to fight with your brain to remember. Your mind was supposed to be the only ally that you always had, and yet Ellie's mind had betrayed her. Had left her alone.

She opened her eyes, her vision locking on mine. Those sapphires pierced me then, showing me their true depth. She was so much more than I knew, than she knew herself.

"My sister's name is Julie," she said. "And my name is Elena Jordan."

CHAPTER 8

Ellie

The gray clouds dulled the whole city as if everything was monochrome, and the rainbow after the storm had never existed. I looked down; the rooftop of Wil's penthouse always made it seem like I was in a different universe, like I hadn't been a part of the 'real' world in a long time. I didn't know where I had come from, and yet I knew this place, this city, wasn't my home.

But where was my home?

It was colder on the rooftop, but I preferred to be outside, looking down at the world, trying to search the streets for clues to my past, as if the cars, the buildings, the street signs, as if everything could tell me a new secret. It was better than being inside of Wil's penthouse. His place was nice; Maddie took good care of it. She came by every other day, asking and chatting about Wil as she cleaned. The entire place had been decorated with a modern, yet masculine vibe. And whenever it was cold, there was a fireplace built into the living room wall that gave off just enough heat to warm my bones.

But here on the rooftop? I had fresh air. A planter box held flowers with petals that wiggled in the wind; Maddie took care of them too. There was even a small square of grass that I sometimes stepped on with my bare feet, to remind myself that life went on outside of these walls. My sister was out there, somewhere.

You must find her, the voice said. *Julie. Where is Julie?*

Her name was heavy on my heart. I held a hand to my chest, thinking of her: that blond hair, her blue eyes bright like mine, eyes we had gotten from our mother. Julie had always been the opposite of me; naturally thin where I was built like a tree, spirited and adventurous when I was rooted to the spot. All I had wanted was to protect her. To give her the safety I wished I had. And instead, she had floated away.

Where is she?

I couldn't answer the voice, couldn't tell it the one answer that would give me peace, the lost answer that broke me in two. Made me feel worthless. Some big sister I was.

Footsteps thudded behind me. I stayed forward, pretending as if I hadn't heard him. I was in tune with Wil's presence now, like an instinctual tick, knowing exactly when he had returned to the penthouse through the shifts in the building, the sounds that came from within. I slept in the other master bedroom, and he locked me inside of there at night, but once it was daylight, I stayed on the rooftop as much as possible.

Unless he called for me. Like I knew he would right now.

"Ellie," he said.

I turned around, meeting his dark eyes. I couldn't shake the feeling that there was good inside of him. He had asked for my name, for my sister's name, and though the voice scolded me *not* to say the words, *not* to give in, screamed at me until I couldn't bear to fight it anymore, the urge inside of me had found her name. And my name. My *real* name. And I knew it had to do with him. All he did was ask. He hadn't required that I did anything for him first.

At least at that moment.

Now, on the other hand, I could tell he wanted something from me.

"There's someone I'd like you to meet," Wil said.

My heart fluttered, instantly thinking of my sister, but based on the closed-off nature of his posture, I could tell it wasn't her. Wil might have had a heart, somewhere inside of him, but he wasn't the type to give in to a desire freely. Wil made you work for it, and he would make *me* work for it. I had to follow his lead.

Don't ever let him own you, the voice said, *Or you'll lose yourself.*

I wouldn't let him own me, I argued with the voice, annoyed at whoever, or whatever it was, even if it was just my conscience. But I had to move forward with purpose, and that meant, at the very least, pretending to be his. I couldn't rely on impulse in a situation like this.

An edge of smoke drifted off of his shoulders as I followed him through the penthouse. To my surprise, two men were seated around the dining table, men I recognized from the picture in his office: his brothers.

"This is Derek," he said, pointing to the slightly older looking brother, with lines around his eyes and mouth. Derek nodded at me. "And Axe," Wil continued, nodding towards the other brother, who had the same almost-black eyes as the other two, but he kept them narrowed, scrutinizing me. There was a dip on his bottom lip, a scar. "My brothers," Wil said.

And between them was a woman with hunched shoulders, wrapped in a blanket.

As she turned, keeping her head bowed, the blanket moved off of her shoulders, revealing scratches in sharp red lines. She lifted her pale face to me, her eyes brick red and blank. Her hair was cut short, all the way to her scalp on the sides, an inch or two longer on the top. Her dry fingers curled around the edges of the blanket, pulling it tighter around her body, to shield herself. She needed protection.

My mouth fell open.

She's just like you, the voice said. I held a hand to my chest. For the first time in a while, I didn't question the voice at all. I agreed completely.

"I'll—" I paused, unsure of what to say. "I'll get you some clothes."

I tripped over my own feet walking to my room, but once I was there, I rummaged through the clothes Maddie had given me. Some were hand-me-downs, stuff she didn't wear anymore, and others were outfits Wil had made her buy for me. The woman in the blanket seemed about my size, so I found a pair of pants and a long-sleeved shirt.

All four of them looked at me when I returned. I motioned to the woman.

"Come with me," I said.

She didn't move at first, but after a moment, Axe cleared his throat, and that startled her out of her trance. We went to the bedroom for privacy, but I knew better than to close the door.

I handed her the clothes. She looked at them, studying the outfit for a second.

She's just like you, the voice said. *Join together. You're stronger together.*

I didn't doubt that.

"What's your name?" I asked.

"I—" she stuttered, her lip trembling. "I—"

"Did they find you in the woods too?" Her focus fluttered, as if she could never make eye contact. She nodded, barely enough to give an answer.

"Who are you?" she managed to say.

This will prepare you two for what's coming, the voice said, stronger than usual, almost as if the man who owned it was standing right next to me, speaking into my ear. *You can trust her. She's just like you.*

"My name is Ellie," I said. "Elena Jordan. But I didn't remember that when they first found me."

Amnesia usually didn't work like this, so whatever had stolen my memories was something else.

"You didn't?"

I shook my head. "But eventually it came back."

She held her head in her palm, exposing her arm. It was muscular like mine, bigger than the average woman's. She shivered and I handed her the clothes.

"I'm sure they'll get you more clothes later, but this will do for now," I said.

Just before I turned to give her privacy to change, I saw a flash of her neck, covered with that same tattoo: four hills pressed together, leaning to the side, in red.

This is the only way you will defeat the enemy, the voice said. *You must work together.*

Once she was changed, I showed her to the bathroom, and she excused herself. The faucet turned on, water splashed in the sink, and when she returned, she had a clean, slightly damp face.

"Do you remember anything?" I asked.

"I'm looking for my daughter," she said. "Where is she?"

"Do you remember her name?"

She held her chin, her eyes unfocused. *She's just like you*, the voice said. *She's searching too.* But that didn't give me comfort. Why had we been let out into the woods, almost as if we had been freed from whatever it was, only to find out that our loved ones were in danger and that we had no information about them? They, whoever they were, had dropped us into a world that we didn't understand.

The woman shook her head. "Can you help me find her?"

I nodded. "Of course."

We went out to the dining area, standing close to one another. *You're stronger together*, the voice kept repeating. And I agreed.

"You found her in the woods, like me?" I asked. Axe, the brother with narrowed eyes, nodded. "Naked and alone?" He nodded again.

"What do you know about her?" the other one, Derek, asked. The strain in his forehead showed his age. I figured he was only a few years older than Wil, but it seemed like a decade could have passed between them.

"She's looking for her daughter," I said. "We have to help her."

"I have no one else," she said. My heart sank, but I straightened my shoulders and reached for her hand, holding it in mine. She flinched at the touch, but then looked at me.

We were stronger together. I had no doubt about that.

"What were you doing in our woods?" Derek asked. He leaned forward. "What was your purpose?"

"I—" she stammered, but she couldn't find the words. She touched her head.

"See?" Derek said, turning to his brothers. "Useless."

"Get rid of them," Axe said.

"No!" I shouted. The three men raised their brows, turning towards me. "That's not right. She knows nothing. She's *not* your enemy."

"If she knows nothing, then she doesn't know whether or not we're enemies," Derek said. "Neither do you."

A chill ran through the air. Wil stood beside me, putting a hand on my lower back, pulling me closer to him.

"Ellie has a point," Wil said. I glanced at him; had that really come out of his mouth? "She's the second woman we've found. Who knows if there will be more." He tilted his chin. "It's better to keep them around, under surveillance, and see what they recover. Piece together their memory."

"Fine," Derek shrugged. "You have the keys to the restraints?"

Wil nodded and got up, heading towards his bedroom. I followed him. I wasn't sure why, but I was going with my instinct. I had hope for once; Wil had stood up for the woman, which meant he had stood up for me.

Ask him to let her stay, the voice said. *You are stronger together.*

"Let her stay here," I said. "With us. You have the room."

He scoffed. "Not likely."

"Please," I begged. "She's all alone. Like me. I can help her."

"I don't doubt that," he said, continuing down the hallway.

"She needs me."

I touched his arm, and he stopped. He looked down at my hand. I pulled away, realizing what I had done—I had touched him on my own.

"Do you realize that you're the first person I've let stay here?" he asked. The silence was heavy between us. I hadn't. "No one has ever stayed here through the night here. Only me." He shook his head, as if it pained him to admit that. I wasn't sure how to take it. Wil seemed like the kind of man who could have had a different woman every night. So why did he choose to be alone? "I'm not going to let another stranger into my home," he said. "That's final."

"But Wil—"

"She'll stay in Axe's workroom," he said. I clenched my fists, and he tossed his head to the side, returning down the hall to his room. "I'll make sure she's treated properly."

I followed him through the doorway. "That's not good enough," I said. "She needs more than that. She needs a friend."

Wil grabbed a set of keys out of one of the drawers, then locked it again. "She needs—"

Family, the voice said.

"She needs family," I said.

Again, Wil stopped. He gazed at me, his eyes flat, his entire expression darkening the longer he looked at me.

He doesn't want you together, the voice said. *He knows. He knows that together, you'll destroy him—*

Destroy him? But why would we do that?

He huffed past me as he went back down the hallway. He looked at the woman and nodded, then turned to his brothers.

"She'll stay with you," he said, turning toward Axe. He nodded. "Not in the cages. A proper bed in the workroom. Restraints, fine. But she will be fed, bathed, and cared for properly."

Axe nodded. How was that even a question in anyone's mind? My heart burned. What kind of animal was taking care of her?

Derek sat up. "Ellie," he said, addressing me, "You'll see what you can uncover?"

At those words, Wil turned to me. At first, I thought it was to test me, to see if I would talk to another man, going against his rules. But then I remembered that his brothers and father were the only exceptions. It was something else he wanted.

I realized he was giving me a chance to speak for myself. And so that's what it was. He was giving me a choice.

But there wasn't any choice to be made. I didn't need a voice to tell me what to do. I didn't even need to think about it. I knew my answer.

"Yes," I said. "I'll help."

CHAPTER 9

Wil

I wiped my forehead, then leaned on the table. Jimmy's was running at a medium pace, and that was lucky for me. I needed to think. Derek and Axe were on the other side of the table, but we didn't have time to screw around and play cards.

Another body?

"How many is that now?" I asked.

Derek gave Axe a sideways glance. "Three," Derek said.

"Seriously?"

"Butchered," he said. "Just like the other two."

It made my stomach turn. There was no clear explanation. But these were the facts: an enemy was hunting us, and it had to do with the women, Ellie and the other two: one dead and one alive. But how did they all connect?

"More naked women?" I asked.

"Not since the one you met."

At first, I had been upset that Derek had insisted on bringing the next nameless woman to my place. But when I realized that Ellie could help and saw the look on her face when she came to understand what the situation was, I knew it was the right decision. I had expected Ellie to resist, to question me. To refuse to help this woman, since she had nothing to do with her sister. Because why would she help her, and therefore, help me? But Ellie never hesitated. She *wanted* to help.

And that surprised me. For someone as closed off as Ellie was, she cared about things other than herself. Other than her family.

She was different from me.

"How's she doing?" I asked, turning towards Axe. He shrugged.

"I set up the cages."

"I thought we weren't doing cages?"

"They're full size. A twin bed. And I take her for showers. House food."

I shook my head, knowing that there was no use. That was, by far, the most Axe would do. He didn't have sympathy for anyone who was trespassing. And to be honest, he lacked sympathy in general.

And me? I should have been like him. Shouldn't have cared about what happened to Ellie. But it was different. I might not have given a shit about that other woman, but I cared about Ellie, at least as far as the fact that she was mine. And unlocking the key to her past would help us figure out what the hell was going on.

Which was why I had to protect her. She was our missing piece.

That's what I told myself, anyway.

"Any word from Ethan?" I asked.

Derek shook his head. "I thought he usually calls you?" he asked.

I shrugged. "But you told him to check out Brackston?" I asked.

"Yep."

"Boss." A man, a foot shorter than me, but twice as wide in pure muscle, appeared at my side. "The men from Midnight Miles are here to see you."

Good. They were right on time. I met them in my office, Derek standing at my side, and Axe waiting at the door. The two men took seats in front of the desk. One with sharp glasses and tattoos, and the other with leathery tanned skin and a ball cap. The tanned one handed over a dime bag carrying a white substance. I immediately lifted a brow.

"Coke," he explained.

"This isn't your typical product," I said.

"Muro wanted you to have it," the tattooed one said.

The substance was uniform, like powdered sugar, not like rocks. I pinched a bit of it and tossed it on my tongue, but I felt nothing. No numbness. No high. *Nothing.*

They wanted us to sell their cocaine, when we already had our own supply *and* they were giving us garbage?

I pushed back the dime bag. "We can't sell this. Give us the heroin and we'll talk again."

One of them laughed and the other shrugged. "No can do, my friend," the tattooed one chuckled. "This is what Muro's giving you."

I sure as hell didn't like the tone he was taking with me. Brackston mother fucker didn't know who the hell he was talking to.

"Tell your boss that this isn't what we agreed to," I said, my jaw set.

"I can tell him whatever you want, but I'm telling you, Muro ain't giving you shit."

I glanced at Derek. He had his arms crossed, sneering at them. He clenched his jaw, his finger twitching against his bicep. But he didn't move to do anything. Was he really trying to follow Gerard's request to keep the peace, right now? The two of them stood up, pushing out their chairs. The tattooed one leaned on my desk, looking down his nose at me.

"See ya, pussies," he said.

No. I wasn't going to let them get away with disrespecting our family like that.

I grabbed the letter opener from one of the mail trays and stabbed his palm, holding him in place. A howl like a wounded wolf split through the walls.

"Fuck! Fuck, man!" he screamed.

The tanned one reached for his gun, but Derek was faster, shooting him twice in the chest, knocking him to the ground.

I knew Derek would have a few words for me about acting impulsively, but I didn't care. Our family's honor was at stake.

I grabbed the tattooed one by the skin on the back of his neck, pinching it tightly in my hand. I lifted up his head, craning my wrist until he could see me. He blubbered, his wails more irritating by the second.

"You're going to deliver a message for us," I said in a low voice.

"Whatever you want, man, please just—"

"Tell your boss that he doesn't know who he's dealing with," I said calmly, "And we don't appreciate his mistake."

I let go of his neck, letting him fall into the desk, the letter opener tugging on the wound with his weight. Then I ripped it out and he cried, his face a mess of snot. He staggered toward the door. Axe stepped to the side, letting him through.

"And take this trash out with you," I said, motioning at the corpse. The tattooed man scrambled back over, picking up his friend by the shoulders, but he grunted and whined. It must have been hard to move a dead body when his hand was punctured.

I locked eyes with Axe. "You want to help this poor asshole out?"

Axe gave a subtle nod, and I let out a long sigh. Damn it. Not only did we have to deal with the naked women and the dead men in the forest, but Miles Muro was deliberately insulting us, sending us his expendable drugs and throwaway henchmen.

The room cleared, and Derek shook his head. "What the hell was that?"

"What?" I snapped. "I'm not going to apologize for defending our family."

"We could have dealt with them later," he argued. "Dealt with Muro personally."

"We do nothing, and Muro sees us as weak. The rest of the crime rings too. And then what do we do?"

Derek thought about it for a moment. His eyes scanned the room, his fingers tapping his chin. He knew I was right. I might have been the most reckless of the three of us, only matched by our half-brother, Ethan, but I still knew that sending a message was something that we *had* to do. There was no way around it. We couldn't keep playing nice like Gerard wanted us to do. We had to make moves *now*, and that meant showing Muro that we were serious.

"I would have done the same thing," he finally said.

Relief filled my chest. I let out a breath. "What do we tell our father?"

"We'll tell Gerard now," he said.

Derek pulled out a burner phone from the desk drawer, then dialed him, turning on speakerphone. We both leaned in, listening.

"Son?" he asked.

"It's Derek and me," I said. "Muro sent lidocaine."

"Not even actual coke?"

"I doubt there was any in there," I said. But hell, I hadn't felt a thing. Still didn't. "And that wasn't what the shipment was supposed to be."

"Right. I was looking forward to the product, the distribution, at least," he said. Sure, he was. I gave side-eyes to Derek; the corner of his mouth lifted in response. With such an easy few decades of running the family mafia, Gerard had plenty of chances to experiment with our products. Leaving us to take care of business.

"We sent a message," I said. He would know exactly what that meant.

He cursed under his breath. "Damn it, you two," he muttered. "You retaliated, just like that?"

"If I didn't, they would have come after us right now," I argued. "Thought we were easy picking."

"Or we could have negotiated with Muro directly," he said. I locked eyes with Derek. He shrugged his shoulders; it was just like he predicted.

"Muro was taunting us," Derek said. "It was his own message. There is *no* alliance, Father."

"You know better," he said. No one wants a war."

"It *is* a fucking war," Derek said. "You've got to open your eyes. He disrespected us."

Gerard sighed loudly. "All right," he said. "Kill any of his workers found in our area. The agreement was to buy their product and sell it ourselves. If that's what the plan was, then we can eliminate the rest. Declare our position."

So he was flipping sides, just like that? What was going on in his mind?

"Fucking hell, *Father*," I said, making sure he heard the sarcasm in my voice. "This isn't about the coke anymore. We've got to be ready. Muro isn't going to wait around for us to arm ourselves."

"And neither are we," Gerard said, his voice harsh. "I'd rather take down the man himself, absorb his empire than be forced to destroy it. But we have to work carefully." He cleared his throat, then adjusted the phone in his ear. "Work efficiently. Killing everyone that has a Midnight Miles logo on their back isn't practical. They're loyal to whoever is paying them. And that could be us."

I sighed. "You want to absorb his company, then?"

"Why not?"

I looked at Derek, who rolled his eyes, closing them tight. Our family had been content to stay in Sage City, slowly expanding into the neighboring areas, with a few casinos and resorts in Las Vegas, so this news was irritating. Gerard had been letting us take over more of the family business in the past years, as he should have, but he hadn't been too hands-on. I wondered if he was going to do anything now, that he had declared his intentions.

My phone buzzed, and I pulled it out: *Kiley* blinked on the screen. We hung up with Gerard and I excused myself to the hallway, finding it empty. Axe, the goon, and the corpse were gone. I accepted the call.

"Hi," I said.

"All right, get ready for this shit. So about Elena," Kiley said, her voice nasally. *Elena*. I loved that name; it sounded majestic. "The sister disappeared about a year and a half ago. Elena about six months after that. Looks like she filed a bunch of missing persons reports, but the police couldn't find anything. By the way, I found an old flyer in one of the databases; I'll send it over in an email now."

How the hell had she managed to dig that up?

"Thanks," I said. "But where did she disappear to?"

"The last record we have of Julie is outside of Pebble Garden University, filling up her gas tank. And Ellie paid late membership dues for a local women's club. I think it was some sort of private gym, actually."

Pebble Garden was a couple of hours away, but not as far as Brackston. Ellie had mentioned that her sister was supposed to start school. That must have been the last place she had looked.

"And her parents?" I asked.

"Gone. Died when Elena was a sophomore in high school."

"Anything suspicious about their deaths?"

"Nothing special. Car accident," Kiley said, her voice mundane. "Unless there's a reason to believe a car accident would be foul play?" I shook my head, even though Kiley couldn't see me. She continued on before I could answer. "Here's the weird thing," she said. "She was part of that gym, right? An all women's martial arts social club."

That didn't surprise me. Ellie was strong. "Right."

"Elena was the first to disappear. After that, a few more. Eventually, people stopped going because too many club members were disappearing. The police suspected the owner, but even after they set up a watch on her, nothing came of it. And still, the women kept disappearing."

"Shit," I said. That did not sound good. Did that mean the women had been hunted?

"I know. I doubt it has anything to do with the owner. But the police didn't know who to accuse." She sighed. "Anyway, something fishy is going on. I hope you figure it out."

"That's about the nicest thing you've ever said to me," I said.

"Don't get used to it," she snapped. "Let me know if I can be of any use."

I clicked off the line, then checked the surveillance footage on my phone. Ellie was in her usual spot, sitting on one of the patio couches on the rooftop, her eyes staring blankly in front of her. Sometimes, her eyes flicked back and forth, as if she was having a waking dream, or she held a hand to her ear as if she couldn't quite hear something.

My chest tightened, thinking of what this new information meant. Someone had been hunting the women from Ellie's gym, and it wasn't clear if it was linked to her sister. The fact that a few other women had been found in the woods made me believe that whatever was going on, had just started.

By the time I returned to the penthouse, it was quiet and dark. I had a habit of staying at Jimmy's until the early hours of the morning, but lately, I delegated the tasks to my men, wanting to go to the penthouse early. I wanted to be around Ellie, to make sure she was safe. Being alone in the world without any of her memories must have been scary as hell.

But perhaps restoring these small memories would help.

Usually, she waited until I spoke, but this time, she turned towards me immediately.

"The woman?" she asked.

My heart sank. She cared for this stranger, a woman she didn't know. Because she saw herself inside of her.

I wasn't capable of caring about someone I didn't know. I would never let myself; I was born to be selfish, to only care about my family's power. Opposite of me, Ellie had nothing in the world, and yet, despite that, she was good. She wanted to help a stranger.

It was hard to understand, but I admired it in her.

"Being treated as well as can be expected," I said. This was Axe, after all. At least Ellie didn't understand the full extent of what that meant.

Her shoulders sank. "Good," she said to herself, lowering her eyes. "That's good."

I watched her, staring off into nothing. Closing her eyes, then opening them again. The moon was full, lighting the rooftop patio in a haze whenever it poked through the clouds, tinting Ellie's skin blue, the red hilled tattoo on her neck shaded purple. She met my gaze and shook her head. Before she opened her mouth, I spoke.

"Your sister, Julie," I said. Ellie visibly perked up. "She disappeared about six months before you did."

Ellie opened her mouth, then pressed her lips together. "That sounds right."

"Do you remember anything about a gym?" I asked. "You had a membership there. A social club or something? Maybe you took classes there?"

She looked down at her fists. "Martial arts?"

"That doesn't ring any bells?"

She paused for a moment, but her eyes flicked away from mine. She couldn't look me in the eyes and say her answer. "No," she murmured. "I don't remember anything like that."

A gut instinct twitched inside of me, wondering if she was lying. Perhaps she was full of lies, and all of the women in the woods were working together, making us think that they were vulnerable, when in reality, they were anything but. And yet another part of me believed one thing about Ellie, and that was that her sister mattered to her more than anything in the world. If I could win her loyalty through her sister, she would be mine. *Truly mine.*

But until then, I could test her.

I fingered the knife in my pocket, coming towards her slowly. She looked up at me, the cloud-covered moon shining in the pools of her eyes. Deep, waiting to burst.

"We're going to find your sister," I said.

"I know," she whispered.

I leaned down, putting a hand behind her back, lifting her up, and pulling her closer to me. Our lips met, full and passionate, my tongue caressing hers, beckoning her on. With one hand on her throat, I licked down her neck to her collarbone, and when her muscles tensed, I savored the moment, enjoying the way she melted to my touch. She might have hated me at first, but attraction didn't lie. She liked being put in her place.

I ran my hands down the sides of her body, savoring her soft skin over that hard muscle. None of that came easily, and I respected her for working hard at it, even more so now that I knew she trained at a gym. She was a strong woman, both in her mind and her body, which made it all the more pleasurable to force her to kneel.

I gripped her shoulders, pressing her body against me, my cock growing hard at the contact. My fingertips skimmed over the top of her shirt, and her nipples hardened. My dirty toy wasn't wearing a bra. I grinned.

"Tell me you hate it," I murmured.

She closed her eyes. "I hate it."

"How much?"

I pinched her nipples between my fingers, ripping through the fabric straight to her skin until her face contorted into a grimace. "I hate it," she whimpered, "so much."

I twisted her nipples until she cried out, then I grabbed her hair and pulled her down to lie on the couch. Holding myself up above her, I put a hand in my pocket, running my fingers over the knife. I gazed down at her lying there, then removed the knife and flicked it open. She held her arms across her chest and looked away.

"Look at me," I demanded. But Ellie inched away, slipping out from under me. My heart rate quickened, my temperature rose until the anger pulsed inside of me. Still, she kept her eyes away from me. "Do I need to teach you a lesson?" I asked. When she said nothing, I let a small sigh escape me. Did I have to do everything myself? "All right," I said. I got off of the couch, stowed the knife in my pocket, then backed away from her. She sat upright, her arms crossed in front, guarding herself.

I should have been sympathetic, should have cared that she was afraid. And the truth was that somewhere inside of me, I did care. I didn't want her to be afraid. She didn't understand that I wanted to protect her, more than anything, but I also wanted to use her how I wanted, and that meant using a knife against her skin, toying with that fear of death that lived in each of us.

But I wasn't Ellie. I didn't put another person's comfort ahead of my own. I knew what I wanted, and what I needed to teach her. She *had* to face her fears. You couldn't survive in my world by running away.

"I'm going to give you a choice," I said. "The knife, or the belt." Finally, she looked at me. She opened her mouth, but I cut her off. "Don't think that just because you're being given a choice means that you won't get the knife. I'm simply asking what you want to face right now."

She bit her lip. "The belt," she whispered.

"Bend over the back of the couch," I instructed. "Remove your shirt." I unlocked the buckle. The leather strap whipped out of my pant loops in a sliding hiss. And when she finally slipped out of that shirt, exposing her back, that rippled skin stared back at me. Keloids and pockmarks, almost as if a person had dug into her skin repeatedly, never letting it heal.

Perhaps she didn't remember because she didn't want to.

My face twitched, the back of my throat dry, but Ellie laid against the back of the couch with ease. As if she knew what was coming, and still, she wasn't afraid. Whatever she had gone through, it had been so much worse than this.

But that didn't stop me.

The first strike went across her back. She didn't move. Didn't make a single sound. Before I did the next one, I moved to the side, so I could see her face. The second strike lashed across her back, the belt wrapping along her side, and she closed her eyes, going to that place where she stared off into the distance, trying to remember.

I struck again, harder this time, but still, she didn't make a sound. Why was I doing this? Why did I want a reaction so much, when it was evident that a belt clearly hurt? The scarred skin didn't color, but the blank sides of her body had turned purple in line with the belt. I wasn't going to get a reaction, no matter how hard I tried.

Not unless I used the knife.

"Look at me, Ellie," I commanded again. She turned around, her breasts supple and smooth compared to her back, and her eyes stayed focused on mine this time, not daring to look anywhere else. "You want to prove yourself to me? Show me how you deserve to be helped? Why I shouldn't kill you?"

I pulled the knife out of my pocket once again, clicking it into place. Her chin shook back and forth, her mouth open, but her words never came.

It wasn't about Ellie's obedience at all anymore. She needed to face her fears, but this? This rage inside of me, it was about Muro. About knowing the fact that everything was about to change. Our criminal reign was in jeopardy, and it was easier to punish Ellie, knowing that I could keep her safe, if only she would obey me and learn to trust me. As if this punishment would make her mine.

She *was* mine, but only in her body. I wanted it all. And for that, I needed her complete trust.

"You're going to fuck yourself," I said. I pointed the knife handle towards her, then offered it. "Show me how badly you want it. How badly you want me." I forced a grin. "And if you put on a good show, I'll fuck you instead."

She didn't take the knife, so I put it in her hand. She lifted her shoulders and face, trying to get farther away from it.

"But Wil, there's—"

"There are no 'buts' when it comes to this," I sneered. "You either do, or you don't. But if you know what's good for you," I leaned down, pressing my nose into her neck, the knife between us, knowing that I was in danger too, letting her hold the knife, "you'll do as I tell you."

I kissed her neck, gently at first, but it wasn't until my teeth met her skin that she relaxed, letting go of her grip on the knife. I pressed my leg onto her pussy, making her grind into me, making sure that she could feel my dick hard against her. Made her moan for it.

Then I stood up and waited.

At first, she was hesitant, not knowing what to do. The knife was on the couch now, between her legs. She pulled down her jeans, revealing those sturdy thighs. She sat back on the couch, spreading her legs, and picked up the knife, biting her lip.

She turned the handle towards herself, but she couldn't move. Couldn't obey me.

I kneeled down, looking at her cunt and the knife's handle right next to it. Those scars on her pussy lips were darker in the moonlight, like strokes of black paint. I didn't know what had happened, but I knew it was terrible. A surgery gone bad, like I had assumed, wasn't even close. This was worse.

I looked up into her eyes. A tear slipped down her cheek. But she avoided me, not wanting to see my disappointment.

But it wasn't that at all. In some way, I understood. I didn't know what had happened to her, but I knew it was horrifying, whatever it was. Something so traumatic, her brain must have forced her to forget.

"What happened to you?" I said, my voice soft.

Her lip quivered. "I don't know," she whispered.

And if I ever found out what had happened to her, if anyone had dared to lay a hand on her, I wouldn't let them breathe ever again. I would make sure of it, bury their face into the ground, until they were one with the earth, ready to decay, being left to the vultures. But what I wanted, right now, was for her to trust me, to know that even if she had to face her fears, that it would be okay. That I would protect her, even if the knife scared her. I grabbed the knife and pressed it down, lower, until the handle was level with her cunt. She gasped, squirming at the touch, but I held her hand there, waiting for her to settle down.

I couldn't wait anymore.

"You can be my good girl, can't you, Ellie?" I asked. Her forehead scrunched, and her scent was pungent, the ripe fear mixed with vanilla lotion on her skin. "It's just the handle, Ellie. I'm not asking you to fuck yourself with the blade. I'm asking you to show me that you're stronger than your fears. That you can get past whatever blocked memory you're repressing, and show me what a good girl you are for me."

Her bottom lip was tucked between her teeth. I let go of my grip around hers, her fingers holding the knife, then I dipped my finger between her folds, the wetness making my eyes roll to the back of my skull. She was so fucking wet, so ready for me. I leaned in closer, wanting to take in her scent. That fear. It was intoxicating. Her breath tickled my face. I put my finger, wet with her desire, against her lips.

"You taste that?" I whispered. "Now, Ellie. Tell me how much you hate the knife."

The small flick of her tongue against my finger made my cock twitch, and I pressed my mouth against hers, both of us licking the juices off of my finger. I kept my hand in her hair, pulling it tight to show her exactly where she belonged. In my arms, letting me protect her.

She moaned, and I looked down. That brave little slut had put the knife's handle in her cunt. All by herself. She fucked her pussy with it, her hips rocking back and forth. I let go of her hair and leaned on the back of the couch, pulling my cock from my pants, fucking myself with my hand as I watched her. The glow in her eyes. The twitch of an orgasm already rolling through her body.

"Don't you dare fucking come," I growled. "That orgasm is mine, Ellie. *You* are mine." I grabbed her hand, making her drop the knife on the ground, refusing her that pleasure. Then I kneeled on the couch, hoisting up her hips, burying my cock deep inside of her. She squeezed me tight, making my cock hurt, as if she worked out those muscles too. I moaned and fucked her hard, each thrust deeper than the last, full of purpose. I wanted it to hurt. I wanted her to endure every inch of me, to know exactly what I wanted. What I was willing to take from her.

"You're mine," I murmured again. "Don't you ever fucking forget that, Elena Jordan."

Her eyes closed, her lips trembling. My dick throbbed, and I knew I was just as close as she was. When her body pulsed with those involuntary reactions, going over that edge, I couldn't stop myself. I came too, hot ropes of come filling her body, marking her as mine, all fucking mine. Body, mind, and soul. Even when fear told her to run, she couldn't help that she wanted this.

Neither of us could deny it. We wanted this, whatever we were, for better or for worse.

CHAPTER 10

Ellie

This time when we went to Jimmy's, I knew the rules. At first, I had thought Wil's rules were a joke, one I would follow along with as long as it kept me alive. But now, I wanted Wil to trust me, like I was beginning to trust him. I couldn't let go of the feeling that I was connected to his family somehow. The other woman they found in the woods was connected too, and who knows how many countless women were out there, connected and confused about what the hell was going on.

And Wil had brought new information, reminded me about Pebble Garden, our home town. I had this instinct too, that though we were connected, he didn't have anything to do with my sister's disappearance. Not in a malicious way.

Wil was standing at a roulette table, talking to a patron, slapping him on the back as they went through a round. I leaned on the bar. There were a few other men sitting at the stools beside me, but this time, I didn't make eye contact. Didn't start any conversations. The more I knew about Wil, the less I considered betraying him. I wasn't sure if I could trust him, but I knew that he hadn't lied. Every word that he said was the truth, which included that he would hurt any man that I spoke to. He might have been controlling with me, but his punishments always came with a purpose.

Like the knife. I knew now, even if I didn't like it, that it gave us more. Holding that kind of faith in each other, even if just for the moment, was like unlocking our souls.

An older man in a suit stood at the bar. He adjusted his cufflinks, then glanced at me and smiled. Gray hair weathered his scalp, thin and bare. A slinky doll of a woman with black hair and eyes, a metal collar tight around her neck, stood behind him, jotting a text message on her phone. I turned away from him, leaning to the side.

"You like rum and cokes?" he asked, his eyes blurry and wide. I didn't say a word. I gripped my glass of lemon water tightly. "You look like a rum and coke girl. How about it?" He hit the bar, and the bartender came to his attention. "Two rum and cokes, please," he said, "And a shot of whisky for me."

He can get you out, the voice said. *You can trust him. He'll free you from the others. And then you can kill your enemy.*

What enemy? I was so tired of the voice. I leaned my chin on my palm, turning even more away from the man. But once the bartender brought him his drink order, he slid one across to me.

"Cheers," he said. I didn't move. He scoffed. "What are you, too good to talk to me?" He tilted his head. "Too good for an old man?" I didn't care how old he was; I just wanted him to leave me alone. "You know, I can take good care of you. Sarah can tell you that." He sounded so pleased with himself. I wanted to throw up.

"Look at me," he barked, his voice loud. The entire room silenced, the music the only noise in the background. I turned toward him slowly, then looked into his eyes. He was drunk. Eyes bloodshot. His gait faulty. Even if it wasn't for Wil's rule, I wouldn't have appreciated this man's attitude. When a woman doesn't want your attention, you leave her alone.

And with all of my might, I held back what I wanted to do. "I'm not thirsty," I said. I was breaking Wil's rule, but the man had to stop.

You're losing your one chance, the voice said. *Ask him for help. Ask him!*

"Stupid cunt," the man said.

I slapped him as hard as I could. His face turned to the side, a red handprint on his cheek. The collared woman finally looked up from her phone, tilting her head at me.

"You fucking—" he started, but I was already past him.

I went straight to Wil. His face was emotionless, his jaw slack. It was clear that he had been watching the whole thing.

"Ellie," he started, "you should've—"

I put my hand on the back of his head and pulled him in for a kiss. I caressed his tongue, going deep, and he moaned. And suddenly, the screaming from that irate man ceased. Wil put a hand on my lower back, pulling me into his body, his cock twitching against me. His suit jacket made his whole body warm; I ran my fingers along his back. He grabbed my ass, squeezing it, as if to say, *Mine. This is mine.*

He broke away from the kiss, holding me at an angle, staring into my eyes. "What was that about?"

"Just wanted you to know," I said in a quiet voice, "that I'm yours."

He glanced behind me at the man, then turned back to me. "Let me take care of this," he muttered.

The collared woman cowered to the side, hiding behind the bar. The older man put up his hands in defense. "N-n-now l-listen, Wil," the man said, "I didn't know she was yours. How could I—"

Wil pulled him by the collar. "Let's deal with this in the back."

I thought I saw Wil give the collared woman a wink as he took the man away. The old man was heavy and gave a hell of a fight.

"We're friends, Wil!" the man shouted. "I've known you since you were in diapers. I was there when—"

His arms and legs swung, but Wil kept wrenching him toward a backdoor that led to a hallway. A few men dressed in plain clothes, helped anchor the older man, getting him into that back room. They must have been staff too.

The door closed behind them. The gambling hall fell silent once again. Someone turned up the music's volume, and soon, the games and conversation returned, as if nothing had happened.

"This is for you," the bartender said. It had celery, a cucumber slice, a lemon wedge, and a meatball sticking out of it. "From me," she said. "For slapping that sonofabitch. On the house."

I didn't get the feeling that Wil would ever make me pay for my own drink, but it was still a nice gesture.

"I don't drink," I said.

"I know," the bartender said. "I remember. It's a mocktail."

I raised a brow, then smiled. I lifted the glass, and she lifted a shot of vodka, and we both took our drinks. The sweet, tartness of pineapple and the fizz of carbonation greeted me. I nodded at her.

"Thanks," I said.

"Thank *you*," she said.

By the time I finished the drink, Wil reemerged from the back, his jacket off, his sleeves rolled up to his elbows, sweat on his brow. He joined me at the bar, then nodded at the collared woman waiting next to me.

"He had a heart attack," he said to the woman. "Drug related, probably. You should get home."

The woman ripped the collar off of her neck and ran towards the door that led back to the restaurant, a wild smile plastered on her face. Then Wil turned to me. A grin spread across his lips like wildfire. He grabbed my hand, pulling me towards the back door.

"Come on," he said.

"I thought you had work?"

He held open the door for me, and I went through, waiting in the hallway on the other side. He followed behind me. The corridor was empty. There were no signs of that old man.

"Don't you have work?" I asked again. "You were meeting someone, weren't you? To talk about a shipment—"

He shook his head, grabbing my shoulders and pushing me toward one of the doors at the end of the hallway.

"I'm not interested in that right now," he said.

We opened the door. A broad, wooden desk, covered in papers, was situated in the middle of the room. Two chairs were in front of it, with one chair in the back. With a sharp movement, Wil wiped his hand across the top of the desk, letting pages fall to the floor. Then he pressed me down, making me lay on it, with my back on the hard surface.

"That was impressive," Wil said. I blinked up at him, waiting for him to explain, but he grasped the sides of my top, then ripped it open, buttons clattering to the ground.

"I don't have another—"

"I don't care," he murmured, leaning down. He sucked my areola into his mouth, swirling his tongue around the nipple, the heat from his mouth spreading across my body in waves. I closed my eyes, grateful that in these moments, I couldn't see or feel anything beyond what our bodies were doing. Even when he made me fuck myself with the handle of a knife, even when he made me want to do it, I didn't see my sister in those nightmares. It was just us. Just Wil and me. No images. No visions. No voices. Just Wil, just me.

"You like showing off that you're with me," he breathed as he switched from one nipple to the other. "Is that it, Ellie? You like showing off."

"I just wanted him to know—"

"That I'm yours, and you're mine," he answered. He sucked my nipple, the nip of his teeth making my back arch, trying to get closer to him. He groaned. He pulled down my pants and underwear, letting them fall to the floor with the rest of the papers and buttons. "Even when you're not in my arms, you know that you belong to me."

He pulled out his cock, rubbing it in his hands as he stared down at me, his eyes glassy, as if in a trance. As if there was nothing in this world that could take him away from this moment. He wanted to fuck me, and Wil, a self-proclaimed criminal god, got what he wanted. I understood that now, and I wasn't afraid.

He pulled my ankles until my ass rested at the edge of the desk. Then he rubbed the head of his cock between my pussy lips, wetting it with my arousal. Then he eased himself inside.

"And you're ready for me," he grinned. A blush crossed my face. "Always ready for me." I couldn't help it. There was an undeniable urge inside of me to give in to whatever urges he wanted. Even when it scared the hell out of me, fucking myself with a knife, it was still an escape from the agony of not knowing where my sister was, what had happened to my memories, why I clung to a male voice inside of me when I didn't know who that voice belonged to. It was an escape to trust Wil. He thrust his hips hard, his cock hitting my cervix, a dull pain spreading across me; I grimaced. He held my hips, digging his fingers into my skin as if he was disciplining me. Punishing me for something I didn't understand.

"This is mine," he said. He thrust again. "You are mine, Ellie."

But the pain wasn't there anymore; it had been replaced by a glowing ember of desire, building in heat. He ran his thumb along my slit, using my moisture to rub my clit in circles. Passion gathered in my body, making me feel I might melt into the desk. And then I realized that this wasn't a punishment at all. Everything inside of me was focused on Wil, on what he could do for me. He could give me my sister. He could give me the answers. And he could give me freedom from my own mind.

And for once, I could just be.

CHAPTER 11

Wil

Most of the papers had been picked up from my office floor, arranged into two giant piles that I hadn't sorted through yet. Not that my office was usually pristine, but there was a method to the chaos, and that had clearly been disrupted. Any time I saw the evidence of the mess we had made, I smiled to myself. Derek caught me once and lifted a brow, but I offered no explanation. It was my secret.

He sat across from me, watching as I dialed Miles Muro's number. On the third ring, he picked up.

"Wil Adler," Muro said, his voice collected and raspy over the speakerphone. "So nice of you to finally call."

The message had been received, then. "I've got Derek with me," I said.

"We're calling to check in about the first shipment," Derek said. "Your men get back to you yet?"

"You mean the one you scrapped?" Muro's jaw clicked through the speaker. I tapped my fingers on the desk. "Yeah. I know."

Why did his response sound so dry? "You don't care?" I asked.

"Now, now, Wilhelm. Those are my men. *Of course* I care," he paused. "But I like to keep things interesting, don't you? Just because one of my men died due to a misunderstanding, doesn't mean we can't be *friends*."

Friends? What was he getting at? I pressed on: "You sent us cocaine. Bad cocaine. I thought you were more of the heroin type?"

"That is just one of our many products," he said. I lifted a brow at Derek, who mouthed 'weapons.' "I figured you could use it to bolster your own stock."

"The agreement was heroin," Derek said.

"Narcotics aren't even my top product, nor is it my concern whether or not you like it. And honestly, those two chumps I sent?" He laughed. "Figured they would be lucky to get out. And either way," he paused for effect, audibly sneering on the other end, "we'll be selling in Sage City."

"With cutbacks," I said.

"We'll be *selling*," Muro repeated. I glanced at Derek, but he pressed his lips together, calculating a plan. "But unless you want to pay for ammunition or artillery, then I've got nothing to add right now."

"You know what that means?" Derek asked.

"I do, and frankly, I don't care. I've got too much to deal with to add the Adlers to the top of the list," he scowled. "We can deal with this later."

The line went dead. Derek sighed, then rubbed his hands over his face.

"What are you thinking?" I asked.

"Muro's got something else going on," he said. "Maybe he's in over his head. But I'm sick of waiting around for him to strike. He hasn't respected our family since day one."

I was sick of it too. "Think we absorb his company? Like Gerard wants?"

"Not without killing him."

I rubbed my forehead. It was possible to kill Muro, I had no doubt about that. But it wasn't as simple as sending Axe or another enforcer. Muro was a boss and had protection that was unknown, at this point, but undoubtedly vast.

"Muro doesn't care about an alliance one way or another," I said. Derek nodded. I thought about Muro's headquarters. They seemed minimal—the white walls, white furniture, everything bare and empty, as if there was no reason to draw attention to any of it, except for the fact that it was stark. But that didn't mean anything. Seeing the sheer size of the place and the particularly arranged structure meant that he likely had an army packed inside, waiting to protect him.

"You think the murders in the woods are connected to him?" I asked. "The women?"

My subtext: Ellie?

"The way he acted just now?" Derek asked. I nodded, and he shook his head. "He's dealing with other shit. Not just us. And honestly, it doesn't make sense." He tapped a fist against his lips. "Why not send a message, one that's loud and clear? Not the silent deaths of our men, but claiming it, actually claiming it, to show us that he meant war? And the women?" Derek shrugged. "Axe said the second one hasn't spoken since he took her to the workroom."

Well, the reasoning behind that was obvious. "She's been caged, for fuck's sake."

"Yeah, but you know. For Axe, he's taking pretty damn good care of her."

That wasn't saying much, but still, it was better than the alternative.

"Any word from Ellie?" Derek asked.

"Kiley called. Said Ellie used to practice martial arts at a women's gym, or club. Something like that," I said.

Derek laughed. "That doesn't surprise me." He must have been thinking about the first night we met when she kneed me in the stomach.

I grinned. "She knows her place now."

"I figured." Derek stood and I did too. "I don't know what to think of this." He ran his hands through his hair. "If it's all Midnight Miles Corporation, then we only have one enemy to deal with. But if it's someone else, someone new?" He squeezed his fists tight. "I don't know what's worse."

I didn't know either. Neither of the options were particularly good news for us. But if I could help Ellie figure out what was going on, maybe we could get closer to finding that answer. Then, we could make a plan.

"Ellie is the key," I said.

Derek nodded. "When you figure it out, let me know. I'm going to talk to Gerard," he said.

"Let me know too."

I walked him out, gave my men instructions, then went back to the penthouse.

***

This time, when I entered, Ellie was sitting next to the fireplace between the front room and the kitchen. It almost startled me. Hearing me, she turned and smiled. I stood still. It was the first smile she had given me, probably ever. It was hard not to smile back.

I took a seat beside her.

"How was work?" she asked.

I shrugged. She didn't need to hear the details about the situation with Muro. "Nothing interesting. Let's talk about you."

She straightened, the top button of her shirt undone, teasing me. The curve of her breast visible in the opening. "What's up?"

"I promised to look after your sister," I started, "but I'm going to be honest. I also need to figure out where you came from, because of what's been going on."

"Like what?"

"There have been a few bodies found," I paused, gauging her reaction. I had mentioned them before, but only in passing. She blinked, but otherwise, had no expression. "We're thinking it has to do with you and the other woman."

"Does she have a name yet?"

I shook my head. "We don't want to lose any more lives," I said. "Those were our men. Good men." We had plenty more, but I didn't like losing good help. Ellie nodded, her eyes never leaving mine, to prove that she wasn't hiding anything. "So let's start with something easy. Do you remember anything else about that martial arts gym?" I traced my memory for the name. "Women's Elite Social Club?"

"Social club?" she asked. "Women's Elite sounds familiar, but not the social club part."

I shrugged. "I guess that's how they got around the laws. But go on. Tell me about Women's Elite."

Ellie touched her chin, her eyes fluttering in front of her.

"Did I start studying there recently?" she asked.

"Looks like you started soon after your parents died."

She touched her arms, skimming her fingers across them. "So it's been a few years then."

"Yes."

She looked up then, her eyes locked on mine. She scooted across the couch, closer to me, then held my hands. "I need you to hold me." She straddled me, sitting so close that the curves of her ass rolled against my thighs. Her pussy was warm, even through her jeans and my pants.

After that kiss the other day, it shouldn't have surprised me, but I still wasn't used to her being affectionate on her own. Without me pressuring her. My cock bulged, loving it.

"And to what do I owe this pleasure?" I asked.

"It's the only way I can think clearly," she said. I opened my mouth to speak, but she moved my hands so that I was touching her back, and I forgot what I was going to say. I rubbed her shoulders, massaging her, squeezing her muscles, letting my hands roam freely, enjoying her softness over the hard muscles.

"When did my parents die?" she asked.

"You were in high school."

Ellie shook her head back and forth, her voice higher in pitch: "Yes. And I had to take care of Julie. She was in middle school, almost in high school." Her head didn't stop moving, as if it was all suddenly coming back to her, and the movement helped it restore. "So it was just us. My neighbor helped me get emancipation, but I had to get a job. Had to prove that I could take care of Julie. Because if no one else was going to take care of us, I had to take care of her. Be her mom and dad. Because if I didn't—"

She stopped, her eyes falling to her lap. A few seconds passed.

"Then what?" I asked.

"Julie wanted so badly to be free, to learn things the hard way." Ellie shook her head. "I just hope I didn't let anything bad happen to her."

Julie, at the time of her disappearance, was almost nineteen and would be close to twenty by now.

"She's an adult," I said. "She's got to make her own choices."

"But I—" Her bottom lip quivered. "I couldn't protect her. It didn't matter what I did. Shelter her. Let her free. Somewhere in between." Her eyes filled with tears. "She still disappeared."

A heavy weight settled in my stomach. I hated seeing Ellie like that. I rubbed a thumb across her cheek. "You can't be with her all of the time," I said. "She might be okay. Off with her girlfriends or a boyfriend. You never know."

"I know the statistics," Ellie said, her voice squeaking. She stiffened, then shook away the tears. "You said it's been over a year and a half, right?"

I nodded, not wanting to say the word aloud, knowing how it might hurt her to hear the truth. Ellie shrunk down, all of that strength I had grown used to seeing in her dissipating before my eyes. I couldn't let her forget that part of herself.

"Hey," I said. I held her chin, and those blue eyes struck me. "We'll figure this out," I said. "You don't worry. Let me worry about it."

And for whatever reason, that seemed to let her relax. The tension in her body released, and she snuggled into my chest.

"My contact also found that you had social media pages," I said, "but, of course, they were taken down after you disappeared."

"Oh?" she asked.

"But that doesn't mean they're gone forever." I winked, then ran the backs of my fingers down her arm. She shivered at the touch, and I grinned. Should I ruin another perfectly good shirt? It was definitely an option on my mind.

But we had other business to attend to. I pulled out my phone and looked at the email from Kiley and read aloud the first post that came into view: "*Classic New Years: The gym is packed, and I no longer have my corner. I'm tempted to ask the yoga pants chick if she wants to fight me for it. On the mat, of course. But I want my window view!*"

Ellie laughed. "That sounds about right."

"Another gem," I said, then I read another, "*Cheat day means I can eat an entire box of donuts by myself, yes? That's exactly what cheat day is. Please and thank you.*" I raised my brows at her playfully. "An entire box?"

She shrugged. "Probably a baker's dozen."

I read another. "*This is not a drill. Seriously. Tequila is on BOGO. Get your margarita-drinking self over here. Then save me a pitcher!*" I tilted my head. "You can really eat and drink, huh?"

"I don't think I've ever had a pitcher of margaritas by myself," she smiled, "But hey, it's possible."

These were too damn funny not to read aloud. "*Even at max volume, these earbuds will never be loud enough for Metalheads.*" I smirked. "Metalheads? I took you as more of a boy band type."

She shoved my shoulder. "Don't you ever insult me again." She quirked her brow. "Unless you sing?"

I chuckled. "We don't usually get voice lessons in the mafia. Though I'm sure my mother would have scheduled them, had I asked."

I turned back to the email, knowing the ones I had actually wanted to talk about were up next. My serious tone leaked out, no matter how badly I wanted to shrug it off: "*Those of you that go to Pebble Garden U, have any of you seen my sister? Blond. Skinny. Bouncy. Way too happy to be alive? Probably has stolen lipstick and sunglasses in her pocket? Tell Julie to call me. NOW.*"

The smile fell from Ellie's face.

"She was always stealing stuff from stores," she said quietly. "Lipsticks. Even a pacifier once." She looked down. "I never understood that."

Based on the records Kiley had found, it didn't seem like Ellie and Julie were hard for money. A modest living, sure, but never behind on bills. Ellie had worked at the local grocery store for years and had worked her way up to a managerial position.

"Why'd she steal?" I asked.

Ellie shrugged. "For the thrill of it, I guess. She just wanted to push boundaries all the time."

I turned back to my phone. "*Please share this. I can't reach Julie. But someone has to know something.*"

I showed my phone to Ellie; it had a picture of her sister, with a phone number to call, as well as her stats: height, weight, hair color, eye color, age. When it came to their facial structure, Julie and Ellie looked exactly alike, the same square face, the same blue eyes. But Julie had blond hair and thin cheeks.

Ellie shrunk down again, and I cupped her face, trying to knock her out of that attitude.

"You can't give up," I said. "We don't know where she is."

"She's out there," Ellie nodded. "But who knows if I'll ever be able to find her. I just want to know that she's okay."

How could she live like this? Not knowing?

And how could I not give her that peace? I had to help her. Not just for my family, but for her. It was the least I could do.

"Is anything else coming back to you?" I asked.

She shook her head. "Not right now. But—" she slid her hand down my chest, then tugged on the button of my pants. My cock filled with arousal and our eyes met.

She was initiating. Again. Those big blues peered up at me.

"What?" I asked, my voice hoarse with lust.

She kneeled on the ground before me. "I want to show you how grateful I am for your help." She pushed apart my knees. My cock thickened against my leg, stretching my pants, and she eyed it, licking her lips.

I should have been thrilled. This meant that I had won her loyalty, had made her see that she *was* mine, that she couldn't fight it anymore. But I couldn't believe it. She had been resistant all of the other times, and had more emotional baggage than anyone I knew. There was no way that this could be real. Because otherwise, what made this moment different? What was to say that this wasn't a trick?

"I know you're grateful," I said in a husky voice, trying to hide the fact that I was turned on. "You have to be." Because she was technically my prisoner.

"This isn't about that," she said, reading my mind. She put her hands on my knees. "You're helping me find my past and my family." She closed her eyes, a smile spreading across her lips. "Family is one of the most important things we have in this life. You—" She paused, rubbing her hands up and down my inner thighs. My cock twitched when she came near it. "You get that. You get me."

My heart ached at those words. Family. How was that the one abstract that tied us together? And how could she be so strong when the entire world was on edge? Her sister was missing, her parents were gone, and I had ripped her from her life and made her a permanent fixture in mine. And yet still, she had found the direct path to my soul and brought a dagger to it—family, fucking family—twisting the knife, to make sure that I could never resist her again.

And why should I resist her?

A god didn't resist what he wanted.

I leaned forward and grabbed the back of her hair, tightening my grip, then quickly unzipped my pants, letting my cock spring out. I shoved it in her mouth until she gagged. I expected her to bite me, and when she didn't, I bent down and played with her nipples. She cooed, pressing against me until I twisted them so hard that she tried to pull off of my cock, but I didn't let her. I kept my hand tight in her hair, pulling her in, my cock in her throat until I heard the gag reflex kick in again. Then I relaxed a little, giving her an inch to breathe. Once she gathered herself, her lips still on my shaft, I shoved it back down again, holding the back of her head.

"Bite me," I said. She gurgled a word and looked up at me, her mouth still stuffed with my cock. "Did I stutter?" I growled. "I said 'bite me,' bitch."

Her teeth pressed into me timidly. "Harder." She pressed her teeth together, but still, I wanted more. The primal craving kicked in. "Harder!"

She bit in as hard as she could, and all of the blood surged to the head of my cock, giving me a head rush, and I growled so deeply that our bodies shook as one. I realized then, that this wasn't about being a god anymore. I controlled Ellie's fate like a god controlled a mortal's, but that was only one facet in a larger world we had created together. Ellie had found a way to snake herself into my soul, corkscrewing herself in until she could never be untethered from me. As a goddess herself, she had forced me to see how powerful she truly was, how she could render me speechless with her vulnerability and stun me with her strength. And I wanted all of that for myself.

Using her hair as reins, I pulled her back and forth, the twinge of pain from her teeth still lingering on my skin even in her wet, warm mouth. She spread her legs and started rubbing herself through her pants. I cursed myself for not stripping her naked before we started, but I wasn't going to stop using her mouth now.

"That's it, you dirty bitch," I said. "Sucking my cock like a hungry little whore." She moaned, and I used her mouth, glaring down as her hips wiggled and she started to get close to orgasm too. I tightened my grip, shoving my cock into her throat again and again until tears bled down the sides of her face.

And with that, we came. What we had was dangerous. Neither of us could resist the urge to destroy each other.

And I knew it would ruin us both.

CHAPTER 12

Ellie

Wil's hands skimmed my lower back as he went behind me into the kitchen. Everything inside of me connected to that point of contact, making it feel as if he could burn a hole right through me. Soft pajama pants rested on his toned hips, and with no shirt to speak of, his abs were rippled like a model from a catalog. His dark hair and eyes contrasted with his features so that he was gorgeous, but normal. No one would suspect that he was part of a crime family.

And for a few minutes, life felt that way. *Normal.* There wasn't a voice anymore. And that worry that held onto my heart, the need to know where Julie was, had been soothed for the time being, because I knew that we would find her together.

"Why don't I cook us breakfast?" he said.

I raised a brow. Wil had a fully stocked kitchen, one that Maddie came to refill regularly, though I had yet to see him cook. My guess was that he usually ate at Jimmy's. Wil kissed my cheek, then motioned for me to sit at the dining table, which had a view of the kitchen. I watched him.

Was Wil really going to cook breakfast for me?

It was weirdly normal. If anyone walked in on us, seeing what looked like a man cooking for his girlfriend, they would have thought we were a regular couple. But that was so far from the truth.

Still, I couldn't help but think of him like that. The longer I was with him, the more the voice dimmed, as if it could no longer fight the power Wil had over me—at least when we were around each other. So it was less work. Less draining. Because Wil made me forget.

Wil laid bacon into the frying pan. The coffee pot dinged, and he poured two steaming mugs. He caught me staring at him, and brought a cup over, placing it on the table in front of me. I thanked him, blushing under his hot gaze.

"Take it off," he said. He gestured at my clothes. My chest burned, thinking of being on display for him. Here it was, the part that separated us from 'normal.'

"I knew there was a catch," I said, my voice teasing.

"Nothing is free," he winked.

As he cooked—bacon, scrambled eggs, toast, hashed browns, even cut up some fresh fruit—he kept an eye on me, his eyes lingering on my breasts, my waist, my hips. And one point, I considered playing with myself, seeing if he would cook faster or give up entirely, but by the time that thought crossed my mind, he brought the plates to the table. I went to put on my shirt, but he shook his head.

"No clothes," he said. "I want to see what's mine."

I blushed, the color creeping across my cheeks and neck. No one had ever wanted me like this. He didn't care if I was posed in a certain way, or if I was relaxed beside him. He wanted me naked. And he just wanted *me*.

I almost expected him to fondle me as we ate, but for the first few minutes, we ate in silence. I gave an occasional interruption to murmur how amazing everything tasted. I was grateful; it had been years since someone had cooked for me, maybe since my parents died.

"What happened to the woman?" I asked. "The woman from the woods."

"She's hanging out with my brother, Axe," Wil said. I had a feeling 'hanging out' was a euphemism for being tortured, but I didn't say that aloud. "If he weren't so concerned with her being a spy," he continued, "I'm sure she'd be living in the main house with Derek and Gerard, but Axe is suspicious. He's convinced that someone is after us."

"Us?" I asked.

"Yeah. My family." He shrugged, forking a knife full of potatoes. "We've got plenty of enemies."

"Everyone has enemies," I offered, trying to downplay it.

"But this has to be a big one." He speared a piece of honeydew, then stared at it, marveling at the shades of green. "Leaving bodies like that. Chopped up." My heart clenched. I had remembered that. He had made the connection between my nightmares of my sister, and the murders of his men in the woods. "No one's claiming it," he said. "Maybe because they're afraid of us." He laughed, then ate the melon.

"Do I have any reason to be afraid of you?" I asked hesitantly.

"Not since you learned the rules," he grinned. "But seriously. Everyone in this state knows you don't mess with an Adler. We conquer. Annihilate. Rule. That's just what we do." He sighed. "Hell, I wouldn't be surprised if—"

A sharp ringing noise pulsed through my brain, making all other sounds fizz out. I dropped my fork, watched it fall on the plate, but I couldn't hear it clatter. All I heard was that wiry noise, pushing everything else away. I held my forehead.

Wil mouthed my name, but his voice was muffled as if he were speaking through a wall. He put a hand on my back, and suddenly, the ringing stopped. I blinked my eyes, trying to make sure that it was really gone, and when I confirmed that, I turned to Wil, out of breath.

"Are you all right?" he asked.

"I'm fine," I said. But something was off inside of me, like I was going to be sick. I could hardly move without wanting to puke.

But I decided to ignore it. Things were finally going right with Wil; I didn't want to ruin it with my paranoia. The ringing must have been in my imagination. Tinnitus. Too much loud music. Everything could be easily explained.

Just like I could logically explain my trust for Wil when I knew I shouldn't have trusted him at all.

But that didn't seem right either.

What the hell was going on?

I picked up my fork, stabbing a bite of eggs, but I wasn't hungry anymore. Still, I wanted to be normal. To pretend. To move on. To look forward for once.

"What were you saying?" I asked. "Something about your brother?"

"Well, it's not just my brother," he said, eager to get back into the conversation. "You see, we've got a reputation," he smirked. "The legacy follows us. So whoever is messing with us, knows that we're the Adlers and that our name carries weight. We can't be scared easily—"

The ringing was sharp, as if it could slice through the tissue of my brain, shredding it until it was mush. I grabbed my head, the fork dropping again, and this time, everything went white. My vision. Wil's voice. Everything was gone.

Kill him.

I blinked it out, trying to wish away the voice, but it was louder. Warmth landed on my back, a hand was holding me there. But then I heard it again.

Kill him.

"Ellie!" a man shouted.

I blinked my eyes. It was Wil. He was holding me against the wall, shaking my shoulders. Trying to wake me up.

"What the hell is going on?" he asked.

I stared at him, trying to find the proof that I knew was there. Who was he?

"What did you say your last name was?" I asked.

"Adler," he said slyly. "You hear about us in Pebble Garden too?"

I blinked my eyes rapidly, trying to get everything back into focus. Yes, I had heard things. I had seen things. Knew the carnage his family had wrought on innocent lives.

Hack his body—

The voice felt as if it were coming from inside of me, building in my heart and bursting through to my brain. Wil furrowed his brows, forcing a smile.

"Are you sure you're alright?" he asked. "Do you need to lie down?"

I shook my head. I couldn't lie down. Not now.

—into pieces.

"I'm fine," I said, though I knew I was anything but. Just when I thought I had it under control, the voice was stronger now. I knew this wasn't over. I had almost trusted Wil. Almost thought I could work with him. As a team. Imagined us as a normal couple.

Cut him like he cut her.

I forced a smile, and that seemed to relax him. His shoulders loosened, though he still watched me.

"You need ibuprofen? Acetaminophen? Something stronger?" he asked.

I shook my head. No. I needed his head on a platter.

But this wasn't the same Wil as the voice had said it was. It couldn't be. He couldn't be responsible for her death.

But he is. He killed your sister.

I followed him to the table, and it was as if my body was someone else's and I was watching myself go through the motions. What was left of my breakfast was scattered on the table and floor: some of the eggs and potatoes, a bite of toast, a quartered strawberry.

"What happened?" I asked.

Hack his body—

"I should be asking you that question. You don't remember?" he asked. I shook my head. "You started screaming, grabbing your head."

"A bad headache," I mumbled.

His forehead scrunched up. "Sure," he said.

—so that he'll never come back.

I kneeled down, picking up a chunk of strawberry. Wil shook his head. "I'll pick it up later," he said. Red juice marked its spot on the floor, like a chalk outline at a crime scene. Like a warning.

The image of her chopped up body surfaced in my mind: the blood on the ground, soaking into the earth. Her eyes gazing to the sky, never to see again.

—so that he'll never kill again.

Wil put our plates and mugs on the kitchen counter. He smiled at me, and I smiled back, but it wasn't real. How could he stand there, acting like everything was fine, as if he was helping me, when he was the reason I was there in the first place?

He killed your sister, Ellie.

I knew that now. Knew that that's what I was doing here. If I took down at least one Adler, even if I died trying, then that would be enough. I could do my part to avenge my sister.

He came towards me, placing a hand on my lower back. The contact made me flinch. I hated that I was naked now. Bare and vulnerable and exposed to him, when he deserved nothing.

But if that's what made him think I was weak, then so be it.

I closed my eyes, holding my forehead again. *He murdered her when she had no way to defend herself,* the words vibrated in my chest, coming from my core. *He murdered her, Ellie. Cold-blooded murder.*

"Let's get you into bed," he said. "You need some rest."

"No." I grabbed his arm, holding him tight. I stared into his eyes and saw two men: the man who I had grown attached to, the one who had fucked me and used me and made me feel more alive than I had ever felt, the one who helped me find memories when I thought I had none, when I thought I had nothing.

And I saw the man who had murdered my sister.

But it couldn't be him. It had to be his brothers, his father—they were all responsible. But it couldn't have been Wil's hands who had taken her life. He wasn't like that.

Was he?

No. He had to pay. All of them did.

Wil cleared his throat, and finally, I continued: "No. I want you to fuck the headache out of me."

"That's an old wives' tale," he said.

Try harder, the voice said. *You must stop him before he kills another. Innocent lives are at stake.*

"Please," I begged, making my voice meek. I squeezed his arm, and finally, he smiled.

"We're going to play my way," he said.

I nodded. Whatever made him trust me.

When he brought me to his room, I knew exactly what he would do. Kiss me, fuck me, force me to take his come, and when the right moment came, that's when I would do it.

The knife was already in his pocket, hard against my skin as he leaned into me. I scolded myself. Of course I couldn't trust him. What kind of person keeps a knife in their pajama pockets, unless they had bad intentions? He guided me, pressing my back against the wall, then held my hands down and sneered at me.

There was another knife on the nightstand.

Get the knife, Ellie.

I nodded to myself, calming the voice. Yes. I would do that.

"You're a filthy whore," he murmured. "My fucking toy. You need to get off all of the time, don't you? You can't get enough of my cock."

Those words would have made me shudder before. To hear him call me his, to know that he wanted me. But the words were empty now. They meant nothing.

I had to force myself to pretend.

Play his game. Then get the knife.

White stars fluttered along the sides of my vision, and I smiled then, giving Wil the biggest, sexiest smile I could muster. His chest lifted, and I inched myself carefully toward the nightstand. I rested my ass on it, slipping the knife under me, the metal cold on my ass.

The knife didn't scare me anymore. Wil had given me that.

And I knew what to do.

Now, Ellie.

As if on command, Wil removed his other knife from his pocket, the blade brandishing in a hardy click. He held it to my throat. I looked him in the eye and saw what was really there.

You killed my sister, I thought, staring into those dark, violent eyes. You killed her. You killed my sister. She was only eighteen.

I blinked as hard as I could, trying to make the urges disappear. But I knew it was true. I had to kill him.

He had done this to her. To me.

I had to kill Wil Adler.

He sneered at me, then dipped down, kissing my neck, biting it. I dug my nails into his skin, wanting so badly to hurt him, but I held back, knowing I had to wait until the right moment.

He pulled out his cock, the pajama bottoms slipping down to his ankles. But when he tried to fuck me, I was dry. I couldn't pretend to be turned on now. Not when I knew his secret.

My secrets. My past.

I could finish this now.

Do it for her, the voice said. *Now, Ellie.*

He raised a brow, questioning my lack of arousal.

"It's the headache," I lied. "Please, Wil. Fuck me."

He spat into his hand, rubbing his cock with the saliva, then rubbed the tip against me, wetting my folds. He slipped into me then, my slit pulling at his skin, trying to stop him, but then he pulled away and rammed back into me, moaning as he penetrated all the way down to his hilt. His cock slammed into my cervix. And I felt nothing.

There was no pain. No pleasure. Only the urge.

This was what I had been trained to do, what I had wanted all along.

His eyelids lowered, sweat gathering on his skin, and I grit my teeth, staring into his soul, unable to blink. This wasn't right. It didn't make sense. Wil wasn't her killer.

But it was a lie. A story he had made me believe. Because he knew what he had done, and I had to stop him.

He pulled my hips closer, and the knife slid underneath me. I carefully grabbed it with one hand, making sure he didn't notice.

This was the only way I could move on.

Now, Ellie.

Wil leaned into me, his breathing growing heavy. He was almost there. Almost completely disarmed by his orgasm.

I had always known that I would do this: wait until the right moment, then strike.

So why didn't it feel right? Why did I want to stop?

A tear gathered at the corner of my eye. His pupils focused on it for a second, watching as the drop of liquid ran down the side of my face.

"I'm sorry," I whispered.

But I had to do this. I had no choice.

"What?" he asked.

Now, Ellie!

I shot my free hand toward him, whipping it around in a circle until I grabbed the knife out of his grip. I lunged forward and stabbed the knife into his dominant hand, aiming the other knife at his throat. But I hesitated at the last second and cut his cheek instead.

I looked down. The knives in my hands. The blades were covered in blood.

Wil's blood.

He stared at me, his chest panting, his hand a wreck. He touched his cheek, the blood staining his fingers, redder than the juice from the breakfast strawberry.

"Ellie?" he asked.

And I knew, then, that he wasn't the killer. Wil was a criminal, but he hadn't murdered my sister. Because she—no, *we*—we never meant anything to him. We were nothing to a crime family.

So why couldn't I let it go?

I didn't know anymore. I never had.

CHAPTER 13

one year earlier

Ellie

The green trim on the blue building would have fit a beach town, but this was Pebble Garden. A college town stuck in the middle of nowhere. The police department, like many of the other businesses throughout the area, had been subjected to the flash deals on cans of paint. And that's what I held onto as I walked through the entrance, using the annoyingness of it all to distract myself from what was actually bothering me. I strode to the front desk. The woman behind the counter recognized me, nodding her acknowledgment. I leaned on the counter.

"Is Officer Shines here today?" I asked.

"Let me check for you," she said, then disappeared into the hallway. I tapped my fingers on the counter, silently pleading that Shines would listen this time. When I had first asked for his help, he had been sympathetic, but now, I was just another case in the middle of the pile. His clean-shaven face came into view. I straightened, holding out my hand.

"Officer," I said.

He took my hand, his grip loose. "What can I do for you, kiddo?" he asked.

I ignored the nickname and held up a flyer. *The Skyline Shift* was written in bold letters at the top. *A perspective scope transformation camp for young women*, followed by an address and acceptance requirements. A logo with four hills squished together, leaning to the side. *Fly toward the horizon today!*

"Have you ever heard about this?" I asked.

He took the flyer and glanced it over. "Is it a bible camp? Summer school? Daycare?"

I shook my head. "I guess the company pays people to stay there while they do modification experiments? Well," I paused, trying to think of the right words, "I guess it's more behavioral therapy stuff. I can't tell, honestly." Shines handed me back the flyer and my shoulders sank. He was already dismissing it. "Keep it," I said, pushing it back toward him. "I've got another in my car."

He folded it, tucking it into his back pocket. "What about this place?"

"What if my sister went there?" I asked. "Her car was found in the same city, and she had their website bookmarked on her laptop." His hands were on his hips, his eyes looking down at a spot on the floor. Waiting for me to finish. I was losing him.

"Why were you looking at her laptop?" he asked. What he meant was that we had talked about this. I couldn't keep obsessing over her.

"I just," I started, but I didn't want to say it. "It's been six months. Six months today, actually, Officer."

"I understand," he said. He tilted his head. "But you've got to understand that some people, you just can't find. Not unless they return on their own. In all likelihood, she probably ran off with a boyfriend. Doesn't *want* to be found, you know?" He shrugged. "There's been no evidence of wrongdoing."

As if finding her car in the middle of a neighboring city wasn't a hint that something had gone horribly wrong. I had told him hundreds of times that Julie had boyfriends, but none that she took seriously enough to elope with. She was mischievous, but she wasn't *that* rebellious.

"I'm the only family she has," I said.

"And as soon as we find out anything about her, we'll give you a call."

There were pen marks on the countertop in a scattered pattern, as if a mother had held her baby while the infant went to town claiming their territory. No one had bothered to clean it up. They had more important things to do, including helping out missing persons cases that were *fresh*. That weren't dead ends yet. I closed my fist, but then opened my fingers and nodded at Officer Shines. This was what I had expected.

But why did it hurt so much if I knew what was coming?

"You're right," I said bitterly. "Thanks."

He put a hand on my shoulder. "It's going to be okay, kiddo."

My heart shrank. The walk back to my car seemed longer than usual, each step forward sinking me deeper into a pit of despair. I slid into the driver's seat, then stared at the wheel. In my peripherals, there was another copy of the flyer, lying on the passenger seat.

The Skyline Shift, it said. The address showed that it was only an hour or so away. The police couldn't help me anymore, and Julie's friends knew nothing. They had moved on too, claiming they missed her, but apathetic when it came to the search.

Which left me.

Why not go to the camp myself? What was stopping me?

Screw it.

I turned the key in the ignition and set the GPS on my phone for the coordinates. A renewed sense of passion washed over me. I turned on the radio, finding a song I enjoyed, then turned the volume all the way up. If no one would help me figure this out, then I would do it for myself. And maybe I would go to my deathbed still trying to find Julie, but I needed to do this. I *had* to find her. For my own sake.

The drive seemed quick. I kept the music up the whole time until I saw a high shrubbed barrier, only exposing the tops of rounded white buildings. I pulled up to the entry kiosk and could see the rest of those domed structures from my car: each was two to three stories high, identical, laid out in rows. Some had shiny glass sides on the flat ends, while others were closed off. But I was too far away to see what was going on.

A security guard wearing all white leaned down from his post.

"Name?" he asked.

"Elena Jordan."

"State your purpose?"

I wrinkled my nose. What was this?

"I wanted to check out the camp. The Skyline Shift?" I lifted my shoulders. "I'm in the right place, right?"

He listened to his earpiece, tapping his finger against it. His eyelids lowered, then he pointed to a building on the far side of the property.

"Dr. Bates will meet you there."

"Dr. Bates?"

He nodded. "Enjoy your flight toward the horizon."

Then the security guard straightened. I shrugged it off. The catchphrase was eerie, but they had to say *something*, and it was probably just me. I had been on edge since Julie had gone missing. But I drove slowly. The parking lot was huge, but there weren't many cars in it, as if they had expected more people. In between the semi-circle buildings, a long line of women dressed in white uniforms walked in a straight line, their eyes forward, their posture straight, disappearing into another building.

A man in a lab coat with a crisp red tie was standing on the sidewalk outside of the buildings. I slammed the car door, and the sound vibrated through the lot. The air smelled fresh, like pine trees and dirt, and I tried to put a positive spin on it. No matter what happened right now, being in the fresh air was good. I could even take a trip to Rubble River on the way back. Finding Julie here would be a bonus. I looked at the flyer one more time, hovering over the words, *a perspective scope transformation camp for young women*. What was a perspective scope transformation anyway?

I guessed I would find out.

I held out a hand. "You must be Dr. Bates?"

"And you must be Elena Jordan. Do you go by Lena?"

"Ellie, actually," I said. We shook hands, and his grip was firm and deliberate as if he was trying to prove something.

"Ellie. So very pleased to meet you. How did you hear about our camp?"

A breeze blew between us, rustling his grayish-brown curly hair. Streaks of white sprang up throughout as if his hair had been brushed with bleach. A metallic odor drifted from him but mixed with the wind, it was hardly noticeable.

"My sister, actually," I said. "Julie Jordan. Do you know her?"

He thought for a moment, but gave a slight shake of the head. "Can't say that I do. That would be a breach of contract, and besides, I'm afraid that I don't get to personally meet all of our recruits." His smile widened, exposing his gums. "But if she is here, rest assured that she's in good hands."

He didn't move. Stayed still. As if he was waiting for me to leave.

"Well," I paused, "Can I have a tour?"

"Ah," he said. "We actually don't allow tours unless we find that a recruit is serious about their stay here."

"You're kidding?" His mouth didn't move: still those same gums, bright red and wet, mocking me in his perfect smile. "How do I know if I'm serious about going here *unless* I take a tour? I drove over an hour to get to this place."

"We recruit from all over the world." What he actually meant? *I don't care where you came from. Go home.*

I clenched my fists, then unrolled my fingers again. It was a habit, a bad one. But I was good about only letting out my aggression at the gym. You had to be purposeful with your emotions. And right now, I couldn't let my frustration control me.

"I am serious," I said. "Give me a tour."

"I'm afraid I can't do that."

I grit my teeth. Did I have to beg?

"Can you at least find out if my sister is here? She's been missing for six months."

He pressed a finger to his lips, as if considering it, but his eyes never blinked, still staring soullessly into mine.

"If she was here, rest assured that she's in good hands. Good day, Ellie Jordan." He motioned toward my car. "We hope you enjoyed your flight toward the horizon. May you have a safe drive back."

I turned toward the car, almost as if he had given me no choice but to leave, but then I froze. Dr. Bates wasn't moving. He was waiting until I left. And I knew, deep down, that I could go back home. Move on. Try interviewing all of Julie's friends once again. I could even visit her professors from her last semester, try to see if they recognized her picture at all. If they remembered anything weird that had happened. And I could mark the Skyline Shift off as another dead end.

Or I could refuse to take 'no' for an answer.

I turned around. "Dr. Bates," I said. Still, that weird smile was plastered on his face, as if he was a skipping record. "I'm very serious about my stay here. I want to prove myself. To you, and to the rest of the camp."

He shifted then, taking a step closer toward me. "Do you know what we do here?" The smile dropped then, his head tilting to the side. I shook my head. "We help lost women find their way into a new purpose. All it takes is a perspective shift, a new way of looking at the world around you. A flight toward the horizon."

Why did that motto sound so demented?

"All right?" I said.

"I'm afraid you're only here to seek your sister." That was true, but why did that have to be a bad thing? "At the Skyline Shift, we give women a new purpose. We provide for them; we pay for their time here, and give them a place to stay. If you wish to have your entire world view changed, then, of course, you may prove it." The smile took over his face once again, and his head straightened. "I assume you've seen the flyer on our website?" I nodded. "Download it. Give it to your friends. And when you've sent us enough referrals, we'll discuss your application to the program."

"Application? Seriously?" I couldn't help it; I raised my voice. "Just accept me now, damn it. You know I'm good for it."

His eyelids twitched, but otherwise, he was still, staring at me with that wide, plastic grin.

"Referrals, Ms. Jordan," he said. "Thank you for your cooperation. We hope that you enjoyed your flight toward the horizon. May you have a safe drive back."

I stared at him for a moment, but he didn't blink. He would have seemed like a statue if it weren't for his lab coat fluttering in the wind. I turned back to my car.

If referrals were what he wanted, then fine. I could hand out flyers for my sister.

***

I should have waited to see if the women from my gym were actually going to go to the Skyline Shift, but I couldn't wait. As soon as I handed out the flyers, I went straight to the camp. This time, once the guard heard my name, he let me in right away. Dr. Bates came out of the nearest building, a clipboard in his hand. But this time he wore a white tie with an embroidered logo, the same one as the flyer: four hills, or lower-case Ns, squished together, tilting to the side.

"Ms. Jordan, you know—"

"Don't turn me away," I begged, my voice raspy. Tears were crusted on my face, but I had nothing left in me anymore. Everyone had turned me away, kept assuring me that Julie would turn up eventually. But she hadn't shown up. I knew that she would never magically reappear. This was the only chance I had left to find her. I needed this to work. "I need this, Dr. Bates," I whispered. "More than anything."

And I was sure, so damn sure, that he was going to turn me away. That gummy grin never faded, and I waited for that creepy motto to spit out of his mouth.

Instead, he shifted, putting a hand on my arm.

"Ms. Jordan," he said. His touch made my skin crawl, but I didn't move. I couldn't back away, not now, not when I needed him to let me in. His lips were pressed together, his curly hair falling across his forehead. "You are welcome here."

My chest clenched. "Really?"

"I spoke with the board. We believe you're ready. We'll have you sign our contract, of course. Please note that our minimum stay is one year."

One year? That was a long time.

But it meant that Julie could still be here.

"I can do one year," I said.

"Good. I'll see to it that you're my personal student," he said. And that smile spread across his face like a half-moon in the sky. "Welcome to the Skyline Shift, Ellie Jordan."

After signing the contract, Dr. Bates gave me a tour of the front buildings. The entire campus was empty; granted, it was night—I had gone straight from one of the evening sparring sessions at the gym to the Skyline Shift—but there were no hints that other women were living there too. Only silent, half-circle buildings, all painted white.

"What about those?" I asked. I pointed to the buildings in the back, the ones with glass walls. From where we were standing, we couldn't see inside, but I knew the glass windows were there.

"When you're ready, you'll go there," he said.

He led me to a building with three floors of individual rooms. Dorm rooms. Mine was on the top floor, a small, but livable space, the ceiling slanting with the curve of the roof.

"Classes start at six a.m. sharp," Dr. Bates said.

"I'll get to sleep then." I slumped down onto the bed, grateful that I had finally made it. It was a step forward.

"And one more thing, Ms. Jordan." He tapped the door frame. "I took the liberty of locating your sister. I hope you don't mind."

My heart swelled. "Not at all." My eyes widened. "Where is she?"

"Once you're ready, I'd be happy to put you in contact."

Once I was ready? What did that mean?

"I'm ready now," I said, my voice meek. "Please."

Dr. Bates paused, but by the plastic expression on his face, I knew that he had already made his decision.

"There are rules about communication between students, Ms. Jordan. I assume you read your contract?" He knew I hadn't. I had signed as quickly as I could, so that we could get on with the tour, with everything. So I could be closer to her. "I'm afraid you're not fully trained yet. But you will be, very soon." He turned to the side. "Enjoy your flight toward the horizon. May you sleep well, Ms. Jordan."

My stomach twisted in knots at those words, but I couldn't figure out why. What was waiting at the horizon?

"Sleep well, Dr. Bates," I said.

He closed the door behind him.

***

That night, I couldn't sleep. A ringing sound filled the room, and when I tried to open the door to see where the noise was coming from, it was locked. That startled me. Adrenaline surged through my veins as I shook the handle as hard as I could, but the door didn't move, as if it was cemented shut with concrete. I shouldn't have been surprised; if the doors had been unlocked, Julie would have snuck out, maybe even come home by now. Maybe that was why they had locked me in; they thought I was going to sneak out too.

The ringing, like a sharp noise from a broken radio, grew louder the longer I was there. I went to the bathroom, sitting in the shower stall, but the sound followed me there too. I rolled up the thin towel hanging beside the door and pulled it over my ears, but I could still hear it. The ringing. It seemed like it would go on forever. I closed my eyes, letting the sound dull into the background.

But then it stopped.

I opened my eyes, looking around, waiting for it to return. But nothing happened. I closed my eyes to sleep.

Then it started again.

"What the hell?" I whimpered. I covered my ears with that towel and squeezed my eyes shut.

In the morning, a knock shook me awake. I don't know how or when I had fallen asleep, but I didn't feel rested. I opened the door.

"Ms. Jordan. Please get dressed," Dr. Bates said, back to his red tie. "Your uniform is on the nightstand."

Uniform? I hadn't seen one the night before, but sure enough, a white shirt and white pants, resembling medical scrubs, were folded on the nightstand. I put them on in the bathroom, then followed Dr. Bates. Lines of women in white uniforms were walking into the buildings, all in a single file line, their heads held high, their mouths closed. Muscular men in white clothes with that same red logo on their shirts were distanced throughout, scrutinizing the women. And in the distance, I saw a naked woman struggling to find her footing. A man jabbed her with a long instrument, shoving her forward. They disappeared into a building.

"That woman," I asked. "Why was she naked?"

"What woman?" Dr. Bates smiled. "We have many women here. All students of the program."

He was avoiding the subject. "That naked one," I answered, a little irritated. "I saw her—"

"I'm sure you saw a flash of skin, Ellie, but there isn't any nudity at this phase."

This phase? "What do you mean, this phase?"

But he didn't answer. Instead, he led me through a corridor, resembling an empty school hallway, to a dark room with a single metal folding chair. Black and white videos played across the screen, blips and dots of black ink making it look like they were old footage, though there was no projector in view.

We say 'no' to unnecessary violence! The only acceptable violence is violence that protects our family. Here, at the Skyline Shift, family is everything. We are all family, the speaker said. *Family.*

"You will be quizzed," Dr. Bates said. I opened my mouth to question him, but he shut the door. A loud click sounded as he locked me in.

Okay. Videos. A quiz. I could do that.

I watched four hours of the same video on repeat. *We are all together in this*, the voice said. I could hear the theme song jingle towards the end, cheery and delightful, but the tone off, like someone who wasn't a musician had created it. *We must work together. We are stronger together.* Women marched across the screen, proud of themselves, of what they had accomplished, but it was always a man's voice instructing them, lecturing the audience, teaching us, teaching me. After some deciphering, that measured, methodical cadence clicked into place; it was Dr. Bate's voice. *Together, we can defeat the enemy.* A woman helping another into a bus. One woman polishing a gun, then handing it to the woman next to her. Finally, the woman aimed the gun at the camera, then the video went blank.

The dock clicked. Dr. Bates went to the back of the room and turned off the video. My stomach growled.

"Is it lunch yet? Breakfast, maybe?" I asked. "I'm starving."

"You have to take the test first," he smiled. "I hope you studied."

This place made you work for everything. I had to work for sleep, and now, I had to work for food? I wanted to scoff at him, but I held it back. All I had to do was get through a few days and find Julie. Then we could leave. Until then, it was better to keep my head down.

The test seemed minimal, but the more I thought about it, the less I knew.

How many years had the Skyline Shift been open?

When was the first graduate released?

What does the motto, *enjoy your flight toward the horizon*, mean?

What does the Skyline Shift give its participants?

That final question was the only question I could answer. *A new perspective*, I wrote.

I was granted a piece of fruit: a single tangerine. It was small in my palm. I could have crushed it if I squeezed hard enough.

I looked up at Dr. Bates, pleading with my eyes.

"This is it?" I asked.

"This is part of the experimental practice," Dr. Bates said. "It was listed in your contract. You read your contract, yes?"

I shook my head subtly, then looked up. Of course, I hadn't read a single word. He *knew* that. Because I would agree to whatever it was, as long as I got closer to Julie. She couldn't be far off now.

"Yes," I lied.

"Good."

This went on for months until I had basically memorized the videos. They didn't have all of the answers, but every once in a while, a new clip would be added to the mix. The faces of men with dark eyes, an older man in the center with peppered gray hair, his three grown sons standing proudly beside him. *Learn their faces*, Dr. Bates's voiceover said. *And never trust them. They must be stopped.* And with these new clips, I'd get another piece of food. A tangerine. A glass of milk. A roll of bread. I ate it all greedily. My body grew thin, my cheeks sunken in, but I learned to live with hunger, learned to listen to the video as if they were a part of me. *You can't trust anyone*, Dr. Bates's voice sounded through the room, *Especially not them. Remember, you must eliminate them.*

I knew that it was strange, this talk of elimination, but I remembered only one line in the contract: *Behavioral Conditioning Program.* I figured it was a government experiment, and though that should have unnerved me, I *had* to listen. Had to obey. Because Julie was there, wandering through the buildings too. I could feel her there, somewhere. She was a student who was more likely to cause a scene, but me? I would do what the video said: *You must play by the rules. Figure out the game. Decipher the protocol. It will give you a new path to follow. A new perspective on life.*

If I listened, did what it said, Dr. Bates would let me talk to Julie.

Then I would get us the hell out.

One day, Dr. Bates gestured for me to follow him like he did every morning, but this time, instead of going to the video room, he led me across the campus between the half-moon buildings.

"You're ready for the next step," he said. "Endurance."

"Endurance?"

On the bottom floor of the building, there was a large empty room with a hardwood floor, and a single man with his arms crossed, wearing a white shirt and pants. I recognized him; he was one of the guards who watched us.

"This is Edward," Dr. Bates said. "He'll take good care of you."

I turned back to Dr. Bates. Take care of me? "How?" I asked.

"In your endurance training, he will be your mentor." Dr. Bates's smile widened and my heart sank. "Julie did this too, you know. Passed it recently with flying colors."

"Strip," Edward barked. His teeth were smooshed together, like the mouth of a shark, but his arms were large and weighty, as if he could smother me between them. I turned to Dr. Bates, looking at him for help.

"Go on, Ellie," Dr. Bates said. "Show him what a good student you are."

I sucked in a breath, then slipped off my shoes and socks. Pulled the loose pants over my ankles, setting them in a pile to the side.

"Naked," Edward added. I closed my eyes and pulled down my underwear too. I shivered, though I'm not sure if it was from the temperature or the situation.

"Shirt," Edward said. I sucked in a breath. A gut instinct told me Edward did not like waiting. I took it off, and since they hadn't given us bras there, I was finally naked.

"Face the wall," Edward said. "Hands behind your head. Legs spread. Knees straight."

I stood as I was told.

A tool slid from a pocket. Then footsteps crossed the wooden floor. A shadow on the ground of a hand being raised.

The whip crashed down on my back, like a lighting strike electrifying my entire body. I yelled out, stumbling towards the wall.

"Don't move," Edward said. "Every time you move, we start from the beginning."

I stared at him, but there was nothing to see. No soul. No heart or mind. No light in his eyes. Only pure violence. I turned to Dr. Bates, who was now standing at the back of the room, but that Cheshire cat grin was still there, fixed on his face.

"Dr. Bates?" I asked.

"Please resume, Edward," he said. "Ellie will adjust accordingly. She is one of our top students."

This wasn't right.

"Dr. Bates, what is this?" I asked. The line on my back throbbed, making my muscles shake. "Beating someone as part of training? How does that align with a flight toward the horizon?"

"The enemy," he said curtly, "They enjoy this kind of sexual act."

"But this isn't sexual," I said, bringing my chin forward. "This is punishment."

"Oh, Ellie," Dr. Bates said, his grin growing. "This is hardly a punishment. This will make you stronger. It is simply an endurance exercise that's been listed in your contract. Like I said, Ms. Jordan, your sister survived it. And I have great faith that you will too." He winked. "Now, show me how capable you are."

I shook my head. "Dr. Bates," I said. But I didn't know what else to say.

The smile drifted from his face. "This is part of your contract, Elena." His voice was stern now, his aggravation growing. "If you want to see your sister again, you will complete the program."

I held my breath. It was just an exercise. Nothing more. All I had to do was survive it, and I had gone through a lot already. I couldn't be that far off. I kept straight, waiting for the sting, and when it came, I bit my tongue. Another strike lashed across my back. I squeezed my eyes shut. I would have taken those mind-numbing videos over this.

"This is for your own good, Ellie," Dr. Bates said.

Soon, the pain became so great that I was completely numb. I couldn't feel another strike, because my brain had taken me elsewhere. I thought of those videos, the mantras they spouted: *They killed innocent children. Children who had no way to defend themselves. And they will kill you too, if you don't end their torment.*

End their torment. This beating was just another way to be closer to those children. I had to survive this, to survive what they hadn't. And then I would defeat the enemy.

When I woke up, I was lying on the floor. Edward was gone. Dr. Bates looked into my eyes, his teeth gleaming. Somehow, his smile comforted me. He stroked the hair out of my eyes.

"You did well, Ellie," he said softly. "Your sister would be very proud."

"When can I—" I stopped, then coughed into my elbow, my back shocking me with searing pain every time I moved, my skin slippery on the floor. Was I sweaty or bleeding? I didn't know. Once I could breathe again, I started, "When can I see her?"

"Soon," Dr. Bates said. "Very soon. But first, you must complete your training."

The days passed in one long blur of videos and beatings. All I wanted was my sister. I looked at those video clips of the enemy, men with families, men with business enterprises, men with angelic smiles when they had committed so much evil. The man with the salted gray hair at his temples stuck out to me, and I made sure to memorize his grown sons' faces: lines around his eldest son's eyes, a scar on one son's lip, and the angular jaw of the youngest. I stared at them and thought of Julie's face, knowing that if she could survive this, I could too. And once we were done, the Skyline Shift would give us a large paycheck, and we would plan a trip together. Maybe Hawaii. Or a Caribbean island. Somewhere different from here.

As I walked between the buildings one day, a flash of blond hair caught my eye. I did a double-take, stopping the line of women. Everyone shifted to a stop. But I had seen her. It was Julie's hair. A glimpse of the same blue eyes. I opened my mouth, but another woman lurched forward.

"Izzy!" she screamed, her eyes locked on the woman behind me. "You have to get out. You have to. They're trying to—"

But a man ran towards her, ramming his gun into the back of her head. Edward came forward too, then leaned down, picking the woman up by her ponytail. Her eyes widened as Edward's knife slid across her throat. The blood pooled out of her like a thick fountain, mucking the dirt underneath her.

A speaker clicked on, and a voice came overhead. "There are *rules*, students," Dr. Bates said. "We obey the rules because the rules keep us safe. We do not speak to other students unless we are given express permission from one of our leaders. Jan was breaking the rules. She chose to resign from the program," he paused, giving a moment of silence. "This program runs on efficiency, and we expect the rest of you to be proper examples. Now, please, continue to your studies."

I stared at Jan, her head lying on the ground, the blood growing around her. The two men, Edward and the other, picked her up, carrying her off to the woods behind the campus. But her blood soaked the earth. I had never seen someone die before. It didn't seem real. My feet were sinking into the ground, into the dirt and blood, like quicksand. And everyone continued on like nothing had happened.

A hand tapped my shoulder. I turned; another woman, a fellow student. Without making eye contact, she nodded forward. She didn't speak.

I caught up with the woman in front of me, glancing at my peripherals, trying to remain unnoticed. The rest of the women kept marching forward. Was it my fault Jan was dead? Had she only tried to talk to Izzy because I had stopped? I had been there for five or six months, but I was the only one who seemed disturbed.

Because it was normal. Because they had seen this before.

It was a resignation. Not murder. Not death. I had to force myself to think of it that way.

And yet one evening, before we were escorted to our dorm rooms, I hid in one of the cafeterias, waiting for the lights to dim. I snuck out, my footsteps silent on the floor. Maybe it was a death wish, but I had to know. Had to find Julie and get her the hell out of here.

I went to the dorm rooms. There would be a sign, I told myself. There had to be. If I walked into her dorm room, I would know it was hers by the smell, by a small trinket. By something. I would hide until she returned, then we would figure out a plan, because we were stronger together.

I walked into a room and a blood-soaked pillow stopped me. A red trail led to the bathroom sink; it must have been a bloody nose. I lifted the extra uniform off of the nightstand, looking for an ID card, a purse, or a wallet, then heard footsteps behind me. I stilled.

"Ellie, Ellie, Ellie," Edward's voice hummed. "Lucky me, finding you here."

I grabbed the base of the small lamp, ripping the cord from the wall as I slammed it into Edward's face. The shade broke off, but he didn't budge. He grabbed me by the neck and twisted hard until the blood went to my head and I couldn't even gasp.

"Little bitch," he muttered, tightening his hands. The world fuzzed-out, and right before everything went black, he dropped me, letting me crash to the floor.

He yanked down my pants and underwear, using his body weight to pin me down. I dragged my nails across the floor, trying to pull myself out from under him, but my nails dug tracks into the wood, and he stabbed me with his cock, pressing between my legs, finding my cunt.

"I knew you were a sneaky little bitch," he muttered.

"Fuck you," I growled.

He punched me in the back of the head, knocking my face into the floor, a headache instantly wrapping its fingers around my skull. I shut down, escaping to that other place. Like a whipping. Like we had done this before. Because I could endure this too. In my mind, I was at Rubble River. Our parents were sitting at the park bench, fixing our picnic lunch. Julie was in the river, holding onto a float, sunglasses on her head, her cheeks sprinkled with water. She threw her hands into the river, splashing my face, and my body moved with the waves, with each thrust of the water. I splashed back, pushing away the masculine body of waves, and I laughed, couldn't stop laughing, because it was easier that way. Easier to be there. Easier to not think. The sun beamed on the surface of the river, blinding me until there was nothing. No air. No water. No trees. No Edward. *Nothing.*

***

For the rest of my endurance training, when Edward beat me until I was bleeding, I never thought anything of it. It was the training, and as long as I obeyed the rules, I wouldn't be forced to resign. I wouldn't have to endure him. What he had done to me in the dorm rooms was a gift; he liked to remind me that it could have been so much worse. I knew that now. The blood dripped down my back, splattered the floor, but I didn't feel anything. It wasn't pain; it was empathy. Knowing what the victims had been through, what I could survive, for them.

When Dr. Bates watched my training for the first time in several weeks, I didn't question it. And when Edward bent me over, making my hands touch the wall again, I didn't think anything of it either. I was too numb to think. Too empty to care. Too exhausted to fight. I thought that there was little Edward could do to make me afraid anymore. The wall was cool on my hands, comforting, but slippery, and at least I could lean onto it.

Edward ran a hand along my back, then reached lower, but I blocked that out. He was superior to me, but he was not my leader.

"Sometimes," Dr. Bates said, his voice cool as he stepped closer to me, "we must use all of our assets to convince the enemy."

Convince them of what?

A sharp jab pressed into my pussy lips, pushing through. I turned back, seeing that Edward's groin was covered in smears of my blood; he had used my sweat and blood to lubricate me. Dr. Bates stared at me, his eyes narrowed as if I was an object underneath a microscope. I turned back to the wall. What else could I do? Uncontrollable sobs unleashed from me, because Julie had been through this too. She had been so daring, so inventive, so much more rebellious than I could have ever been. Yet I couldn't think of her in this position. How it would ruin her spirit. How it was my fault.

Tears wet the ground beneath me, growing into a reddish-pink puddle. Using my endurance training, I blocked out the motion of Edward's hips. Washed them away. Went to another place, like I always did.

When Edward finished, Dr. Bates brought me a towel.

"Thank you," I murmured, barely able to get out the words. I didn't meet his eyes.

"Sometimes, we have to do things we don't like," he said. "Remember that, Ellie. You have to play the game. Figure out the players." His voice grew softer then, like it pained him to put me through this. As if, no matter how hard he had tried, he couldn't stop it. "He might think you're weak. That you're helpless. And he'll prey on you like he preyed on her."

Her? Who was he talking about? But I had no energy to ask.

"But you are strong, Ellie. If you hack his body into pieces like he cut hers, then you'll be able to end this. For everyone."

I blinked up at him, that smile gleamed across his face. Exhaustion rocked through my body, and I begged the universe that my training was done for the day. That Dr. Bates would be my comfort. A tangerine. A bread roll. Milk. My bed. Sleep never felt as good as it did in the Skyline Shift; I could even block out the ringing at night. Some students were taken in their sleep, never to return, and I begged the universe that if I was forced to resign too, that I could at least see my sister first.

"I am so proud of you," Dr. Bates said, breaking me out of my thoughts.

"You are?" I asked. A warmth swelled inside of me. I hadn't heard those words in years.

"You are truly gifted," he said. "Not many make it through what you've accomplished. I think you're ready for the next phase of training."

I bit my lip. What could be harder than this?

Luckily, after a few more weeks had passed, when the next phase began, it wasn't as treacherous as I had expected. But still, seeing another woman, a fellow student of the Skyline Shift, standing across from me, naked, her fists raised with wooden sticks in each palm, ready to fight, was confusing. I recognized her—the short brown hair, spiked with wax at the top, reddish-brown eyes—but I didn't remember her name. I opened my mouth to ask, but Dr. Bates interrupted me.

"The only time we talk is when we are given express permission, or when our leaders address us," Dr. Bates reminded me. Both of us turned and nodded. Giving up our privilege to talk was better than the alternative. Jan's resignation wasn't the first, nor would it be the last. "You must fight each other."

"What?" I asked. "Fight her?"

"You trained at Women's Elite Social Club, did you not?" he asked. I remembered that name, but that life was so far away now. It seemed unreal. "So did she. You will fight each other, and see who wins."

This was, by far, the most normal thing in the Skyline Shift, if 'normal' was even a concept anymore. I could fight her, simply because I had done this before, and would do it again. It would prepare me to fight for her. My sister.

"She's just like you, Ellie," Dr. Bates said. "You have to fight her. This will prepare you two for what's coming."

The woman ran at me, her fists raised with rattan sticks, her arms whipping around like a fan, then slicing forward, hitting me on the return. Nothing hurt anymore, but her strike woke me up. She stepped back, waiting for me to respond.

"This is the only way you will defeat the enemy," Dr. Bates said. "You must fight for your sister, Ellie. Just like this student must fight for her daughter."

I gave him a curt nod, taking the set of rattan sticks from his hands. This was the only way I could avenge my sister.

But what had happened to my sister?

I adjusted my grip on the sticks, then lunged forward too, swinging my wrists around, blocking the woman's hits, then using my sticks to disarm her dominant hand. She sneered at me, a smirk hidden inside of her, amused at having a worthy opponent, then we crashed back into each other. Our sticks cracked like the beating of a hammer, both of us not giving the other the chance to breathe. She blocked my moves, then reached forward and punched me in the jaw with her empty hand. I used that moment to disarm her other stick.

"Good. Very good, Ellie," Dr. Bates said, clapping his hands. "You've been well trained. We are so lucky to have such bright pupils in our program." He beamed at the woman, then turned to me. "I think you're already ready for the next test. But first, we shall practice."

Our days and nights passed like that. In the bedrooms, the ringing never stopped, and still, I counted the tangerines, ate them with care, learned to eat the peels, saving one sliver of rind to count the days I had been there, the days that I had been given food. I learned to see the tangerine, small at first, as a wealth of nutrition, and dreamed about the day I could see my sister. Eating tangerines at the river, juice dripping down our chins. One more beating. One more fight. One more peel. I told myself that Julie, wherever she was, had gone through this. She had likely thrived from it. And we would be stronger, more equipped to take down the enemy when the time came. If only we finished the program.

During that time, the wording shifted in me. It was no longer about seeing Julie, but about avenging her, making sure that the enemy paid. I didn't know what I was avenging her from, and yet I trusted the program to illuminate those answers for me.

***

Dr. Bates took me to another dome-shaped warehouse. In this one, the floor was concrete. Dr. Bates gestured for me to remove my clothes, and when I saw Edward in the corner, I sucked in a breath and did as I was told. I knew not to argue. It was easier to follow the rules the way they wanted me to. But this time, Edward had a bullwhip in one hand and a slender metal device in the other, the black handle thick and sleek.

I would do whatever they wanted, as long as he didn't touch me.

I got in position with my hands against the wall. Then he struck the whip against my skin. I didn't move. My skin had turned to leather, scarred and stable, tough enough to withstand the whippings. Another strike. Each lash must have hurt, but I escaped, transported myself to another realm, and reminded myself that I would experience this with the enemy. Another strike. This was for endurance. For my survival. But then Edward pressed the metal contraption against me, the two thin prongs jabbing my skin, electricity pulsed through my body, twisting my bones into contractions until I collapsed.

Dr. Bates motioned for me to get up, his eyes narrowed, disappointed in me. My heart sank.

"You want to see your sister, don't you?" Dr. Bates said.

"I do," I whispered.

"Then get up," he barked.

"I can't," I cried. My body trembled. I had gone through so much; when would I find her? When would I be able to hug her, to know that she was okay?

Why did I have this feeling that she wasn't okay?

Of course she wasn't okay. We had to escape this program.

But how?

"Typical," Dr. Bates sneered. "I knew you weren't ready."

"I am," I cried, desperate to please him. I needed, more than anything, to see her. "I want to see her. Please."

Edward's feet walked to the corner. Then Dr. Bates came forward. He slipped a knife into the ground, the handle locking into a contraption built into the concrete. The knife stood straight up.

I kept my eyes on him. Not the knife.

"When it comes to our enemies, you must be willing to put yourself through even the most gruesome situations," he murmured. "You want to see your sister?"

"Yes," I whispered.

"Prove it." Those words coursed through me. I remembered the first time he had spoken them to me. What did I have to do now? "You must sit on the knife. Penetrate yourself with the blade. Your sister did this too, Ellie. And you're so close. So close to seeing her again. But you must endure this. You must prepare for the enemy."

I closed my eyes, my head still resting on the floor. "I can't. I can't. I can't," I muttered, not sure if I was actually saying the words. How could I? How could I deliberately cut myself?

"You can, and you *will*, Ellie. The doctors on site will make sure that you don't develop an infection. But you must prove yourself, that you're stronger than your fear. Stronger than your desire to flee. Your sister could do it, and so can you." He kneeled down, holding my chin, making it rise so that I had to look into his eyes. He licked his lips, his eyes staring into me, seeing what I needed so badly. "You're just like her, Ellie. But better. Stronger. More beautiful," he whispered. His eyes lingered on my lips, and for the first time, I wondered if he was attracted to me. But he was like a father to me; I didn't see him that way.

And yet I knew that if that's what Dr. Bates wanted, I wouldn't have a choice.

"Now, get up," he said. My legs shook as I stood slowly. "You will survive this. This is nothing compared to what you will endure. For your sister. In her honor."

Her honor?

My lips trembled, and I shook my head. "Dr. Bates, please," I whispered.

"Don't make me tell you again."

I closed my eyes, standing over the knife, thinking of my sister in that same position. Why had she endured this? What caused her to think that this would be okay? That it was better to hurt herself than to try and escape?

Had she run away, before or after she completed this task?

Was she trying to protect someone too? Who had brought her here?

How could I find her when I was so alone? So trapped.

But I could do this. To save her. To rescue her. If I endured this, then maybe she wouldn't have to do it ever again. I could get her out. I just needed to figure out where she was.

I slid onto the knife. It cut my lips like butter and I shot up, unable to do it anymore.

Blood ran in spirals down my thighs. "Please," I cried.

"Elena," Dr. Bates said, his voice booming. He came forward, grabbing my shoulders. "Do it. For your sister." A smile gleamed across his face. "Trust me, Ellie. I won't let it kill you."

You?

Had it killed someone before?

I closed my eyes, bending my knees again. The knife hit my ass, and I jumped up, then quickly hit it again. Then I slid off, falling to the floor.

"That's it," Dr. Bates said, rubbing my back. His fingertips soothed the scarred skin. "Edward?" he asked.

Footsteps returned. His shadow drifted over us. I clenched every muscle in my body. Not him. I couldn't endure more of this.

My throat clenched, my body achingly full of tears. I was so close to giving up, and I felt guilty, disappointed in myself. But I couldn't let go. I had to keep going. For her sake.

Because if it meant seeing Julie, what wouldn't I do?

When would all of this stop?

"You may stay like that, Ellie," Dr. Bates said. He pulled his fingers through my hair, moving it off of my neck. "Edward is going to give you a tattoo, to mark your time here at the Skyline Shift."

I could have objected. Should have said 'no.' Should have gotten the hell out. But I was tired. All I wanted was a tangerine, a glass of milk, a roll of bread, my bed, Julie. The tattoo gun hissed, muffling the constant ringing. I could sleep.

Those four hills, or a double M, the same logo that had been on Dr. Bates's ties, was now on my neck. If I looked hard enough, I could see it on every woman's neck. At least, those who had earned it.

***

Right before the one year mark, a knock sounded on my door just past midnight. I put on my uniform and tried the door, expecting it to be locked, as always, but for once it wasn't. My heart sped up, thinking it might be Julie, but instead, it was a man, dressed in a button-up shirt and pants. That grayish-brown curly hair was unmistakable.

"Dr. Bates," I said. "Come in."

I was happy to see him. He was my only connection, and though I exchanged facial expressions with other students when no one was looking, Dr. Bates was the only person who I conversed with regularly.

Edward wasn't a person I *wanted* to know, but Dr. Bates was like a father to me, guiding me until I became a better, stronger soldier.

"Your contract is almost up," he said. I blinked, waiting for him to continue. "Are you ready to return to the outside world with your new perspective?"

"Absolutely, sir," I said. "I will enjoy my flight toward the horizon."

He sat on the bed next to me. "I have one more task for you," he said. His fingertips touched my shoulder, his warmth penetrating the fabric. His eyes lingered on my lips, and it was clear to me then, that he wanted me. But during this whole year, he had never touched me. Looked at me, yes. Authorized my beating, yes. But he had never done it himself.

It was almost as if he could protect me.

My heart clenched, thinking of the words he had said. One more task? Sweat gathered on my brow.

"But I—"

He held up a hand, and I immediately fell silent. "I promised you your sister. I won't change that. But I need you to do one last assignment for me. One last contract," he sighed. "She would have wanted it."

Would have? I stared at him, trying to read what he meant, what he wanted me to endure, but I couldn't understand his expression. It never changed.

So I thought about his words: *would have*.

Like she didn't exist anymore.

But that couldn't be true.

"Anything for Julie," I said. And for the Skyline Shift," I added quickly.

"Good."

Without his lab coat on, he looked almost like a university professor. He was kind that way, maybe even gentle. He put a hand on my shoulder.

"Let's go see your sister."

At the back of the campus, the trees stretched up, so much higher than the buildings. Sometimes, we heard noises coming from the forest, but we never questioned it because we couldn't speak. My heart swelled with excitement, but I kept it all in. Dr. Bates led me to a garden, but there was no one there. I wrinkled my brows, but I trusted Dr. Bates. His methods were unique, but he always knew what was best for us.

The stench of rotten eggs and fertilizer filled my nose. I pinched my nostrils shut, but Dr. Bates seemed undisturbed, like he was used to the stench.

"She's just past these trees," he said.

I followed him, but once my eyes settled on a head, lying on the ground, I recognized her immediately. The soft cheeks. The blond hair, tangled and brown with dirt. Her nostrils stuffed with clumps of earth, as if she had been suffocated with it. Her body sliced into pieces. The blood pooling in her skin, making her cheeks purple. Her eyes still open, yellowed, blotched with thick, red vessels, looking up and seeing nothing.

Julie.

I don't know what happened, exactly. I blacked out. I couldn't breathe. It felt like my soul was being crushed from within. And when I finally came back to my senses, it was still nightfall. I was sitting on a bench in the garden, facing the campus. Dr. Bates was beside me.

"I hate to do that to you, you know," he said. "Julie was a good girl. One of our best students. But even she fell victim to the Adlers. And she deserves to be avenged, doesn't she?"

I blinked back the tears. "Of course, Dr. Bates," I said.

He put a hand on my back, rubbing my scarred skin, his eyes studying me.

"When you wake up tomorrow," he said, putting hair behind my ear, "you won't remember me. You won't remember anything. But I will be with you, Ellie. I will always be with you. And as long as you do what I say, I will protect you. And you will end the monsters who did this to your sister. Won't you, Ellie?"

"Of course," I whispered.

"And if you fail," his voice grew stronger, "if you try to escape, you will die, Ellie. Just like your sister. So it is imperative that you end the Adlers. It's for your own good, and for the good of the program. Can you do it, Ellie?"

I nodded. "I will do it."

His smile stretched across his face, his teeth shining in the moonlight. "Julie would be proud of you," he said. "Let's commence the final phase."

Inside of a lab, white light surrounded me. The phrase, *Kill the Adlers*, filled my core as if Dr. Bates's words were coming from within, until I felt nothing but those three words.

Kill the Adlers.

When I awoke, I was in the woods. A man with dark narrowed eyes and a scarred lip looked at me, his voice like an echo drifting away.

For my brother, the man had said. *He'll take care of you.*

Take care of me?

I blinked my eyes. I was back in the bedroom. One of the rooms in Wil's house.

Wil.

Wil Adler.

Wil held his cheek. Blood dripped down onto the wood floors. I must have cut him. But I felt nothing. No remorse. No guilt. Only anger. Only rage that I hadn't seen his true self sooner.

He had done this. He had killed Julie.

"You killed my sister," I said, my voice shaking. But it didn't feel true. Didn't feel right. Was it possible that Wil had known Julie? Could he have killed a woman like her?

He always killed for a reason. And there was no way he would have a reason to kill Julie.

You will end the monsters who did this to your sister, Dr. Bates's voice said.

But what if Adlers hadn't killed Julie at all? What if their actions had put the entire Skyline Shift into motion, but the act itself, her death, wasn't by their hands at all?

He wouldn't be the first person I've killed, but it would be for a far lesser reason than the rest, Wil had said. Could he have murdered my sister?

And I realized that under the right circumstances, he could.

"You killed her," I repeated, my voice a low growl.

"Ellie?" he asked.

CHAPTER 14

Wil

Ellie dropped the knives, then looked down at her hands. "Wil, I—"

I raced forward, taking her wrists and twisting them behind her back until she was bent in half.

"Did you kill her?" she yelled.

"Why would I kill your sister?"

I pulled her into a headlock, then dragged her to the window. Once she was passed out, I shackled her wrists and ankles to the restraints behind the curtains. You never knew when you would need restraints, and this proved it.

When she roused from unconsciousness, she was hanging limply from the cuffs. She sneered at me and straightened.

"You killed her," she barked.

"I didn't kill Julie," I said. "Why would I kill her?" The irritation leaked through my voice. "And why would I try to hide it? And when would I ever run into her? You lived in Pebble Garden. That's hours away from here."

She studied me, her composure strong, but then she gave out, and her lips trembled. "I know," she whispered. "I know. Please. Hold me."

"Are you going to try to kill me?"

She shook her head. "I'm chained to the wall, right?"

I stepped forward, expecting her to pull against the restraints, to try to attack me, but she stayed still. Her skin was pale, and her shoulders had gone rigid. I rubbed the back of my fingers along her cheek, her soft skin, smooth compared to the rest of her body. Blood dropped down from my hand, hitting the floor. The adrenaline had made me forget I was cut.

"What happened?" I asked.

"Please," she whispered. "Help me."

I tried to think of how to help her in a way where it could be just me alone, but I knew that I had to ask my brothers. I lowered my eyes. A trickle of blood ran down my neck. I had to take care of that first, then figure out what the hell was going on.

"I'm going to leave you here," I said. "Try to stay safe."

"What do you think I'm going to do? I'm chained to the wall!"

I gave a small smile, then shrugged. At least she was up to questioning me.

"I don't know. But I can see now that you're capable."

I wrapped my hand in gauze and pressed a small towel to my cheek. I dialed my brothers, telling them to meet me at the Adler House.

Gerard and Clara, our parents, were out, so we took the study. A fireplace roared in the corner constantly, and I cursed my family. Always with the fireplaces. Ever since Ellie had tried to attack me—hell, that wasn't an attempt, she *had* attacked me—I had been sweating. I released the towel from my cheek; it had finally stopped bleeding.

Derek immediately saw my wounds. Axe raised a brow.

"The fuck happened to you?" Derek asked.

I raised my hand, showing him the bandage. "Ellie," I said. "She attacked me."

"You kill her?" Axe asked.

"No, I didn't kill her. Are you serious?" Axe stared at me. I was shocked, but I shouldn't have been. If someone attacked you, then you killed them, especially in our line of work. "There's something wrong with her. She didn't mean to attack me."

Derek pointed at my palm. "That's a disarming technique. Making it so you can't fight."

I scowled. "I figured that out. Thanks." I rubbed my forehead. "This was different. It's like another being took over her body, forcing her to fight."

"A demon? Possession?"

"Something like that." I wasn't sure what the hell it was, but I was at a place where a demon couldn't be ruled out. Not with the way she had looked at me, her eyes flickering with disgust, loss, and pure hatred, then those emotions disappearing in an instant, as if she was scared and helpless.

"What happened?" Derek asked.

I thought about it for a moment. What had happened? This morning had seemed fine. Ellie was her usual self, and so was I. But then she snapped.

"We were at breakfast, but she got a headache," I said, "Started screaming out of nowhere. Then she tried to seduce me."

"Tried?" Derek asked.

"It worked," I shrugged. I couldn't deny that. "But then we were fucking, and she grabbed the knife."

"What were you talking about?"

"We weren't talking, we were fucking."

Derek scoffed. "Before that, at breakfast. When the headache started."

I thought about it. Everything had been mundane. We had been talking about the other woman, the one with Axe, if she had been a message from an enemy. Then Ellie had shifted.

"Maybe she remembered something," Derek offered.

"I'll go talk to her," I said. "You two, see if that woman knows anything." They both nodded.

I drove back to the penthouse, weaving in and out of traffic. It would have been practical to have them meet me at my place, but I didn't want them near her. Axe had an instinct when it came to these things, and there was no way I was going to let her anywhere near him or Derek until we had a plan.

In the bedroom, Ellie's shoulders hung down, her body limp, wrists dangling. She didn't look up when I entered, though by the twitch of her chin, I knew that she heard me.

"Did you get your memories back?" I asked. "Is that what happened?"

"Dr. Bates," she said. Then her words became quicker. "Dr. Bates. He trained me. Promised I would get to see my sister. But then I had those visions where she's dead and I'm here and I don't know what the hell I'm supposed to do." Her breathing neared hyperventilation. "She's not dead," Ellie cried, a tear slipping down her face. "She can't be. It was a trick. Everything I went through, it can't be for nothing. She's still alive. She's not dead."

My heart rate increased, thudding in my chest. "What happened?" I asked, my voice low. I clenched my fists. I had a feeling I didn't want to know the answers.

"They tortured me," she cried. "Ruined me." Hanging against the wall, I couldn't see them, but I knew what she was talking about: the scars on her labia and on her back. The bumpy skin. The black lines. Then I thought of her headaches; were those linked to her past too? "Dr. Bates showed me proof that you had killed her. Her body cut up in the woods. Told me that I had to stop you before you did it again." She shook her head. "But it's not true, is it?" she stammered. "Julie's not dead. She can't be. She can't—"

"Ellie, listen," I said. "Breathe with me."

For the first time since she had attacked, she locked eyes with me, and we took deep breaths together, our chests heaving in and out, her body shaking in between each attempt. Once she had stilled, I took a step closer. "I want you to listen to me very carefully. I have never seen your sister before, nor has anyone in my family." I waited, making sure that she absorbed that information. "We want to help you find her, and find out who killed her."

"She's not dead."

"Are you sure?" I asked. "If your memories aren't—"

"She's not dead!" Ellie yelled, her cheeks red, her bloodshot eyes glaring at me, daring me to say it again. "She's not dead," she repeated, her voice quiet. "Those were just visions. Nightmares. I'm mixing things up."

Staring into her blue eyes, I could see the pain etched inside of her. Whoever had done this—this Dr. Bates—he hadn't only marked her body. There was so much inside of Ellie that was torn, that was broken. That I didn't know or understand.

I rubbed a thumb across her cheek, trying to be gentle. "Someone put you in the woods to hunt us. But they don't own you."

Her eyelids fluttered, then tightened in anger. "Because you do," she said, "Can we really compare cages?" Her words drifted off. She was nearing sleep.

Pain in the back of my throat congealed. I shouldn't have felt guilt; Ellie had been in the woods, on our property, and by being gifted to me, she had been given a second chance at life. If it weren't my birthday, Axe would have killed her instantly.

But if she had been put in our woods against her will, what did that mean? What did that make me?

"You're an Adler," she said, her voice tired. "That's what you do. Conquer. Annihilate. Rule."

I clenched my good fist, then wiggled the fingers of my bandaged hand. I wanted to ram my fists into the wall until my hands were a bloody pulp. But what good would it do, besides releasing my anger?

But then it struck me. *Adler*.

"Stay here," I said. And this time, she didn't have a comeback about how she was already stuck. "I'll keep an eye on the surveillance."

At the family house, I found Axe and Derek still in the study, discussing Midnight Miles.

"Workroom. Now," I said.

Derek raised a brow, but they both followed me. We went through the woods to the side of the house. We came to Axe's workroom, surrounded by trees and camouflaged by vines and dirt to make it look like an overturned rock that had been reclaimed by the earth. It was soundproofed, so you never knew what to expect when you went in. Inside, the woman was sitting on her bed inside of a cage, still naked, though a pile of clothes was to the side of her bed. Her short hair messy, her eyes red and filmy from exhaustion.

"The trigger is our last name," I said in a low voice to my brothers. "Watch. Say it to her. Tell her who we are."

"We're the Adlers," Derek said loudly. The woman's shoulders rose, her eyes unblinking as she stared at us.

"What did you say?" she asked.

Axe raised a brow. "She never speaks."

"That doesn't mean she's homicidal," Derek said.

But at those words, the woman gave herself space, then catapulted her whole body towards the wall of the cage, moving the whole thing forward.

"Shit!" Derek said.

The two of us ran forward, holding it down in spots. Axe went to one of the locked cabinets on the opposite wall of the room.

"I'll find a tranquilizer," Axe said.

"You killed her. You killed her! You fucking monster!"

She slashed at the cage, but the bars were too close together for her to make any impact. I held the walls of the cage, lowering them into place, then Axe tossed us padlocks to anchor it to the metal loops in the concrete floor. Once the cage was latched, the two of us stepped back. The woman paced back and forth. Axe held a syringe in the air, the liquid dripping down the sides of the needle.

"I will kill all three of you," she murmured.

"You won't," Axe said.

"Where are you from?" I asked. The woman glared at me, her eyes shooting imaginary spears. "We're in Sage City. You must be far away from home."

"Fuck you," she hissed.

"Who do you think we killed?" I asked. "Is it your sister? A mother?"

"My daughter, you asshole."

My chest tightened. What the hell was going on?

"We don't know who your daughter is. We didn't kill her. You've been tricked."

"Liars!"

She jumped backward and threw herself at the bars again, the whole cage shaking. I sucked in a breath, then gestured towards the door. The three of us started heading out, but at the entrance, Axe lifted his gun from the holster, showing the woman that he was armed. Then he stepped out.

We waited outside in silence, trying to process what had happened. I had always figured that the women and our dead men were related, but I had never thought that the women would be responsible for the deaths. They were too vulnerable. Naked in the woods. No memory. As if they had been wiped clean.

Perhaps being close to Ellie had messed with me. I didn't want her to be sent by an enemy, knowing what that would mean. I wanted us to work. I didn't want to kill her.

But that didn't matter right now. Ellie was chained up, and so was the woman. And now that we knew the trigger, if there were any more women, we'd be able to keep our surname silent, to prevent any further damage.

"They've sent soldiers," Derek said.

"To kill us," Axe said.

"The dead one must have killed our men."

"We'll get rid of them."

"Wait," I said. "Killing them won't solve our problem. Whoever it was will just send more of them, and we'd lose these two as a resource." I shook my head, waiting for them to object, but neither of them did. I continued, "Right now, we have them under our control. We can try to learn from them, see what they know. Figure out who sent them."

"Or we can kill them," Axe said. "Trap the next one. Use her instead."

I met his eyes and I clenched my fists. My cut palm hurt like a mother fucker, but I narrowed my eyes through the pain, to prove a point.

"I won't let you lay a hand on Ellie," I said slowly. "If anyone kills her, it will be me." I lifted my chin. "Ellie is mine."

Derek put a hand on Axe's shoulder. Derek didn't care who killed Ellie, as long as she was taken care of when the time was right. "No one will touch Ellie," he said. "Right, Axe?"

Axe nodded. "If she needs to die, that's on your hands."

"As it should be," I said. But for now, we had to give her—and the other woman—time to come around, and to be useful to us. "No one dies yet."

"Not yet," Derek said, nodding his head.

"Not yet," Axe said.

I excused myself, heading back to the penthouse. I hadn't been back and forth between the two places this much since I had first moved out years ago, but it was necessary. I wanted to see the woman's face when I said our surname, to see that change within her with my own eyes.

By the time I returned, Ellie's wrists were bright red, as if she had been yanking on the metal cuffs. Her ankles were swollen. Damp light brown hair hung in front of her face, covering her eyes. As my shoes tapped the floors, she snapped up, baring her teeth at me, as if she planned to bite me in half.

I stepped forward. I touched her cheek, and she leaned into my touch, her defenses melting away at the simple gesture.

"I don't know what's wrong with me," she whispered. "I can't fight it."

"You can, and you have," I said. I leaned my forehead against hers.

"I'm ruined," she cried. "I can only think straight when you're here. Right here with me."

Testing it, I stepped back, letting her go, leaving her there alone. The monster returned, taking hold of her limbs, lighting her with fire. She sneered at me, spit flying from her teeth. I reached to put a hand on her throat, but she bit my finger.

"Fuck!" I yelled. I looked at my hand, expecting to see bone, but it was only red with teeth marks. She cackled like a maniac. This wasn't her. I tried again, but this time, I didn't hold back. I squeezed her neck tightly. The rage faded from her face but she was still wild, still twisting in her restraints. I gently released her, giving her a chance to breathe.

"Yes," she growled, snarling at me. "Fuck me," she squirmed. "Fuck me like a rag doll. Show me how much you want to dominate me. Punish me."

It came to me then: even when I took her agency away, sex was the only time that Ellie had control, the only time she was truly free. I squeezed her neck, watching her face turn red from the lack of oxygen, the red then shifting to a light purple, my dick twitching. She was brutal, and maybe even crazy. A dangerous soldier packed into a dynamite body, and yet, I still wanted her. I wanted to fuck her. To conquer her. To destroy her. To free her from the agony that burned her each day and night, until she had her own mind. To ruin her again, and again, until she was truly mine.

I let go, and she coughed, choking on the air. I pulled out my cock, stroking as I watched her compose herself. The anger started then, coming up from her toes, seizing her core. Her lips open, ready to scream, and I shoved my cock into her, thrusting so hard inside of her slit that we both grunted.

"Yes," she cried. "Do it. Give it to me."

"Give it to you when you tried to kill me?" I whispered into her ear. I rammed my hips into her again, her whole body crashing into the wall. "Damn it, Ellie." What the hell was she doing to me?

No matter how hard I thrust, Ellie begged me for more.

"Fuck me harder," she screamed. I fucked her so hard that I thought I might knock the wind out of her. So hard I could have killed her. But still, she wanted more. The scars on her pussy lips were hard, rubbing against my shaft, and I reached a hand down, rubbing her rosebud, the scars there too. I knew so little about Ellie. There were things I could read on her skin, those scars, her back, her pussy lips, her ass, but I didn't know how she was broken on the inside. I needed that brokenness. Needed to set it free. Needed to find her, the real her, and cage her all over again, so that I could protect her, make sure nothing ever hurt her again. Fucking her was a release for both of us, but then tension inside of her was what needed to escape. Her body clenched around me, taking me in as if my cock were a dagger that could fuck until she died.

"Fuck me harder, Wil! Please!"

My fingers skimmed over her back, then I found her hips and dug my fingernails into her skin until she beaded red. I fucked her harder than I ever had until her whole body twisted in need. This was something we both needed. To feel each other. To remember that we were more than our base urges, more than her desire to kill, more than my lost desire to control her fate. Together, we could be lost in our minds and forget everything else in the world. And I came, I came so hard that I let out a howl, my come shooting inside of her, and Ellie twitched around my cock, coming too. And even still, she pressed her body against me, as if she was afraid to stop.

As soon as we calmed down, I couldn't look her in the eye. Night had descended, reminding us that our monsters lurked, even when we wished them away, when we banished them through our bodies. I might not have killed her sister, but the people I had killed? They had brothers, sisters, mothers, fathers. Why couldn't Ellie be one of the people left behind?

I shook the thoughts away. This was different. I couldn't change who I was. I was born an Adler. I would die an Adler.

But I could change her fate. Make sure that she lived. That no one hurt her ever again.

Being a god had its purpose, and I could use it to help her. But it wasn't about using her anymore.

A tear ran down her cheek. "I don't know what's wrong with me," she whispered. "I don't know how to fix it."

"We'll figure it out," I said, cupping her cheek. My words wavered, because I wasn't sure how we could change anything. "We'll figure it out," I repeated. Because I wanted to believe it too.

CHAPTER 15

Ellie

The four of us sat around the round table in Wil's office; Maddie, the other two women found in the woods, and me. The newest woman was shorter in stature and afraid to look up. Axe had found her that morning. The short-haired woman from before stared at me, then Maddie, waiting for someone to speak. Maddie was the only one who had free hands. The rest of us had our hands and ankles cuffed. But I knew, deep down, that this wasn't the only way we had been chained down. It had been much worse.

You're stronger together, the voice said. I looked at their faces, then closed my eyes and let myself agree. I knew that was true; for once, there was no reason to fight that.

I turned to the woman who had spiky hair on top of her head. "What's your name?" I asked.

"Billy," she said.

I knew, now, that she was from Pebble Garden too, and that we had gone to the same gym. But did she remember me?

"I'm Ellie," I said.

"I don't remember my name," the third one said. That made sense; it had been foggy to me at first too. Sandy blond hair covered her head, reaching her shoulders. She was smaller than Billy and I, but just as built. Her green eyes were piercing. If it hadn't been for her eyes, I might have wondered if she was Julie in disguise.

Julie was out there. Somewhere. She had to be.

I didn't know what I would do if she wasn't.

"Is there a name you like?" Maddie asked.

The woman shrugged. "Not really."

"Let's call you Jane, then," Maddie said. "It's simple, and we'll remember it."

If I didn't think of my sister, I still would have thought that Jane looked familiar, like I might have known her in a different life. But even if I had known her at the Skyline Shift, we wouldn't have spoken to one another. Communication amongst each other was considered dangerous; the only person we were permitted to speak to was Dr. Bates.

And that's where I would start.

"Do you know Dr. Bates?" I asked. Jane rubbed her forehead, shrinking down even further in her seat. "You don't remember a lot, right?"

She shook her head. "Not a thing."

Axe had found Jane in the woods by their parents' house, like Billy and me. But the difference was that this time, Jane was closer to the house. Where Billy and I were found deep in the surrounding woods, Jane was only a quarter of a mile away. Billy touched the back of her neck, her fingers running over the tattoo.

"Do you remember getting the tattoo?" I asked. She had the same one as me.

"Yeah," she said. "You mentioned Dr. Bates?"

"Yes?"

"He was there, wasn't he? When they marked me."

I nodded. If her experience was anything like mine, then he had been there for all of the tests. He may not have watched us for every training session, but he was an ongoing presence, always present during the important transitions. And if wasn't there in body, then his voice carried over the speakers, constantly reminding us of what to do.

Like he was doing right now.

You can work together, his voice said. *Kill the Adlers together. Kill them right now.*

I locked eyes with Maddie. My forehead wrinkled, trying to fight the pain. But any time I ignored his voice, the ringing started, and it was so hard to fight.

"The voice?" Maddie asked. I nodded. She squeezed my thigh under the table, as if to say, We will work through this. Together. "All right, so that's good," Maddie continued. "You both know Bates. And Jane, does that name sound familiar?"

She shrugged, her eyes never meeting ours. Her eyes closed, as if she was trying to blink away a vision. Maddie put a hand on Jane's shoulder. She flinched, then looked at her.

"Do you remember anything?" Maddie asked.

Jane blinked rapidly. "I can't trust you," she whispered.

Maddie gave her a sad smile. "Well, I'm not here to hurt you," Maddie offered. "Anyway," she turned to the rest of us, "whoever this Dr. Bates was, he must have been a psychopath. Do you remember what he did to you?"

"It was a program," I explained. "Training us to fight."

"To endure," Billy said.

I nodded. "To let the worst take us."

"What do you mean by that?" Maddie asked. "Was he preparing you for something?"

"To fight for my sister," I said. I couldn't talk about it too much or I would see her face. Those visions would come flooding back, memories that I preferred to keep buried. And I hated seeing her like that, rotting in the woods alone.

Because it wasn't a memory. It was a nightmare. Nothing more. Another way for Dr. Bates to manipulate me.

"My daughter," Billy said.

"My mom," Jane said.

The three of us looked back and forth between each other. We were all searching for someone, and they were all women too.

"So, what? I know your sister is missing," Maddie said, making eyes with me. She turned to Billy and Jane. "But what about your daughter and your mom?"

"I don't know," Billy said. "She's gone."

Jane wouldn't answer. All she could do was nod.

"You two don't have criminal backgrounds," Maddie said to

Billy and me. "So unless you were sneaky about it, there's no reason for you to know the Adlers." Maddie then turned to Jane. "Not so sure about you, though." Maddie shrugged. "We need your name to know more."

I knew how to help Jane find her memories, but Wil and I had agreed that using the trigger word wasn't wise. It was hard enough having Billy and me activated.

I tried to think of why the Adlers would be compelled to kill our family when none of us had any connection to them.

But that was it; there wasn't any reason.

The ringing pulsed between my ears, shooting to the bridge of my nose.

"Skyline Shift!" I shouted quickly. The ringing stopped. Billy's eyes lit up. Maddie pulled back from the table. "Did you go to the Skyline Shift?" I asked. "That's where you know Dr. Bates, right?"

"He recruited me shortly after my daughter went missing," Billy said hesitantly, "saying he knew the answers about where she was."

My heart sank. "Did you ever find her?"

She shook her head. "There was an emergency. I had to start the final task early."

Maybe Dr. Bates had known that I was captured by the Adlers, and knew that they had to send more soldiers. How many women would he send?

"What do you remember about the Skyline Shift?" Maddie asked.

"They taught us that we had to take down the enemies," I said.

"The enemies?" Maddie asked. She flicked her chin to the doorway, where the three brothers were waiting on the other side. "Just them, or others too?"

"Just them," Billy said.

Jane looked up, glancing at the window in the door. "Who are they?"

"No one," I answered.

Tell her, the voice said. *She deserves to know. She has a right to know. Let her make her own decision.*

I scoffed aloud. That fucking voice. Dr. Bates, telling me to let her make her own decision, when I hadn't been allowed to make any for myself. The ringing started again, pulsing in my head, growing until I could hardly think. Maddie raised her brow at me, and Billy pursed her lips. But it wouldn't stop. I held my head in my hands. *Make it stop. Make it stop. Make it stop.* But the sound was enormous, expanding until it seemed like my brain would pop. I breathed deeply in staggered breaths. I could be stronger than this. Stronger than the voice. I could—

A warm hand on my back startled me. Maddie smiled, her voice dimmed. "You okay?"

Sometimes it felt like it would be easier to accept Dr. Bates's voice than it would be to fight it. The pain was like nothing I had experienced, as if my entire existence could be wiped out with one headache.

"I'm fine," I said. But I wasn't fine at all. I needed to figure out what the hell was going on. "Where is the Skyline Shift?" I asked. "Do any of us remember?" Billy shrugged. "You ever heard of it?" I asked Maddie.

"Brackston," Jane said. The three of us looked at her curiously, wondering how much she remembered now. "The program was in Brackston," she repeated.

"Right," I said. Brackston. I remembered that. Brackston was only an hour or so away from where Julie and I lived. "Yeah. It was in Brackston."

"Brackston?" Maddie asked, her voice higher-pitched. "Are you sure it was Brackston?"

"Yeah," I said. "Why?"

She bit her lip, then looked down at the table. "Fuck," she muttered. "Brackston?"

I nodded. "What's wrong with Brackston?"

She turned towards the doorway, looking at the window. Wil and Derek were visible in the glass, talking to each other. I assumed Axe was down the hallway.

"Let me talk to Derek," Maddie said. She stood up. "Keep me posted if you figure anything else out."

Maddie excused herself from the table, then locked us in the room. I looked up at the walls. I had stopped coming in here after I decided that it wouldn't give me the answers to my past, but as I looked at the black and white photo of Wil's family on the wall, I realized it was there all along.

"Are you sure we can trust her?" Billy asked. Jane perked up, nodding her head too. "She seems cool, but she's with them, isn't she? Which means—"

"She's not with them," I said, raising a hand to remind her to stop. We couldn't say the trigger word in front of Jane. In the window, Maddie was talking frantically, raising her hands above her head, while Derek nodded, scratching his chin. Wil was off to the side, sighing.

"She's not with them," I repeated, knowing deep down that it was true. "She just works for them."

"Which means—"

I shook my head. "No." I turned to Billy. "I mean she literally cleans for them."

"Oh," Billy said. Jane looked down at her shackled wrists. Derek put his hand on Maddie's shoulder, looking into her eyes. She shook her head, turning away. Then Wil spoke to Derek. I tried reading his lips, but I couldn't make out anything.

You'll never be able to trust him, the voice said.

"Fuck!" I yelled. I pulled on my restraints, the cuffs digging into the bruises on my wrists. "I am so sick of Bates's voice in my mind all of the damned time." Jane looked up, her eyes wide. I breathed out hard, letting the air take my anger with it. "Aren't you?"

"You hear him too?" Jane asked.

"We all do," Billy said. She shook her head, the brown hair shuffling on her scalp.

Maddie came in abruptly, slamming the door behind her.

"You do realize that Brackston means whoever owned the Skyline Shift could have been working directly with Midnight Miles Corporation, right?"

My chest tightened. She seemed so scared now. What did that—

"Miles Muro," Billy said, rubbing the back of her neck. Maddie glanced at Billy's neck, then moved her hands out of the way. "Hey!" Billy yelped. But Maddie stared at those markings, shaking her head.

"Not just working with," Maddie said to herself. "He probably owned it. Built it, even." Her voice was grim, her head hanging low. She nodded at the tattoo. "Not hills. Not a curve. MM. His initials. A logo."

I rubbed the back of my neck, knowing it was there too, marking me with his name.

"What does that mean for us?" I asked.

Billy looked up. "You don't know?" she asked.

"Know what?"

She studied me, those muddy red eyes shifting across my face. "I don't know much," she started slowly, "but I know Miles Muro is not someone you want to mess with."

"Muro owns the company, Midnight Miles. He's a crime lord. But not just that. He owns a corporation," Maddie explained. "He's growing quickly. And he's…" She shook her head, thinking to herself. "Fuck!"

"Like them?" I nodded towards the door, hinting at the brothers.

"Kind of," Maddie shrugged. "The family here," she said carefully, eyeing Jane, cautious of saying the brothers' surname, "They have rules. They murder. They gamble. They deal drugs. They protect. All of that. They're criminals too. But they don't traffic." Fear was in her eyes, as if she had seen the terrors first hand of what Midnight Miles could do. "Muro? He ripped you guys from your lives. Made you his personal weapon. It's a different form of slavery." She shook her head, her eyes downcast. "At least the family here has loyalty. Midnight Miles?" She shrugged. "Family? He doesn't care about family. Not even his wife." She crossed her arms. "He has no loyalty."

"What does that mean for us?" I asked, looking down in my lap, afraid to hear the answer.

"It means you were sent to kill the brothers," she said. "In all honesty, Derek thinks the best decision is to get rid of you guys. But I will *not* let them harm you." Her voice was forceful. "And Wil?" She nodded towards the door. "He's with me. It's just Derek and Axe that need convincing."

How the hell was Wil on my side, when it came to this? I was just supposed to be a toy he could discard whenever he wanted, but this? I had tried to kill him. Had bitten him. Had cut his face and hand. And yet he was helping me.

Did he actually care?

I looked down at the metal links surrounding my wrists. The ringing filled my head again, and I closed my eyes, trying to make it go away.

Kill him, the voice said.

But I didn't want to hurt him.

I turned to Maddie. "Will you adjust my cuffs?" I asked. "Make them tighter?"

"Of course," she said. "You want to talk to Wil?"

I nodded. She tightened the bands connecting the two cuffs, so that my wrists were close together, making it harder for me to fight. After she did the same for the other two, Derek and Axe led them out of Wil's study. I stayed behind, sitting at the round table.

Wil's footsteps surged through me, awakening my spirit. I had told him everything I knew, and he hadn't run; he was still here, still willing to help me, even when he knew that the easiest solution would have been to get rid of me.

He took a seat beside me. I looked into his deep brown eyes, seeing more than a criminal. I saw a man who wanted to protect his family. And a man who wanted to help a stranger, a woman who had tried to kill him. Me.

"If you didn't kill her," I asked. He stared at me, waiting for my response. *You know his answer*, Dr. Bates said in my mind. *Lies. All lies. He will never be honest with you.*

I squinched my eyes together, trying to drown out the voice, but then the ringing started. A tear went down my cheek, but as soon as Wil touched my hands, everything went silent. My head throbbed, but at least the noise had stopped.

"If I didn't kill her," he said, nodding for me to continue.

"If she's not dead," I corrected, "will you help me find who hurt her?"

"I will kill any fucker who touched her," he said. My heart rate increased, and the pressure swelled in my head. I wanted to believe him. I wanted so badly to trust him. But the ringing started and I had to concentrate on thinking.

Why shouldn't I trust him? He had kept to his word every single time.

Lies. All—

"I'm afraid," I whispered, the tears making my throat ache. "They lied to me. Made me believe them. And it's so hard not to believe them, not when you know what they're capable of." Wil's features tensed, remembering what I had told him. "If I fail my mission, they'll kill me, Wil. And I can't kill you. I won't let myself." The tears streamed down now, and I couldn't stop them. "You've got to believe me."

"I believe you," he said.

And those words struck my soul, hitting me where everything was shattered. It had been such a long time since anyone believed me. Officer Shines hadn't. None of Julie's friends did.

But Wil believed me. How could that be true?

"How can you?" I asked, breathless. "After what I've done."

He put his hand on the back of my head, his fingers tangling with my hair. That softness made me melt, made me feel like I could be whole again, but it only lasted for so long. I knew the urge to fight would come back, and then, what would I do? I couldn't hold onto Wil's touch forever. I needed to be on my own.

"You're mine, Ellie," he said, locking his dark eyes on mine. "I'm not going to let anything happen to you."

I wanted to believe him, but I didn't know how. If I had let my sister down, let her be captured by the Skyline Shift, losing the one person I cared about more than anything in the world, then how could I trust anyone? How could I trust Wil to protect me?

My heart sank with my body, drifting down, heavy, as if nothing would ever bring it back up.

CHAPTER 16

Wil

The closer we drove to Muro, the less confident I was that we would get answers. With each passing minute, I only had more questions. Was Ellie's sister truly dead? And if so, who had killed her? And why was Ellie able to fight the programming from the Skyline Shift one moment, and let it control her completely the next?

I didn't understand the switch between being mine, and being my enemy. I wanted to trust Ellie, but she and I both knew that she wasn't wired to trust me. She had been conditioned to kill me.

She was mine, and yet, she wasn't.

"We need to figure out a way to help the women," I said to Derek. He adjusted his grip on the steering wheel, then checked his speed.

"How do we do that?" he asked.

"I called Ethan," I said. "He's going to take a look at the camp they were in." Derek nodded. "But is there a professional that can help?" I asked. He pressed his brows together. I shook my head, gazing out at the faded green hills passing to the side. "This is some weird cult shit. I don't like it."

"None of us do," Derek said. Our phones buzzed at the same time, likely a group message from Axe. Derek nodded at me to read the text and I checked my device.

Another one of Muro's women, Axe sent.

"Damn it," I muttered.

"What is it?"

"Axe found another one."

"Another woman?"

"Yep. Another female soldier."

I rubbed my forehead, scowling to myself. I had the space to protect Ellie, and hell, if I wanted, I could house two or more of the women in the extra rooms in my penthouse. But I couldn't babysit, run Jimmy's, *and* deal with a war, and I sure as hell didn't have any loyalty to the rest of the women. Ellie was different. But even with Ellie, I couldn't keep her in handcuffs for the rest of her life. There had to be another way. A way to fight this. A way to unearth Ellie's soul. To free her from everything. Perhaps even to free her of me.

But that wasn't a possibility I was willing to accept right then. First, we had to figure out Dr. Bates and Miles Muro. Then we could figure out the rest.

"This is bullshit," I muttered.

"Focus on Muro," Derek said. "Then we'll figure out the prisoners."

The building to the Midnight Miles Corporation was sleet-colored against the overcast sky. I always knew I hated the bastard—Miles fucking Muro—but the fact that he had ripped Ellie from her life, conditioned her to be his undercover soldier, erased her memories, had her tortured *and* raped her, made me sick. I had grown up in the Adler mafia; crime was in my blood. But I couldn't fathom this. I wanted to squeeze the life out of him.

And yet I knew I was just like him. Muro had trained Ellie for his own ends, and what was I, if not doing the same thing?

The difference was that Muro didn't care if Ellie lived or died. But I would protect her, forever and always.

Which was another damn problem.

Instead of letting us pass through the gates, the security team checked our car twice. After discussing the situation on their headsets, maybe with Muro himself, the guards' eyes cast up to the skyscraper, then they returned our pistols. I glanced at Derek, who gave a subtle nod. We had guns hidden inside of the seats too, ones that they hadn't found, but Muro didn't care that we were armed. Almost like he *wanted* us to bring our weapons. To play a game. And that made me uneasy.

"The hell was that about?" I asked, looking at Derek as he parked. I checked our guns, making sure they hadn't messed with them or the ammo. To my surprise, they were still completely intact. "They let us keep the guns?"

Derek shook his head, glancing at the building. "I don't like this."

The rest was the same; we crossed the empty entrance lobby, passing the white furniture with the bright red orchid in the middle of a table. That flower caught my eye. It was delicate and utterly feminine, but the color was violent, being the only smear of color on the entire floor. It reminded me of those women from the woods, of Ellie. Each of them was dangerous, but mysteriously so, wrapped up into a package that was hard to resist. Like a light bringing us closer to our deaths, those women lured us in. And Ellie lured me.

The guard let us up to the top floor without a word. As the elevator cart clicked to a start, my stomach sank. Derek sucked in a breath. The elevator rushed to the top in an electric hum. Stepping out of the cart, we exchanged a glance, then opened the office doors.

"My favorite brothers," Muro said. He clicked a button on his wireless earbud, then smirked and gestured to the two of us to come in. I glanced around his office; this time, there were no beefy guards pouring shots of whisky in the corner, but there was a woman kneeling to the side of him, her head bowed. Derek studied her for a moment, as if he recognized her, but he shook it off.

"One of these days, I'll have to make the trip to Sage City myself," Muro said, his tone nonchalant as if we still had a good relationship. "But alas, business keeps me here, in the headquarters. You know how it is."

I got the feeling he was saying that to mock us. In comparison, we, the Adler family, controlled Sage City, our state's capital, and had footing in Las Vegas, as well as other businesses in different states, a legacy that had taken us generations to build. Muro, on the other hand, had spread throughout the entire United States quicker than a weed, stretching his greedy fingers, caring more about his growing power than building his foundation that would last.

But civilizations were built and destroyed like that. Muro would find that out soon enough. And the best part was that he hadn't covered Sage City yet, the only other major city in our state. *We* stood in his way.

The only reason we were there was for Gerard. He had insisted that we try to work it out. Negotiate. Reason. I wouldn't have agreed, except for the fact that we knew Muro had to do with the women from the woods, and by seeing him, Derek argued we might be able to figure more out.

"You've come to discuss purchasing artillery, correct?" Muro said. I glanced at Derek, who shook his head.

"We came to discuss our recent orders," Derek said.

"Ah, that's right. I hear there was a misunderstanding with my men," Muro asked, looking at me. "You came to apologize?"

I couldn't help it. I laughed in his face. "Actually, we wanted to make sure you understood that there *will* be cutbacks."

"Cutbacks," he said. "I see. Because a home is a home." He shrugged his shoulders. "And we don't like it when people touch our things."

I lifted a brow. *Our things*? Why did it seem like he was talking about Ellie? Muro calling her a 'thing' made me feel like shit. How could I consider myself any better than Muro when I had captured her? Forced her to my will? Became her god?

"What are you talking about?" I asked.

Muro smiled, his mouth pulled wide. "And what do you think I'm talking about, Wilhelm?"

I stared at him, daring him to make a move. "Women," I said. Because he was right. I hated when other men talked to or touched Ellie, but she wasn't a 'thing.' I glanced at the kneeling woman, but she hadn't moved. "Women," I continued, refocusing on Muro, "especially *my* woman, deserve more respect than that."

"Your woman," Muro snickered. "What an interesting concept. Do we ever really *own* anything? Especially people. Every being has a mind of its own. Unless, of course, you get rid of that mind."

Get rid of what? Their minds?

Just like he had manipulated the women at the Skyline Shift.

The woman was as still as a statue on the floor, waiting for Muro's demands.

"We know you sent those women," Derek said. He adjusted in his chair, then put his hand on his gun.

"What women?" Muro asked, a playful grin on his face.

"We found five naked women in the woods. Two of which tried to kill us." Derek left his arm loose at his side, ready to fight. I wrapped my own hand around my gun, a flicker of pain from the cut still healing there.

Muro's eyes scanned my face, lingering over the scab on my cheek. "I see you've been having fun, then," Muro smiled. "Tell me. Does she like getting her cunt fucked with a dagger?"

How did he know about that?

"Watch it," I growled. Derek hit the back of his knuckles on my leg, warning me to stand down.

"So there are feelings, then?" Muro laughed. "It's no matter to me. You know that if I raise a finger, you two won't make it out of this building."

But there was a chance that we could take Muro down with us, and he knew that possibility as well. He even let us keep our guns—perhaps he wanted a fight. I rubbed my pistol in the holster. Muro eyed my movements the entire time.

"We're here to negotiate," Derek said.

"Not to kill more of my men?" Muro said. I sneered, and Derek hit my leg.

"My apologies," I said, gritting my teeth. I had to trust Derek to know what he was doing. "We want to set things right."

It was a lie. Muro snickered, and I knew he knew it was a lie too.

"But that's the thing, isn't it?" he said. "Were things ever *right* between us? First, you let the Knox girl go free, nearly letting Oliver escape in the process. Word has it that you were in possession of the Pink Diamond before we retrieved it. Now, you shut my men out of dealing in your territory, all because of a misunderstanding?"

How the hell did you call skipping cutbacks, insulting us with shitty cocaine, and sending undercover soldiers to kill us, a misunderstanding?

"Your men didn't pay the cutback fees," Derek said.

Muro shrugged. "That bothers you, doesn't it?" He leaned back in his chair, lacing his fingers together in thought. "I suppose if a person *was* to extort women into being experimental soldiers, the first thing I would do, if it were me personally," he held a hand to his chest, "would be to go after you. You notorious Adlers, with your hold on Sage City. Messing up my plans for the rest of the state." He shook his head. "I hear you all have a penchant for obedient women."

I swear he was eyeing me, as if he knew that Ellie was mine. I took a deep breath, controlling myself so that I wouldn't strangle him on the spot.

"We can work together, Muro," Derek said. He was as calm as ever, unattached to the situation. But I wanted to punch Muro in the face. "It doesn't have to be like this."

"And what's the alternative? Having lunch together on the weekends? Pool parties at my estate, trading black market secrets, creating an alliance between our two groups?" Muro smiled. "I don't make alliances. I conquer."

Conquer. Annihilate. Rule. We had our own ways too.

"Ruling without cooperation will only rally your enemies to join forces and wipe you out sooner," Derek said.

Muro leaned forward. "Then go for it," he said. "But I don't have time for this dance anymore." He sighed, then leaned back in his chair and scratched the bolt tattoo on the side of his face. "I know this is what the family mafias might call a war, and I suppose," he grinned, "that it just might be one. But let's call it a truce for now. We can figure out the logistics after I return from abroad."

The man was mocking us. I clenched my fists.

"Gerard would like to work together, rather than create an enemy of you," Derek said.

The woman on the floor sniffed, and Muro snapped his head at her, offended that she would make a sound. Then the smile on Muro's face fell, leaving behind a blank expression. He tapped his chin and turned to us. "Funny, isn't it? I have yet to meet the infamous Gerard Adler himself. Almost like he doesn't *want* to meet me. Sending his sons instead. The coward." Muro tilted his head. "And I'm afraid it's too late." Muro stood. "Nothing against you. Just your father, and his unwillingness to make room for bigger fish."

I adjusted my jacket, staring down at Muro, shorter than me, and yet completely pompous. He smiled. "If you want a job, Wilhelm, feel free to come here," he said, winking at me. "I hear you're rather good at navigating a dealer's room. I'd like to expand into that arena eventually."

What the hell?

"I will *never* leave my family," I said.

Muro clapped slowly, the smile cheapening his every move. "Bravo. Good for you and *your family*."

I gripped my hands tight, and Derek knocked the back of his hand into mine, and we turned towards the door.

With each step, anger surged inside of me. Muro's corporation was bigger than our mafia, but we still controlled Sage City. What the hell were we doing here?

Were we just going to walk away?

No. Fuck that.

I snapped around, grabbing my gun and pulled the trigger, but Muro already had that kneeling woman strapped across his chest, using her as a shield, his gun keeping her in place. At the last second, I moved and the bullet skimmed her cheek, searing her flesh and leaving a wound in its wake.

Derek immediately aimed his gun at Muro too.

"So you *do* have some fight in you," Muro laughed. His gun jabbed into the woman's chin. The lines around her mouth shimmered in fright; now that her head wasn't lowered, I could tell that she was older, maybe even as old as Muro. And her green eyes were full of panic. She knew this might be her last moment.

"Please, Master!" she cried.

Master?

"Your father likes them like this," Muro said. "I heard you two do too. But I want to hear it for myself. Do you like them obedient? Compliant?" He dug the gun deeper into the woman's chin and she flinched, tears running down her cheeks. How the hell did he know about that? "It's easier, isn't it? Keep them like this, like submissive pieces of trash, and they're easily disposable."

"Drop the fucking gun, Muro," Derek ordered. I glanced at him quickly; he was staring at Muro, his head reeling as if he was trying to figure out how to protect the woman. What the hell was he defending this stranger for?

"Who cares about her?" I yelled. "Let's kill them both!"

But Derek didn't move.

"Tell me, Wilhelm," Muro said. "What's this girlfriend of yours like, anyway?" He smiled. "Ellie. Isn't that her name?"

"She's not a girlfriend," I quipped, but I knew saying those words didn't make it any better. But I had to protect her, and that meant pretending she wasn't mine. She couldn't become Muro's target. But how did he know I had Ellie? "She's—"

"Your woman," he smirked. "One thing is clear to me. You care about her," he nodded. "Be careful now, Little Adler. Love is dangerous, my friend. It misguides us."

I lifted a brow, then adjusted my aim. What was worse, Muro calling me a friend, or giving me advice about love?

"What are you talking about?" I asked.

"I'm asking you: what could be more reckless than falling in love with a dangerous woman?"

I stared at him, the smile still painted on his face. I didn't understand him. If he had sent Ellie, then why warn me about the very woman he wanted to kill me?

"What the fuck?" I yelled, tilting my head towards Derek. "Let's shoot them—"

"Lower your gun too, Wil," Derek roared, his eyes still resting on Muro.

"Fuck playing nice," I said. "It's over. Gerard can—"

"Lower your fucking gun," Derek said.

I waited, watching Muro's face. The lightning bolt tattoo pulsed with his heart rate, and yet Muro's cocky smile never dropped. He was having fun with us.

He was playing a game, and it was bigger than Derek and me.

The woman groaned in fear, her lip quivering, and I saw Ellie in her. The woman might have been under Muro's spell, but she wasn't there by choice. She had been coerced, taken from her life. And just like Ellie, she didn't deserve this.

I lowered my weapon, and Muro shoved the woman to the side. She fell to her hands and knees and began sobbing, a relieved cry that echoed through the room. Derek lowered his gun too, but clenched his fists.

"My issue isn't with you," Muro warned. And I had a feeling I knew who he wanted. Gerard.

"Good luck, Muro," I muttered. "You're going to need it."

"Likewise," he said.

It took all of my energy not to slam my fists into the walls of the elevator, not to toss that red orchid across the lobby until the vase shattered into a million pieces on the white tiled floor. Muro was a cocky piece of shit, and I hated him down to his bones.

Derek checked his phone, then started the engine.

"What the hell was that?" I yelled. I hit the dashboard with my fists, cursing myself for the ache in my palm. "Who cares what happens to Muro's slave?"

"Gerard asked us not to fight," Derek said.

"This is war, Derek. It's not just a disagreement. We've got to—"

"Sometimes," he said, his voice booming so loud that I shut up. "*Sometimes*, there are issues that we can't see." He glared at me. "This isn't just about Muro and the drugs, or the soldiers. And if Gerard asks us not to start a war—"

"Our father doesn't know—"

"Our father is doing what he thinks is right," Derek said, his voice loud again. "I respect my family. I stick by them, even if I don't understand what's going on." His eyes were bloodshot, as if he had been thinking about this for a long time too. Ethan, our half brother, crossed my mind. Even though Derek and Ethan had hated each other, when Ethan asked for our help, Derek never hesitated. He was always loyal to his family. "If our father asks us to wait on a war, then I will respect his wish as best I can." *As best I can*, meaning until that time had passed. Why wasn't that *now*? Derek shifted back into his seat. "You ought to do the same."

I turned forward. I could do my best too. For now. "All right," I said. "The hell is going on with Gerard then?"

"I don't know," Derek said, sighing. He started the engine and the car rumbled around us. "But I know it's important to him. He's our family. He raised us." He let out a long sigh. "We stick by him."

Raising us didn't mean Gerard was a goddamn saint, but I understood. "We stick by him," I repeated.

Derek checked his phone, then pulled out of the parking space. "Another one," he said. The women? My hurt palm twitched.

"That makes it six," I said. Five alive, one dead. We'd have to start setting up cages in the woods, or even mine and Derek's places. "What the hell are we going to do with all of them?"

"You remember Dr. Mercia?" Derek asked.

I shook my head. "Who's that?"

"She used to work with Axe," he said. "Maybe she can help."

CHAPTER 17

Ellie

Through the night, I laid on my back, watching the shadows creep across the ceiling. The metal restraints dug into my wrists and ankles, so to be comfortable, I had to lay in this position, still and quiet. Most of the time, the voice was silent now, but I still heard that ringing whispering in my brain. Wil was asleep beside me, but his breathing was quick. He never settled throughout the night. He wanted me to feel safe, to know that he had my back, but at the same time, I knew the reason he was restless.

A flash of an image: bringing the cuffs down on his neck until I crushed his windpipe.

You're mine, he would gasp with his last breath.

His face would turn red, redder still, until he fell apart and disappeared into nothingness.

My mind filled up with these visions, imagining his death over and over again.

And so, neither of us slept.

The next time I heard him stir, I turned to him. "Go to your bedroom," I said. "You'll sleep better there."

You'll feel safe, I wanted to say. And you'll be able to relax. Without me.

"No," he said. He put an arm around my stomach, holding me from the side, then linked his thumb inside of the cuffs.

His arms around me. Holding me. Trying to tell me we were safe.

You're mine, Ellie, Wil had said. *We'll figure it out.*

Because we had no other choice.

I will kill any fucker who touched her, he had promised.

But not if I killed him first.

***

When I finally opened my eyes, the sun was blinding. In the window, the clouds were gone, and the blue sky was alarming. How late had I slept?

Had I actually fallen asleep?

My wrists and ankles were crushed pins and needles, so I rolled them awake as best as I could. I glanced beside me, but Wil wasn't there. I pushed myself up on the bed.

"Good morning, princess," Wil's voice sang out from the doorway. I raised a brow, then lifted my cuffed hands to scratch my forehead. "We've got a visitor," he said. "Dr. Mercia. Ever heard of her before?"

I shook my head. "Should I have?"

"Nope." He grinned. "Let's get you freshened up."

In the bathroom, Wil took a wet washcloth and wiped my face, then rubbed a bar of soap between his hands, using the lather to wash my skin. I suppose he could have had a guard come with me, or maybe even Maddie, to help me clean up. But knowing him, he wouldn't let anyone else do this. His tone seemed cheery, but the false kind that was hiding a secret, like he had gotten bad news that he didn't want to share with me yet. A crease ran through his forehead, a new one, as if the stress of the situation made him ill. But his lips were soft, open, waiting for me. His breath landed on my cheeks, warm and sweet, and it was intimate, being vulnerable enough that he had to help me.

"I can do this myself, you know," I said as he wiped the washcloth over my face again, rinsing off the suds. "Even with the handcuffs."

A subtle hint of a smile fluttered across his mouth, then disappeared.

"I want to do this," he said in a quiet voice.

Warmth filled me, but I blinked it away. It couldn't let those emotions inside of me anymore. Being with Wil was an impossibility. I knew that now. He was an Adler, and I had been trained to kill his family.

But what if I could undo the training?

No. I couldn't dream about that. I had to think realistically.

At the dining table, a woman in a gray blazer and matching pants stood when we entered the room. Blond hair was tied into a low bun at the nape of her neck. Wil put his hand on my lower back.

"Dr. Mercia, this is Elena Jordan," Wil said.

I glanced to the side; Wil's brother, the older one, Derek was sitting on the couch at the far end of the room. The other brother was gone.

"Ellie, right?" Dr. Mercia said. "I've heard a lot about you."

She held out her hand, and I stared at it for a moment. She saw the handcuffs, and yet she was acting like treating a captive patient was a normal thing.

She must have known the Adlers were a crime family, then.

I lifted my hands slowly, shaking with one, letting the other hand dangle.

"I wish I could say the same," I said, "But you're news to me. And the rest, I can't remember anyway." I sighed.

"Humor. That's good," she said, smiling. She nodded at Wil and Derek. "We'll be fine from here. Thanks."

Wil pursed his lips together, then shrugged. The two of them left.

She's one of them, the voice said.

I squeezed my eyes shut. Just. Fucking. Stop it.

The ringing started again, like a giant bell always vibrating, never coming to a stop. I leaned forward, resting my elbows on the table, my head collapsing in my hands. This woman was not the enemy. *Not* the enemy.

"Tell me what's going on, Ellie," Dr. Mercia said.

Gray hair grew out from her roots, but otherwise, she dyed her hair into a yellowish blond. Laugh lines surrounded her eyes, spreading down her cheeks, and there was a mole above her upper lip. She seemed kind, but professionally so.

"What do you mean?" I asked.

"Wil mentioned you had an experience with a cult."

Was it a cult? Hell... I had been led to believe it was an experimental program, like a course of study. Maybe even a college program. Not a religious belief.

Though the Skyline Shift *did* have a belief system.

"I was trained by a doctor to kill the Adlers," I said. "I always hear this voice, you know? His voice."

Don't tell her.

"And no matter how hard I try," I closed my eyes, "He comes back. Tells me what to do. Dr. Bates's voice."

"Who is Dr. Bates?"

Don't tell her.

"I think he ran the camp," I said quickly, trying to think back and say it before the voice stopped me. "Anyway, he made me believe that if I did whatever he said, he would tell me where my sister was."

Don't tell her, Ellie.

"And did he tell you where your sister was?" she asked.

"He made me—" but I couldn't bear to say it. "He showed me—" I stopped, then, because what was it, really? "He showed me a video of her body decomposing."

I will kill you myself, Ellie!

"A video?"

"Yes," I snapped. Her tone was as if she didn't believe me. But that's what it was—it had to be. "A video," I repeated.

I grit my teeth together, feeling the pressure all the way down my neck. The metallic taste of blood traced my tongue.

"Do you want to hurt the Adlers?" she asked.

It was a yes or no question, but the answer wasn't that simple. Did I want to hurt the people who murdered my sister? Yes. I wanted to kill them. To force them to pay for taking an innocent life away from this world when she deserved so much more. When I deserved to see her grow up.

But I knew, deep down, that the Adlers hadn't hurt her. And yet it was hard to accept the reality, the one that had always been there, lurking beneath the surface.

It was a video. Just a video. A nightmare. A vision.

Julie was out there, somewhere. She had to be.

"Ellie?" Dr. Mercia asked.

"No," I said. "*I* don't want to hurt them."

But the voice did.

"But you hear voices, telling you to hurt them?"

It was just one voice, but that one voice was enough. I closed my eyes again, then nodded.

"All right," Dr. Mercia said. She waited until I opened my eyes. Her hands were folded in her lap, her eyes beaming into me. "You're having trouble breaking away from your experiences with the Skyline Shift. Does that sound correct?"

"Yes."

"And you want to think for yourself, but you're having a hard time being independent, especially in a situation where you were held hostage. Does that sound accurate?"

So she *did* know the exact situation. That didn't make it any more comforting.

"Yes," I said.

"I'll be honest with you, Ellie. What we're dealing with isn't simple. But I can do my best to help you." She leaned forward. "But you have to *want* to break free. This isn't about me helping you, but about you wanting to help yourself."

Anything to get Dr. Bates's voice out of my head. "Fine."

"All right," she smiled. "Let's do the quick version." She tucked a loose strand of hair behind her ear. "So when you get these violent impulses, you need to delay your decision-making. Give it as long as you can. Especially the big decisions, like whether or not to harm someone. And after a cup of coffee, a hot shower, whatever it might be, you *still* want to murder this person, then yes," she laughed quietly, "It's probably your actual desire. But don't kill someone on an impulse."

"What kind of doctor are you?" I asked. "Condoning murder?"

She shrugged, the smile fading for a moment, then returning.

"I don't practice anymore, but I am your doctor right now," she said. "Call me a fringe doctor. I deal with unique psychiatric cases."

None of it mattered anyway. I just needed the voice to stop. And I needed her help.

"All right," I said. "Don't make quick decisions. I can do that."

"Wil says you've become friends with Maddie? And the other women?" she asked. I nodded. Billy and Jane weren't exactly my friends, but I had been talking with Maddie fairly regularly, even after Wil restrained me. She was one of the only people that came to the penthouse. "That's good. Keep talking to them. And Wil. Talk to as many people as you can. Share your experiences. Hear what other people have to say. Don't force yourself to be alone. You need to branch out and understand the world for yourself."

Those seemed like conflicting ideas. How could I think for myself, and yet listen to what others had to say? But I guessed the difference was that when I was alone, Dr. Bates's ideas took hold of me, but when I was with other people, like when Wil wrapped his arms around me, I could think for myself.

So I could get behind that advice too.

"And?" I asked.

"And you need to think critically about your experiences," Dr. Mercia said.

"Think critically?"

"Were you accepted into the Skyline Shift, or was it different than that?" I thought back, tracing our interactions. "What did they promise you?"

I saw a vision of my sister, running through a field of green grass, laughing as she jumped into a large water fountain. Even then, the haze of light made everything feel like a dream. I hurried to her, muttering to myself about how I shouldn't have had to be her mother and father, how angry and hurt I was at our parents for leaving this world when they said they would always be there for us. I yelled at her to stop making a scene, that I was tired of chasing her. But then she splashed me and I was wet. There was no point in fighting it. I got in and splashed her right back, and we laughed and played until security escorted us out of the park.

I thought of my sister's corpse, lying shadowed beneath the trees. Not her, but her body, lying there, her blank, yellow eyes looking up and seeing nothing.

"They promised me that I'd be able to see my sister again," I said quietly.

"And did they fulfill that promise?"

In a way, they had. Dr. Bates had shown me her body. But I told myself that was a video. It couldn't be real. Not with what I had endured, with everything we had been through. Tears welled up in my eyes, and Dr. Mercia handed me a tissue box. I wiped my nose then crumpled the tissue in my palm.

"Did you think your sister would be alive?"

I stared at her. "She *is* alive, Dr. Mercia."

"She might be," Dr. Mercia paused. "But they made you think that the Adlers killed her, right? In order to use you for their purposes."

I clenched my fist, raising my narrowed eyes to meet hers.

"I am not your enemy," she said, her voice stern. "You need to learn to accept these truths. These are the facts: we do not know who killed your sister."

"She's not dead."

"But if she is—" Dr. Mercia stared at me, daring me to interrupt her again. "If she *is* dead, then we don't know who did it. But the Skyline Shift used that information to coerce you into doing their bidding. You were used."

She put it in plain words, forcing me to consider my situation. Used. Coerced. It sounded clinical. Like it was easy to pull back the layers and see exactly what had happened to me, when experiencing it was so much harder than that.

"If she's dead," I whispered. She wasn't, but I had to ask. "Who killed her?"

"We might never know," Dr. Mercia said quietly, "But you need to accept why this happened the way it did so that you can move forward and think clearly about your past."

I had begun to do some of those things she had mentioned already, and they had helped. But the tinnitus and the headaches screwed it all up and made me want to give in, to let Dr. Bates take over once again. It was easier that way.

"What do I do for the ringing?" I asked. "The headaches?"

"I can get you Vicodin for the headaches," she said. Was that how she knew the Adlers, by supplying them with prescription drugs? "As for the tinnitus, an antidepressant might help, but it might not. Your best bet is to wait it out."

Which was frustrating, but after all I had been through, I could try.

"One more thing, before I go," she said. She nodded at the bedroom doors, where Wil and Derek's voices were lowered. "Be careful with the Adlers."

A shot of adrenaline ran through me. I thought she was on their side?

"What?" I asked.

"Don't replace one system with the other," she paused, studying me as she did so, as if to make sure that I was actually listening to what she was saying. "The Adlers may not have killed your sister, but they've done plenty," she whispered. "If the situation called for it, they wouldn't have thought twice about taking her life, and yours." She stood and gave a curt nod. "You need to think for yourself. And *only* for yourself."

Wil and Derek emerged from the room, and Dr. Mercia's concerned expression transformed into a warm-hearted one. She held out a hand again, and this time, I shook it without questioning her.

"It was nice to meet you, Ellie. Tell Wil to get in touch with me if I can help you in any way."

Wil put an arm around me, and calmness settled on my chest. Once she and Derek left the penthouse, Wil turned to me and nodded at the handcuffs.

"You want to try unlocking those?" he asked.

I waited for a moment, thinking about what Dr. Mercia had said. I had to think for myself. I had always assumed I *did* make decisions for myself. But had I let Dr. Bates control me all along? Had Wil controlled me too?

Had my situation with my sister, being her parent for the last of our teenage years, had that controlled my decisions as well?

I didn't know if it was the best idea to let me go uncuffed again. Not yet.

"Let's wait," I said. As much as I hated it, I needed to believe it was the right thing to do. I didn't want to hurt him unless I meant to do it myself. "For now," I said. Wil put an arm around my shoulder, pulling me in tight, and I let go of those worries, trying to concentrate on accepting the truth.

Dr. Bates had lied to me.

But Wil? He had always been there.

But then I thought of Dr. Mercia's words.

None of his truths meant that I could trust him.

CHAPTER 18

Wil

My driver rode in the front, while Ellie and I rode in the backseat of the SUV together. It was easier that way; I could stay with Ellie and keep an eye on her. Driving put a person in a vulnerable position, and as much as I hated it, I couldn't trust Ellie yet. Not completely.

"The others will be there too?" she asked.

I nodded. "Wil and Axe are bringing them."

"And why are we taking them to a brothel?"

The Dahlia District wasn't *exactly* a brothel. It was technically an entertainment club for billionaires, who happened to buy sex. But the owner, Iris, had an arrangement with our family. We protected her club from law enforcement *if* she paid the price. But since we had separate deals worked out with her husband, we gave her a reasonable fee with the understanding that there may be a future day where we would need her help. Like today.

"They aren't going to work there, are they?" Ellie asked.

I shook my head. "The club has a few extra rooms in the back. They can stay there. That way, they're away from our family, but still protected."

Ellie lifted a brow, but I didn't offer any explanation. Iris would explain it herself.

After parking, my driver got out of the car and lit a cigarette. In the stillness of the backseat, I turned to Ellie, then looked down at her bruised wrists, still tight in the cuffs.

"Remember what we talked about?" I asked.

"Think about my decisions. Don't listen to the voice."

"Listen to *yourself*," I said. "Not Bates." She nodded. "If you actually want to kill me, then by all means," I smiled, "Do it. I'll fight back, but..." I shrugged, and a tiny smile flitted across her lips. "But don't do it because a man from your past told you to."

Her eyebrows twitched, criticizing my words. "You hate that, don't you?"

Hated that a man from her past controlled her moves now? Of course I hated it. I hated that a man had violated her, ruined her trust, exposed her to the worst tortures imaginable. That I couldn't protect her, or for fuck's sake, do those screwed up things to her myself.

Because at least then, if it had been me, I could take responsibility, and see how it changed her life.

And screw it. I would take responsibility, by torturing that mother fucker until he wished he had never been born.

I punched in a code on the side of the cuffs, then inserted the key. The lock released and the restraints fell into Ellie's lap. She looked at me with a questioning look in her eyes. I tilted my head.

"You're going to have to trust yourself someday," I said. Those words were meant more for me than for her, but I knew we both needed to hear them. I had to learn to trust my own instincts, to believe that I was right about Ellie. That she wasn't a pure killer. She was more than that. I had felt it inside of me. I had to trust that feeling too.

But Muro's words haunted me: *What could be more reckless than falling in love with a dangerous woman?*

I blocked them out, shaking my head, then motioned for Ellie to move to the edge of the seat. Opening the car door, I hopped to the ground, then undid the restraints on her ankles too. Ellie *was* dangerous. There was no doubt about that. I might have been stronger, but Ellie was faster, and if I wasn't careful, she would kill me. And love, as stupid as it sounded, would make me more likely to trust her. To look past the red flags. To see only the good inside of her.

Like I was doing right then. I hoped that I wasn't making a mistake.

I let go of the thoughts, staring past Ellie to the brick buildings of the Dahlia District. Ellie jumped down and rubbed her wrists. We walked to the side entrance on one of the attached buildings. Derek's SUV and Axe's van pulled in, parking beside mine. I nodded to them and their drivers then turned back to the building. Before I reached for the door handle, it opened.

A tall woman in twelve-inch platform boots with chink-length black hair popped out. Her arms, legs, and neck were covered in tattoos. She sneered at me, her black eyes rounder than ever.

"You're late," she said.

I had already checked my watch; we were actually on time. Iris tended to be kinder to Derek than she was to me, because I ran the gambling hall where some of her customers lost money that they could have spent on her girls. Her husband was out of town, working on a new business venture, or I would have suggested we dealt with him directly. Hell, I knew Iris would have agreed.

"We're right on time," I said.

She rolled her eyes. "Your brothers?" she asked.

I nodded behind me. "Bringing in the rest of them."

When I was in my mid-twenties, Gerard had paid her to whip me with a single tail in front of the entire club as a birthday present. Oh, the joy of birthdays for the youngest son in a mafia family. I was in a position where if I ducked out of it, she wouldn't get paid, so of course, I played along with the joke. She didn't go easy on me, even when it was clear I was not happy about the situation. To this day, she still put a bad taste in my mouth.

"Hi," Iris said, turning to Ellie. "You must be 'his.' Is he at least treating you like the queen that you are?"

Ellie cracked a smile, then looked between me and Iris. "Excuse me?"

"Wil said something about one of the lost female soldiers being 'his' woman, emphasis on the 'his.'" Iris glared at me, then snapped her head back to Ellie. "I just want to make sure you're getting the treatment that comes along with being owned. Or," Iris smiled at Ellie, "I can see to it personally that he has an attitude adjustment."

I chuckled, and Iris glared at me. Ellie backed away from us both slightly.

"Ellie is with me," I said. Hell yes, she was mine. "But we need you to hold the other women here until we figure out what's going on with the woods and Muro, and—"

"Don't tell me," Iris said, cutting me off. "Honestly, I don't want to know why I need to hold your hostages here. I know I don't really have a choice. So please," she forced a smile, turning her attention to me and putting a hand on her hip, "Could you let me protect your hostages, so I can move on with my life?"

"They're not hostages," I said. 'Prisoners' was the more accurate term.

"Not completely," Ellie muttered.

Iris glanced at Ellie. "At least she tells the truth. But yes, I *will* help them. Not you, but *them*. Now, if you'll excuse me."

She shoved past us and went to the parking lot, reaching for the four women with her outstretched hands, spouting off at Axe, and being polite, but volatile, to Derek as well. Axe never missed a beat, that stoic expression never fading, even when it came to Iris. But Derek scowled at her.

"You're lucky we're—"

"Actually, we're even." Iris narrowed her eyes. "I'm protecting your girls, and you're protecting mine."

I sighed, laughing to myself at the absurdity of it all. If it weren't for her husband, I doubt we would've helped Iris.

Iris took the four women through the kitchen to the dorm rooms at the back of the club, calling a few entertainers out of their bedrooms to introduce them to each other. Ellie leaned on my shoulder, closing her eyes, a pinched look on her brow. I squeezed her shoulder.

"You okay?" I asked.

She shook her head. "The headaches," she said.

I pulled one of the pills from Dr. Mercia out of my pocket.

"Take one," I said. "That's what they're there for."

Ellie shook her head. "It makes me foggy. I can't."

What irritated me the most was that the other women didn't have the same problems Ellie, perhaps because they weren't fighting the voice like she was. It made me angry. Why should she have to suffer when she was trying to fight? Wasn't fighting the urge to obey her fucked up programming hard enough?

Ellie walked past me, her gait staggering from the pain, but as she met the women in the hallway, Ellie linked arms with the short-haired woman from the woods, leaning into her. With all of the women next to each other, I realized that they were all Ellie had. No matter how much pain Ellie was in, both emotionally and physically, she still tried to help them. She still tried to trust me.

I couldn't understand how someone could be selfless and trusting, even after everything she had been through. It didn't make sense. She should have hated everyone around her, should have been running as far away as she could, never speaking to another person again. But she still wanted to help. And that, among other reasons, made me want to protect her, to give her a space where no one could hurt her ever again. Not even me.

I hovered behind them, listening from the doorway.

"So you'll get to sleep in here. Private rooms," Iris said, then patted the door. "But know that once you step foot into the hallway, there are cameras. And you will be watched." She cleared her throat. "The Adlers have security throughout the club, as well as the parking lot and the surrounding woods. There's actually a ratio of four to one. So, you know, you can't leave the premise. At all."

"You're refreshingly straightforward," one of the women said.

"I've learned the hard way about keeping secrets from friends," Iris said, tilting her head. "I'd rather you know exactly what's going on."

My chest tightened. Was it stupid of Iris to be telling them the truth? Besides Ellie, each of them was wearing restraints and couldn't run away. And with our extra security watching the perimeter and the interior of the Dahlia District, there wasn't a chance that they would get very far, even if they didn't have cuffs.

"You're really just here to help us," Ellie said, her voice quiet, but reassured.

"Right," Iris said. "I want to help you."

Iris showed the other women to their rooms, and Ellie helped one of the women—I think her name was Billy—settle in. She brushed Billy's hair, then spoke to her in a quiet voice. Billy's forehead had the same pained expression as Ellie's, and I wondered if Ellie had convinced her of the truth too. That we weren't the real enemies. Perhaps Billy was fighting it after all.

Ellie's light brown hair dusted her shoulders, her bright blue eyes choppy and full of pain, but lurking behind them was the urge to fight for what was right. She stroked her friend's arms and hair with a gentle touch, trying to give her comfort in a world that must have been terrifying. Ellie was beautiful, but she was strong too, stronger than she knew. Even when the world tried to control her, tried to bring her down, Ellie had fought hard for her family.

A pain swelled in my chest. I knew I wasn't helping Ellie. I was part of the problem.

Iris appeared at my side, staring at Ellie inside of the room too. I rubbed my hands together, then turned away, heading back to the kitchen where my brothers were waiting. They were in a heated discussion, and because I couldn't be bothered to care about what they were talking about right then, I went to the kitchen sink and splashed my face with water. The sounds of women in the dorm rooms steadily increased in volume. A few of the entertainers came to the kitchen to see what was going on, what Derek and Axe were arguing about, missing the fact that there were cuffed women occupying the once-empty bedrooms.

It seemed simple here. The club wasn't full of dead men butchered to pieces like it was out there.

Iris leaned against the counter, then crossed her arms. "You're pretty into her, aren't you?" she asked.

I raised a brow. It was such a seemingly simple question. But coming from Iris, someone I barely knew, it meant a lot more than that.

"So it's that pathetic already," I scoffed.

"No, actually," she said, dropping the bitter tone from before. "She seems like a good woman. It'd be hard not to fall for someone like that."

That was only the start of it. There was much more to Ellie than what Iris could see from the surface.

"So what's the problem?" Iris asked. "Besides the attempted murder and all."

I shrugged. It was hard to explain. Had I met Ellie before the Skyline Shift experiments, she might have been exactly what I was looking for. A woman untarnished by the world, who had a dirty mind and a will to fight.

But now, I would never be able to trust her to be faithful to my family, to be loyal to me. She had been conditioned to kill me, and I would always have to sleep with one eye open, waiting for a new trigger to set her off.

And in the end, I had forced her to be mine. My dreams of being her god seemed so insignificant now. There was no reason for her to be loyal to me.

"She's not the problem," I said. "I am."

Iris shrugged. "At least you realize it," she said. "That shows improvement, doesn't it?"

I smiled; there it was, the Iris I had come to expect. She smiled at me though, showing that the comment was not an insult, but said with sincerity.

"Thanks for helping them," I said.

"Anything for my girls," she said.

I turned towards the hallway to find Ellie. Maybe there was a better alternative for her, than being forced to stay with me.

CHAPTER 19

Ellie

Wil appeared in the doorway. Billy tensed beside me, her cuffs jingling.

"It's okay," I whispered. "He's not going to harm us."

"But what if he harmed them?" she asked, her voice loud. I glanced up at Wil. He swallowed hard. His eyes were on me, but his focus was somewhere else, as if he was looking past me, remembering a hard memory.

"He didn't," I said, confident in my words. I had no proof, but I knew it was true. The way he held me, pressing his body into mine. The headaches and the voice were becoming dull as time went by, replaced by my feelings for Wil.

Was it about him, or about what he did for me? The silence that he gave me. The stillness.

"I'll be back," I said to Billy. She nodded, her fingers clenched so hard that her knuckles turned white.

I followed Wil out of the room, and we walked down the long hallway to a door on the other end, which opened up into an unoccupied nightclub. Harsh fluorescent lights lit the main floor, exposing the slips in cleaning—a ripped napkin, a stain from a spilled drink, a garter belt on one of the chairs. To the side, there was a stage with a polished hardwood floor and beams of light fixtures hanging from the top. And on the other side, a bar with no one behind the counter. We sat on the stools anyway.

It was quiet between us, but I never stopped touching him, afraid that once we broke contact, I wouldn't be able to make it stop. But then I thought of Dr. Mercia's warning. Was I just replacing Dr. Bates's voice with Wil?

"Does your family own this place?" I asked, breaking the silence. Wil grinned like I had asked something amusing. What the hell was I supposed to think? He was part of the Sage City mob. For all I knew, he could have owned everything in the city.

"We protect it," he said. He swiveled his stool so that his back leaned against the counter, his arms stretched out, his posture facing the stage. "Are you okay with leaving them here?"

What other choice did we have? Even if there were more armed guards here, I knew it was better than keeping them caged in the woods.

"Yes," I said.

Wil turned to me, holding my hand in his. I sighed deeply, trying to relax, to remember that we all had lives outside of this. The stage was empty, and though the spotlights seemed like they would be bright, I wondered about the women here. Did they have to deal with this kind of danger? Or was it purely an Adler thing? Was I just lucky?

"What do you need to feel safe?" Wil asked.

His words snapped me out of my daydream. The question puzzled me. Hadn't we already discussed that? "Well, since the women are here, they can—"

"Not them," Wil said. "You. What do *you* need?"

His dark brown eyes were pure, with light reflecting in them. And with his lips pressed together, he waited for my answer. For once, this wasn't about him at all; he simply wanted to give me safety. But it had been so long that I didn't know what I needed anymore.

It had started once my parents had died and got worse when Julie disappeared. If Julie had run away with a boyfriend like the police believed, it would have been so much easier to deal with. Easier to contact her. Easier to accept. But running away to an experimental camp? How I hadn't talked to her, even after Dr. Bates promised me? How could I accept that?

I waited for that image of her body to show up in my mind, the waking nightmare. But it never came.

She had to be out there. Somewhere.

She had to be.

"I need to know what happened to my sister," I said. "I know she was at the Skyline Shift too. But maybe she escaped," my voice squeaked. I shrugged. "Who knows. She could've eloped with a boyfriend. Maybe fell in love with one of the guards, who ended up saving her. Or maybe she's in jail in a foreign country." I forced a laugh. "I wouldn't put it past her."

But Wil didn't laugh. "You mentioned those dreams," he said, his voice calm. "The ones of your sister's body?"

"Sure," I said. The ones I was actively trying to suppress at that moment. I squeezed his hand. "What about them?"

"You know that some of our security team died in a similar way before the women showed up."

A raised area held booths spread out along the edges, with round tables in the middle. Divots in the blue walls were hung with tiny light bulbs.

Wil started, "There's a chance—"

Don't say it, I thought. Please don't say it.

There was a kitchen in an area off to the side of the lounge, with dining chairs and candles on each table. I let my eyes focus on anything but him. This place had everything, it seemed.

"—that your sister—"

The kitchen. The dining area. The booths. The stage.

Don't say it.

"—is dead."

I let go of his hands, and the ringing started again, ticking back and forth, each click shaving a sliver off of my sanity. I held my hands over my face, forcing it back inside of me, because I didn't want to deal with it.

But I sucked in a breath and sat up.

Then it stopped. I wasn't even holding him.

"She's out there," I said.

"She's out there," Wil repeated, "But the people who sent you could have killed her."

"Don't do this." I reached over and tightened my grip on his hand, but Wil didn't move. He stared at me, asking me with his eyes to say more. "Don't do this." I couldn't live with the idea that I had given up so much, and yet she wasn't there, and never would be. *Let's go see your sister*, Dr. Bates had said. The trees stalked the edges of the campus, hiding everything from us. *She's just past these trees.*

I closed my eyes, trying to blink that dream away.

"We don't know for sure," he said, squeezing my hand back. "But I promise you. I will find her, and I will find anyone who wronged her."

Wil's eyes held mine, taking me in, knowing that I had problems, and yet he was desperate to help me fix them. There was so much wrong with us, wrong with me, wrong with *him*, but I wanted to believe him. I knew how protective he could be, how loyal he was to his family. I wanted to believe every word he said.

I hate to do that to you, Dr. Bates's voice drifted in my mind. Tears formed in my eyes. *Julie was a good girl. One of our best.*

No. Not now.

"Maybe you should stay here," Wil said. "Iris likes you, and you can keep an eye on the others too." He glanced at the door leading to the kitchen. "And Dr. Mercia said you need to have more relationships. There's no shortage of people here."

"No," I said.

He straightened his shoulders. "What?"

"No," I said again. That must've been strange for him, a self-proclaimed god being told 'no.' "I'm staying with you."

His eyes bore into mine, searing me to my soul. Maybe he thought that this was another ploy to get him to trust me.

But I could turn on him right then if I wanted. As far as I could tell, we were alone in that part of the building. But I wasn't going to kill him.

"Are you sure?" he asked.

I blinked back the tears. "At least until we figure this out."

When he stood, I grabbed his hand, and we walked out of the main entrance to the parking lot. In the car back to Wil's penthouse, the trees zipped past us, and I stared past the trunks to the flashes of water on the other side, the sun shining down on the ocean in a blinding streak. We were going back, where we could be alone. Where I knew the rules. Where I was okay with them. We were going home.

Maybe I felt safer with Wil. Maybe I didn't need anything to feel safer, because I had him.

Once we made it to the front door, he held it open for me. I think he expected me to go to my bedroom and to leave him there, but when I stood beside him, still touching his arm, he pulled away.

"You can't hold onto me forever," he said, his tone pained. "You need to be able to be by yourself. To make your own decisions."

And for once, I let myself feel it. The emptiness. The voice had stopped. The ringing was gone. And I wasn't holding onto him anymore.

"I am," I said.

He scowled at me. "This is fucked up, Ellie," he said. "You were coerced into being here. It's just like the Skyline Shift. All I've done is fucked everything up for you even more."

"And I'm still here."

I dared him to say more, to argue why I should have been running away. But the truth, honest to my soul, was that I wanted him. Even if the voice was gone. Even if the nightmares were repressed. Even if he was speaking his truth, I knew that there was a heart inside of him. A piece of his soul that wanted to protect me.

"I know what I want," I said.

I stepped forward, putting a hand on the back of his neck, then kissed him, pressing our lips together firmly, letting him understand that everything I felt was real as our bodies. Even as his cock twitched against me, he let me kiss him, let me make a fool of myself as he resisted, because he wouldn't give in, wouldn't tell me with his lips that he felt that way too.

"Trust me, Wil," I whispered. "This is it. This is just me."

A sigh escaped his mouth, and finally, he pressed into mine, holding my back tightly against him. His mouth opened, and his tongue searched me for the answers. Warmth surged through me, tingling in my arms and face. Swooping me up by the ass, he carried me, bringing me to his bedroom, our tongues twisting with each other the whole time. He slammed me into the bed, then gazed down at me as he undressed. Lying against the mattress, I slipped out of my button-up shirt, gazing up at him. Dark hair. Sculpted shoulders and arms. A firm stomach. His lips open, waiting. A scar on his cheek, a mark from me. His brown eyes darkened then, but were always focused on me.

"You deserve better than me," he said.

I wanted to shake him and scream that I needed to be able to make a damned decision for myself and that this was it. *This* was what I wanted. But I reeled in the frustration, and spit out those same words again. To show him that he needed to believe me.

"I know what I want."

He climbed on top of me, his strong arms pressing against me, his cock heavy and weighty on my thigh. He peered down into my eyes, seeing more than I could ever know.

Trust me, Wil, I thought, Please, trust me.

"You're beautiful, Elena Jordan," he said. "You know that?"

Tenderness crashed in waves through me. I put a hand on the back of his neck and pulled him into me, kissing him again. Letting it all go. Wil might have forced me to be his, but I knew he would do everything he could to find my sister. To help me let go of the past. To move on. To help me get through this mess we were both drowning in.

His cock penetrated my pussy, slow and hard, his eye contact never breaking from mine. His body rubbed against my clit. His hands held me, not holding me down like so many other times we had fucked, but held me up, supporting me. And for once, it didn't matter where we were or what was going to happen. As long as we were like this, I could forget. Because it was this. Just me. Just him. Just this moment with Wil.

CHAPTER 20

Wil

Ellie had fallen asleep after we had sex. The selfish bastard that I am, I had woken her up a few times when she responded to my touch. The idea was that if I had enough orgasms or exhausted my body enough, I could fall asleep too. And while she fell asleep easily, I stayed awake, staring at the ceiling, at her. A light snore escaped her. I wanted to kiss her forehead, but I left her there. She trusted me, and hell, I wish I could trust her too. But I couldn't sleep, no matter how hard I tried. No matter how hard we fucked.

The next morning, around four a.m, my phone buzzed. A burner number. It was probably Ethan. My stomach twisted, and Ellie turned over from hearing the vibration.

I answered the call. "Yeah?" I asked.

"That camp?" Ethan asked, purposefully keeping it vague, "It has about a hundred women. Maybe more." I pushed myself up, sitting in bed. "All of them are going through the same training as her."

I quietly let myself out of the room. Once I was alone, I asked: "Did you see the actual training?"

"I saw some of it. But I stayed away from the rest," he said.

"What kind of training?"

"Beatings. Fighting each other too."

I pinched the bridge of my nose. "A hundred women?"

"Maybe more," Ethan said. "I'll send you the address."

The phone clicked off. I rested my head against the wall, trying to figure out how the hell we were going to get out of this one. A creak in the walls signaled movement. I turned. An oversized t-shirt hung on Ellie's shoulders, covering her ass. Fuck me. If we weren't in such messed up circumstances, I would've scooped her up and locked her in my bedroom, not letting her come out until we were both deeply satisfied.

Instead, I leaned against the wall.

"What's going on?" she asked.

I could have said it was work, and that could have been close enough to the truth. But I knew she needed to know.

"The Skyline Shift," I said. "There are more women. Maybe a hundred or more."

Ellie's smile disappeared. "Damn it," she muttered.

Neither of us knew what to say. How would we save that many? And hell, how could we fight all of them, without killing them?

Axe and Derek likely didn't care about what happened to these women. And to be honest, part of me did, and part of me didn't. I only cared because of Ellie. Because those women were like her, and I hated knowing what Ellie had gone through.

I turned back toward the bedroom and Ellie followed me in, pausing at the bed. But I went to the bathroom and started the shower.

"Where are you going now?" she asked.

"We've got to go there, right? Figure it out ourselves," I said. "Get dressed."

About an hour later, we were on the road, heading to Brackston. Axe came with us. The sun was rising, covering the road in a soft glow. I drove, Ellie in the seat beside me. Axe was in the backseat, watching her closely. I knew trusting her might be the last mistake I made. If her stories about her training were right, it didn't matter if she died, or when she was able to kill me. Here, later, or anywhere. As long as I died.

Perhaps it was a death wish, knowing that whatever the hell we were, it wasn't going to last.

Three hours later, we drove past the main entrance of the camp, the dome buildings visible through the gate. According to Ethan's directions, parking a few miles down and trekking through the trees was our best bet to observe without being seen. We went a few hundred yards into the woods, then went in the direction of the camp, following Axe's lead.

The trees spread like fingers, revealing flashes of white-domed buildings. Women were ushered between the buildings, some in single file lines, their heads turned down, and others alone. Naked or in white uniforms. Every few feet, a man dressed in white had his arms crossed, his finger in his holster, as he watched the women walk, keeping them in line.

"That's him," Ellie whispered. "Dr. Bates."

She pointed to a man looking down at his clipboard. He flicked a lock of hair out of his eyes. A mix of brown, gray, and white curls. He was shorter than I expected but more athletic than I had anticipated too. He knocked on a door to one of the dome buildings, then smiled when a naked woman came out, his eyes never falling to her breasts as if her nudity was completely normal. They were simply specimens.

From afar, we could see through one of the glass walls. A woman had her hands in front of her as she stuck out her ass, her legs spread apart. A stocky man dressed in a tight white shirt and pants raised a bullwhip in the air, then brought it down on her back, lighting a dark red streak across it. Her body shuddered, but then she stiffened, trying to stay still.

A flash of red on her neck—those marks, the Ms.

I scanned the rest of the perimeter: all of the women had that same tattoo, the same one Ellie and the other women had on their necks. It must have been a branding, to mark them as the property of the program. Of Miles Muro himself.

Axe went forward, towards the back of one of the buildings.

"The hell is he doing?" Ellie whispered.

"Axe?" I asked. But Axe kept going, keeping his head high as he walked straight into the building. Ellie bit her nails, and I held my breath. When he returned, he walked back into the woods, as if he had always belonged there.

"Let's go," he said, going past us. "They'll realize we're here soon."

So he had stolen something, then. "What did you take?" I asked.

"A flash drive."

We followed him back to the car. This was closer to Axe's usual line of work; he knew what he was doing. The camp seemed to continue on as usual, despite our likely known intrusion, probably for the students' benefit, so that their training would not be disrupted. We hiked quietly, going at an average pace, but when Axe started going faster, we did too.

On the return home, Axe drove. He handed me the flash drive, and I flipped it over, looking at it in my palm. The same red logo. No matter what happened in the coming days, even with lasers and cover-up tattoos, Ellie would always wear that mark. Nothing could change what she had been through. I pocketed the flash drive.

We stopped at the Adler House. Though I knew that if Ellie could handle being me and Axe for that long without trying anything, that it was very unlikely she would attack Gerard, we didn't go in. But when Axe gestured for me to step out of the car, I left her inside. We stepped away from her, and Axe kept his voice lowered.

"At the very least, she should be restrained," Axe said. I grit my teeth.

"She didn't try anything that whole time," I said.

"No, but anything could happen. Another trigger word. A hidden command." His jaw relaxed. "Another reason to kill us."

I stared at him. Axe's eyes were darker than mine or Derek's, almost as if his pupils blended in with his irises. He had always distanced himself from us but never strayed far enough to leave our family for good. He had his work, and he kept to himself that way.

Axe usually brought up one solution. A final one. An option that I would never allow for Ellie.

"At least," he repeated, reminding me that there were alternatives.

"Mercia helped her," I said. Axe visibly pulled back, as if the name shocked him. "Ellie hasn't had headaches or the voice in a while." It might have been a day or just a few hours, but that was better than nothing.

"Do you have proof?" Axe asked.

Proof that she was cured. I gave a subtle shake of my head and turned back toward the car.

"I'll talk to Derek," Axe said. I closed my fist. That meant that Axe was set on the final outcome, what he thought would best protect our family. He wanted Ellie and the rest of the women gone for good.

But I would never allow it.

At the penthouse, Ellie went to the rooftop and I dialed Mercia from my office. I turned on a tablet and watched Ellie on the surveillance footage, her legs tucked beside her as she stared at the cityscape. But peace was written on her face this time, an expression she hardly had when she was up there. She usually looked distant. Distraught.

But she was calm, somehow. How could I destroy that?

"Wil?" Merica asked. "What can I help you with?"

"I need proof that your methods worked," I said. Damn. That hadn't come out as eloquently as I had hoped. "Ellie hasn't been having headaches. Or hearing voices."

"But you don't believe her," Mercia said, trying to understand. "You want proof."

"Sure."

What 'proof' was I looking for? It wouldn't comfort Axe; he'd still want to kill her and the rest of them, to be done with it so that we could take care of the next problem: the camp itself. To Axe, they weren't worth saving; no one was. But I couldn't let her go. It was already bad enough that Ellie had to go through the brainwashing that the Skyline Shift put her through. I couldn't become her enemy too.

But perhaps I had always been her enemy. Who could blame her for hating me when I had held her captive and trained her for my own selfish desires?

"Wil, I apologize for this, but I can't provide you with proof," Merica said, her voice resolute. I sighed. I knew that answer was coming. "The truth is that I could do an in-person examination of her. Try some other methods to see if I could stir up any hidden aspects of her training. But it won't change the situation. It wouldn't be definitive proof." The phone crinkled as she adjusted, then Mercia continued, "You have to trust her."

My phone beeped; I checked the screen. This time, it was Derek calling. My jaw twitched. What was going on now?

"I gotta go. But thanks," I huffed. "We might have some other patients for you."

And by some, I meant at least five. Derek could have been calling to add to that situation.

"Looking forward to it," Mercia said.

I clicked over to Derek, scratching my chin. "Yeah?" I asked.

"Another one showed up," he said, out of breath. Just like I had expected. "The bitch nearly killed me."

That wasn't good. "You didn't say our name, did you?" I asked.

"I'm not stupid," he said. "She attacked me, screaming that she knew I was the Adler who had killed her mother."

So now they were attacking us based on something else, not just a trigger word. Fuck. Fuck. *Fuck*.

"What did you do?" I asked.

"Knocked her out. Cuffed her," he said. "Might have to transfer her to the Dahlia District in a cage. I'm not kidding; she was fucking feral. Didn't act all innocent like the others did."

"She could be from a different group. Completely separate," I tried.

"Or Muro's changing tactics."

After more discussion, I hung up and watched Ellie on the screen, her sweet eyes gazing at the clouds. To Axe, she was a killer, ready to attack us. To Derek, she was another experiment gone wrong. But what was she to me?

She was a woman. A woman with more strength than I would ever understand. And she was mine.

But the choices were becoming clear. If the women were attacking us without a trigger, I had to choose what was right for my family. And that made me sick.

For now, I would deal with the issue at hand. I put the flash drive in the USB port of my computer. The drive was encrypted, but after sending it through a decryption program, I was able to access a few of the files. Most of them were broken, but eventually, I could see that each file had a set of numbers, which was attached to a woman. I had to click through several before I found what I was looking for.

172966: Julie Jordan: Deceased.

Action Line 13: Transferred to Shadow Hills.

Action Line 12: Transported from SS campus to woods.

Action Line 11: Resigned during endurance training; Alexandra Mink assisted.

Next to Action Line 13, there were coordinates for her location.

How the hell was Ellie going to take this?

On the tablet's screen, Ellie stared off into the distance, her lips pressing together in a pattern. She wasn't talking to herself; she was singing. Carefree. Happy. I wanted to sneak up to the rooftop's doorway, to listen to her voice. She was finally comfortable with her life here, her life with me, and I was about to screw it all up. I had a feeling all along that her sister was gone, but Ellie? Had she secretly realized what had happened, and hadn't accepted it? Or did she really believe Julie was still alive?

How the hell would I tell her?

Axe sent a text: *I know she was a gift,* he started out, *But this needs to end.*

And I knew that in his mind, there was only one way this problem would be solved.

CHAPTER 21

Ellie

The air shifted as the door behind me opened. Usually, since I knew it was Wil, I would wait for him to join me on the couch, letting myself stay lost in my thoughts. But for some reason, instinct—*my* actual instinct, and not just a voice in my head—told me to look at him. His shoulders were slumped, and there was a grim twist to his lips. My breath caught in my throat.

"What is it?" I asked.

He sat beside me. "You know that file Axe got?" he asked. I nodded. "There was a file there."

He was dancing around the subject. It wasn't like them, and the more I thought about it, the more it made me dread what was coming. I don't know that my situation could have gotten any more messed up, but the way he was carrying himself told me that it was about to get worse.

"What?" I asked. "Just say it."

And with three words, he broke me even more.

"It's your sister," he said.

I stared out at the gray sky, wondering why the hell I was still there. I could have gone into the camp, kamikaze style, and this torment would have been over sooner. But I had held on, for her, for Wil, and yet he was about to take that away from me too.

"She's—"

I shook my head furiously, my eyes burning with anger. "She's not," I insisted. "She's still out there."

"Ellie," Wil whispered. "She's—"

"Lost," I cut him off. "She's just gone somewhere. Just because there's no record of her doesn't mean that she doesn't exist."

"But there is a record." He held my shoulder. "Ellie. Your sister. She's—"

"Missing."

"Dead," he finished. "She's dead. She's not here anymore."

My head dropped, my gaze falling to my lap. I stared at my hands. My sister and I had different fingerprints, but we had gotten our long fingers from our mother.

And now they were both gone. My mother. Now, my sister. And even my dad.

I was the only one left.

No. That wasn't possible. Not after everything I had been through.

But as I turned to Wil to argue, I saw her instead. Her head looking to the side, those blank eyes, her yellowed skin, her body decomposing. The scent of rotting meat. The flies that hung around us. The dirt inside of her nose. Her lips and skin blotchy and purple. The dried up blood on the edges of her cut flesh. The dirt underneath her, darkened with her insides. And Dr. Bates's heavy hand on my shoulder. As if his touch could make it better.

As if Wil thought he could make this better.

"I don't believe you," I said. Wil's eyes pleaded for me to understand, but I couldn't. I wouldn't let myself. He might have always told me the truth, but this was different. This was my life. My purpose. The only thing that I had held onto since our parents died. Making sure that Julie was safe.

So no. I wouldn't accept it. She wasn't gone. She wasn't dead. She was—

"Ellie," Wil said. He held my shoulder. "You're right. That's just what the records say. We won't know for sure until we—"

"What do the records say?" I hissed. "Tell me. The exact words."

He narrowed his eyes at my tone, but I didn't care. Kill me now, I thought. I didn't care. If he was telling the truth, then what difference did it make?

"Deceased," he said. His features softened, and he let go of his grip on me. I rubbed my shoulder where his hand had been. "Resigned.

Like I said, that's just the record. But you're right. We won't know until we find her."

What he meant was that we wanted to find her body. I bit my tongue until it bled, and I tasted the copper in it, knowing that I had so much blood, and that if Wil was right, if those nightmares were real, then Julie didn't have any left.

"Let's go find her," he said. He stood, then held out a hand for me. "The file had coordinates for her last known location."

Those woods. The tall trees. The sprinkles of light shining through the branches.

I felt empty. I wouldn't let myself feel anything. Not until I knew for sure.

I hated myself for accepting his offer, but I had to know.

I took his hand.

Wil tried to make conversation on the way back to Brackston, but I couldn't stomach the words; they made me nauseous. At one point, he put a hand on my thigh, his hand inching closer to my pussy, but when he saw that I wasn't interested, he stopped. Maybe he thought it would be a welcome distraction from the pain like it had been in the past. But this was different. This was a truth that I wasn't sure I'd ever be prepared to handle.

The sights of the town were familiar, cast in the golden light of sunset. But instead of going past the camp into the woods like he had that morning, Wil took another freeway off to the side, then drove for ten minutes, before taking the off-ramp. A splintery wooden sign stated *Shadow Hills* in white paint, the frame cracked, showing the park and the surrounding area hadn't been kept up in years. The hills were covered in dusty white stalks of grass. And there wasn't a shadow in sight.

We parked in the small lot. Wil walked forward, his eyes searching the ground. I went past him, knowing instinctively where she was. Wil followed closely behind me. And I thought that maybe if I saw her there, everything would make sense. That this was all just a bad, messed up dream, and Julie was actually safe. She might have gone to the Skyline Shift, but she wasn't stuck there forever. She was here. Sneaking out with a friend. And this was all just an elaborate prank. She had gone too far this time, and I would scold her for it.

In the distance, there was a hill followed by a patch of short, but thick trees. My steps grew quicker until I ran toward it. When we got there, I lifted the branches and crouched underneath them.

A long, gray bone, with dark dried up flesh. Another. One broken in half. A set of ribs darkened like the rest. A skull with vacant cavities.

I kneeled down and touched the skull, stroking the brittle flesh. The texture was like dried up food, left to decay in the trash. Had animals scavenged this body? Had the insects had their fill? I picked up the skull, turning it over a few times, observing the shape of the head, the chin, the forehead. Those empty eye sockets. This wasn't my sister. These were just her bones.

They were her bones.

I held her face close to my chest, hugging it there. A tightness ballooned inside of me, and I screamed, the sound echoing around us. Wil's shadow stretched to the side. I couldn't stand it, this silence. Julie had been such a talkative person, and now, her tongue was gone. Decomposed by bacteria and insects and ravaged by animals until there was nothing, absolutely nothing that I could do to save her anymore.

It should have been me. Julie was young, so damn young, and yes, I was young too, but she had so much to give this world, so much to explore, and all I had wanted to do was to keep her safe. To guard her against the horrors. And I had completely failed. She was the one who was supposed to explore. Who was supposed to see more of this world than I ever cared to see. And now, she was gone.

Arms tightened around me. I don't know how long Wil had been holding me, but I held her skull against my chest, afraid it might disappear too, then I loosened, afraid I might crush what was left. I buried my head into Wil's arms and cried so hard that I couldn't breathe. Snot in my nose. The unbearable ache in my chest. Wil held me close, and his touch was safe and suffocating at the same time.

I turned, gawking up at him, my mouth hanging open since it was the only way I could breathe. I pushed his arms away. He scooted back, still crouching on the ground too. Tiny pieces of her flesh crumbled off as I picked up her bones, gathering her in my arms.

"Help me," I managed. He didn't move, so I repeated myself, my voice louder, and my tone harsher than before. "Help me carry her. She deserves more than this."

In silence, I gathered up what I could, and when I turned to scowl at him for not helping, he came forward, picking up the pieces I couldn't carry. Wil hit a button on his car fob to open the trunk, but I opened the door to the back of his car, placing her on the seat. She wasn't a piece of cargo. She was a person.

She was a person.

A small piece of her bone fit in my palm, and I carried it with me, clutched in my hand, sitting in the front seat with me. Dark streaks of dirt and purple flesh covered my shirt. Wil glanced at me, then dusted his clothes off before getting in the car. Pieces of my sister fell to the ground.

Because this was nothing to him. They might not have killed her, but death was always around the Adlers. It meant nothing to Wil.

"What the hell is your problem?" I asked as he slipped into the driver's seat. He didn't look at me, refusing to make eye contact.

"What?"

He was so cold. So damn emotionless. Holding me one minute, knowing how messed up this was for me. Then not even looking at me the next.

It was easier to blame him. To think that this was his fault. His fault that I had been too late. Because maybe if the Adlers hadn't been a problem, if the Midnight Miles Corporation had different enemies, maybe Julie would have survived. Maybe I would have gone in her place.

And then it would be my bones. Not hers.

"You're just like them, you know," I said.

"Like who?" he asked, his tone dry.

"The Midnight Miles Corporation, that company that owns the Skyline Shift. You're just as fucked up as they are."

Wil started the car engine, and he sped off onto the road so fast that Julie rattled on the back seat, her bones thudding against the cushions. I stuck out a hand, holding them back, making sure that none of them fell off the seat.

"Slow down," I said. "You're going to break her."

"Why didn't you buckle her in, then," he sighed, the sarcasm so damn irritating in his voice.

"Fuck you," I said.

He kept driving. Thirty miles over the speed limit. Then forty. I shook my head.

"You don't care about anything, do you?" I asked. "It doesn't matter if someone like Julie dies, because it doesn't affect you or your family's business. That's all you care about. The bottom line. What makes your family money. Who cares if the rest of us suffer?"

His hands tightened around the wheel, and his lips pressed together, but he didn't deny it. That was the worst part. I wanted so badly for him to tell me that I was wrong. That I was so damn wrong. That the Adler family had a code. That he was better than that. Better than I could imagine. But he didn't say a word.

So I pressed further.

"Fuck, Wil. You used me. A person, just like Julie, as a fucking birthday present. Your personal toy. And you think you're so much better than *them*?" I hissed. "You're not. You're just as bad as Bates." The car hummed faster, but I kept going. "You're just as bad as Muro. You're just like them."

He ran the car off the road, slamming on the brakes. Everything flew to a stop, and a few of her bones fell to the ground.

"What the hell, Wil?"

"Muro, Bates—" he started, staring at me, his face red, his breath panting, "They didn't care if you lived or died. They didn't care about your sister."

As if to imply that he did.

But I knew better.

"Neither do you," I muttered.

We stared at each other. His eyes flicked across my face, and I knew that he was weighing his good and bad deeds, as if letting me *live* as his sex slave was so much better than risking my life as a soldier, like Bates had. But they were the same. Bates had created a killer instinct inside of me, molding me to be a perfect soldier.

Wil had taken me from the woods and given me a place to live in, but he had used me too. Molded me to his sexual whims. Made me fuck a knife. Just like Bates had.

But this was my life. And I knew I was right. They were the same.

And as much as I wanted to believe him, I wasn't going to let him tell me that I was wrong.

CHAPTER 22

Wil

The next day, we took Julie to Rubble River State Park, a river in Pebble Garden where their family had often visited during the summer, and a place Ellie kept promising to take Julie again, but could never quite find the time. And once Julie snuck out to meet a boyfriend there during high school, Ellie was even less interested. She even made a point *not* to go to that river.

"It seems so stupid now," Ellie said, staring out the window.

These were the stories Ellie told me about while we drove. She said them to break the silence because someone needed to know about Julie. But I couldn't get her words out of my head.

You think you're so much better than them? You're just as bad as Bates.

And I was. There was no doubt in my mind about that. Some might even argue that I was worse. Even if he did rush them to sign it, at least Bates gave the women a chance to look at a contract. With me? I dealt with people's savings, their livelihoods, made them think that with just one more pill, with just one more round of poker, then maybe things would be better. But they never were. The house always won.

The shore of the river was covered in jagged stones, so we stayed off to the side, where the terrain turned to dirt. A park bench was a few yards away, and on the other side, a metal trash can. I had a shovel in my car already, so I dug a hole in the exact spot. Ellie said their family used to put picnic blankets and towels down during family trips.

Ellie gently placed the bones into the hole. Her chest heaved, but so much of that energy had been expelled in Shadow Hills, where we had found Julie. Perhaps it was a relief to give Julie a proper resting place. I wasn't sure. Funerals were second nature to my family, but they never brought any comfort, only a day's break from work.

So what did this mean to Ellie?

Ellie sat beside the upturned dirt for a long time, a steady stream of tears trailing her cheeks. She loved her sister, just like I loved my brothers and parents. And I knew that as heartless as I was, I would have been devastated if anything happened to them. I knew how broken she must have been inside. Any time I tried to touch her, I scorned myself. Ellie didn't deserve the fucked up love that I had. She wasn't meant for my world, nor was she ever meant for Muro's. Perhaps death would have been a mercy to her.

But I kept her from that. Selfishly. Because I couldn't live with her death on my conscience. Not when I wanted her for myself.

And that was what was holding me back.

I made a decision then, as the sun crowded behind the treeline. I wouldn't kill Ellie like my brother insisted. I would make sure that she lived, at least when it came to us.

But she needed to leave. I couldn't keep her anymore.

***

"Wake up," I barked, standing in the doorway. Ellie rubbed her eyes, then blinked up at me, adjusting in the bed.

"What?" she asked.

"Get your shit together," I said.

"What? Right now?"

I crossed my arms, leaning on the door frame. I wanted to be a dick, to make her see why staying with me wasn't an option, so that she would make that decision for herself. But it wasn't easy. With a knife in my hand, holding it against her throat, I could be a beast. But this? I didn't want to let her go.

But I had to.

"You can't stay," I said. "Your best option is to go to the Dahlia District. Be with the others until we figure this out with Muro," I said.

Ellie shook her head. "I'm not going there."

"Why?"

"Because it's no different. If I go there, I still can't leave," she snapped. "What is wrong with you? Why can't I stay here?"

"Because I don't want you anymore," I said. Her facial expression went slack, and my whole body tightened, trying to predict what she wanted.

But Ellie didn't fight me. There wasn't a question in her body. Only acceptance.

She sunk down into the bed, her arms limp. "So where do I go?" she asked in a voice so quiet I could barely hear her.

"I don't know," I said. "But you have to leave, or we'll kill you."

We hadn't made official plans to kill them yet, but I knew it was a very real, near-future possibility. Ellie did too. She bit her lip, then stood, gathering the few belongings she had collected during her stay. Her hand grazed the side table, skimming over one of my knives. She glanced at it, then shoved it in her bag too. Good; she would probably need it. I shoved a bottle of water at her, and she snatched it out of my hand. She didn't say another word to me, and I didn't say anything either.

I took her to the woods behind the Adler House. I don't know why I did. I guess I thought that if I could put her back there and erase everything that had happened, then maybe I could give her a chance to live for herself.

As expected, Axe and Derek didn't care for the idea, but this was my decision. They knew not to mess with her. If anyone was going to kill Ellie, it was going to be me.

I drove further back than I had in a long time, likely deeper in the woods than where Axe had found her. Then I stopped, leaned across her, and opened the car door.

Ellie put her bag's strap on her shoulder and slid out.

I started, "Good—"

The car door slammed shut. Ellie kept moving forward as if she had walked out of her own dream and into the real world. Into a place where she could do what was right. Where she could do what she wanted, without thinking of her sister. Without obeying Bates's commands. Without me holding her back.

I drove back through Sage City, aimlessly taking off-ramps, going down side streets, returning to the highway, but never finding where I was supposed to go. I ended up back at the Adler House, parking next to all of the other extra cars, staring into the woods. She was out there, somewhere. And she was better off that way. I could protect her from afar. She didn't need me.

But I wanted Ellie. I loved her spunk, her desire to fight. How equally possessive she was of me. How she was brave, even when she faced her worst fears. But most of all, I wanted to protect her. To shield her from this world. To make her mine.

But I knew I couldn't do any of that. It wasn't realistic for us.

I went to Axe's workroom, sighing as I opened the door. Axe was sharpening his knives, while Derek punched numbers on a laptop, his chair leaning against a standing cage. For once, the place was empty. But a fresh bloodstain was in the corner. Someone had just left.

"How'd she take it?" Derek asked, the legs of the chair clanking to the concrete ground. I grunted in response, taking the chair between the two of them, sitting on the opposite side of the table, facing them. "That good, huh?" I gave another grunt. Axe glanced over at us but kept the knife sliding back and forth on the whetstone, the shiny metal gleaming in the fluorescent lights.

"Now that we're all here—" Derek started.

I interrupted: "Gerard isn't here."

Derek shrugged. "We need to figure this out ourselves."

"Fuck. Are we finally taking the reins?"

Derek clenched his jaw, and I straightened. Yeah. I should shut up. It was a jab at Gerard's fickle attitude over giving us control. But Derek had already made it clear that we had to stand by our family. And this wasn't about Gerard, but about us. I knew that.

It just didn't make giving up Ellie any easier.

"We'll fill him in later," Derek said. "But what do we do about Muro? He's a big problem."

How simple it sounded, coming from his mouth.

Axe's knife slid across the stone in a sharp hiss. "Take him out," Axe said flatly.

Derek slammed the laptop shut. "That's an option," he said. "But we need a plan to make that happen. That, and a way to convince Gerard that it's the right thing to do, no matter what his hang-ups are." Derek held his chin, staring off to the side. I got the feeling he knew more about Gerard's 'hang-ups' than he was letting on. "Muro has too many people surrounding him."

"I thought he was abroad?" I asked. "Could be easier to take him out in a foreign country."

"And easier to take us out," Axe said.

That was true. But honestly, it was hard for me to care about what happened. Family was my life, and I had always made decisions that were in line with what was best for the family, but that wasn't enough anymore.

I could go abroad, take Muro out, and hell, if I died in the process, then so what? Ellie had been forced in each direction for so long: always thinking of her sister, then doing what the Skyline Shift wanted her to do, and finally, what *I* wanted her to do.

And then there was me. A man who only ever put his family first. Even when it came to love.

Fucking love.

So why couldn't I let go of Ellie, if that was what best for my family?

Ellie had always lived her life for others, never getting to decide what she wanted for herself. Had I been like that too? Letting the mafia run my life, because I was an Adler by blood? Conquer. Annihilate. Rule. It seemed pointless now.

What did I want?

"I have an idea," I started. I picked up a handsaw, my eyes resting on the jagged tooth edges. "Why not use me as bait?" I pressed my thumb into one of the blades, letting it prick my skin. "Get the rest of the women to come out. Then you can kill them like you want." I forced a smile at Axe. He would like that. "One by one."

He didn't acknowledge what I had said, just kept sharpening his knife. Yeah, it might have been a low blow. But I didn't care. I was out to ruin everything.

"And what will happen to you?" Derek asked.

"Who cares?" I said. "The gambling hall practically runs itself. You guys can take care of it."

Derek let out a long sigh, then crossed his arms at me. "You feel sorry for yourself," he said, narrowing his eyes. "Is that it? You lost your woman, and now you want us to feel bad for you?"

Like he understood. He was worse than I was. He lived and breathed the family business because he was obsessed with becoming the next boss. The oldest brother to the very end.

"I lost the only thing I ever wanted for myself," I growled.

"And there's your problem. Thinking of her like an object," he said. "She's not a 'thing,' Wil. She's a woman." He shook his head, never letting his eyes trail from me. "A woman who tried to kill you. And that's not an exaggeration." I rolled my eyes. He put his hands on the table, bracing himself for his next words as if it pissed him off to deal with me. "You need to think of her for the person that she is: an assassin sent to kill us. If we had known, Axe would have killed her on the spot. We never would have gifted her to you." He slammed his fists into the table, the tools shaking against it. "So stop the fucking pity party."

He was right, but I couldn't stop myself. I hated myself so much right then. And I wanted him and Axe to feel it too.

"Use me as bait for Muro," I said. "Offer him a trade. Then as he's taking care of me, you can ambush him." I forced a chuckle. "At least I'll be of some use."

"Fuck, man. Get over yourself," Derek said. "You turned the gambling hall into a profitable venture. Uncle Jimmy *never* had it that packed, and you know it." Derek's eyes flicked towards the ceiling, as if he could see Uncle Jimmy's soul floating above us. And he was right; I had proved myself to the family. But that didn't matter.

"What's the real problem?" Derek asked.

"Ellie," I said without hesitation. It was as simple as that.

"She's on the no-kill list," Axe said. As if that was the only problem.

"Just like you said," Derek added.

"You forced me to get rid of her," I said.

"No one is forcing you to do anything," Axe said.

That was a lie. We had a code, an honor to stick by. Family came first, and if the two of them thought that Ellie needed to go, then she needed to go. But instead, they held up my request to keep her alive, as long as she wasn't around anymore. It was supposed to be a fair exchange.

"We agreed not to harm Ellie," Derek said, reading my mind. "And that's not going to change." He patted his pocket, reminding me that he had a strong tranquilizer there, should they run into each other and she became violent. "But we've got to make a decision together when it comes to the rest of them." Derek lifted his shirt, revealing a bright red and black bruise on his ribs. "Those women?" That label didn't do them justice. He shook his head, then corrected himself, "Those *soldiers*? They don't screw around."

I cringed away. The woman must have broken ribs. Like Axe and me, Derek wasn't a small man. If it had been Axe, he probably would have killed the woman, but Derek wasn't like that. He had more deaths on his belt than I had, being the next in line for Gerard's role as boss, but he still felt things, especially for women. Had a conscience. Axe didn't.

But that didn't mean that Derek would protect all of them.

"So let's think this through before we go to the boss," he said. Our father. I hated calling him that, especially with everything he had been pulling lately. "What's best for the family business?" Derek said.

"Being alive," Axe said.

"So let's kill everything that gets in our way," I muttered. "Kill everything that breathes within ten feet of us."

Finally, Axe shot a look at me.

Derek snarled. "Come on, man. Listen to yourself. It's—"

"It's the programming," I said, interrupting him. He stared at me blankly. Axe stopped his blade too. "They've been trained to do this. Tortured beyond belief. You saw them," I said to Axe. He gave a subtle nod. All of those women had scars across their bodies. We would never understand what they had been through. "There's a good chance that most of them led normal lives, but somehow were led to the Skyline Shift."

We were all silent for a while. The lights flickered above us. Derek shifted in his seat, the chair creaking underneath him. Axe held the knife still against the stone, waiting for us to decide.

"It's not the women," I repeated.

"It's the programming," Derek said, repeating my words. "I looked up the names on that flash drive, and none of them had links to us. They might have known our names, or at the very least, Muro's business. So," he shrugged, "I can agree with that. They were regular people."

"Regular people can still be evil," Axe argued.

I shuffled my feet. Axe was hard to change.

"What about Ellie? She was okay by the end, right?" Derek asked. "Which means whatever Mercia did, helped."

Mercia might have given Ellie direction, but Ellie had fought for herself on a daily basis. I had seen her on the rooftop, her lips always moving, her ears twitching as she listened to the voice in her mind. And even when the violence took over, she had fought it *hard*. Resisted it. Apologized for what she was about to do.

"We drove to Brackston and Pebble Garden," I said, lifting my chin. "She didn't try a single thing."

"No driver?" Derek asked. I nodded. That was one of our rules with the women, and I had forced myself to let it slip, to give Ellie a chance to prove herself. "Then perhaps there is an alternative," Derek continued.

"The quickest solution is eliminating the enemy," Axe argued.

"But we can't go in there with brute force," Derek said. "We have to take down the Midnight Miles Corporation one step at a time. Starting with the Skyline Shift." Derek turned to me. "What do you want, Wil?"

I thought about it. For years, I had thought that I wanted a toy, a woman with fight inside of her who eventually surrendered to me, becoming mine, and mine alone, forever. And part of that *was* Ellie. She had surrendered, more than any woman ever had, and that kind of vulnerability stuck with you. Even if she was the only one giving up power, it had marked both of us. And I wanted more now. It wasn't just about playing god. It was about trust. I wanted her to choose me. To trust me.

And I wanted to protect her, even if that meant that she chose a different life for herself.

"We destroy the camp," I said. I weighed the saw in my hand, then settled it back on the table. "We can deal with the rest of Muro's men later. But first, we start with getting rid of their secret weapon."

"Now that," Derek said, grinning, "I can get behind."

Axe even gave a hint of a smile. "Welcome back," Axe said.

Invigorated by their support, I leaned forward on the table. "We'll eliminate Bates first. He's the head of the operation. We take out him, then get Mercia to help with the rest."

"But how the hell do we kill him when he's surrounded by all of his trainees?" Derek asked.

I didn't know. Hell, I didn't know a damned thing about taking out an army like that. But I knew that this was what we needed to be done.

Somehow, we had to get through this. We had to form a plan together.

"Let's figure this shit out," I said.

Axe put down the knife and the three of us brainstormed, thinking of the best way to take them down. We had to do it swiftly and efficiently, and in such a way that Gerard was on board. The woman would live, and with Mercia, we could give them back their lives. Perhaps even hire them as our soldiers. It didn't make up for what they had gone through, but at least they wouldn't be dragged down by a life they didn't choose for themselves.

Because I may not have chosen to fall in love with a soldier who was sent to kill me, but I would choose to stand by her. To protect her. To do everything I could for her.

I had to do this for her. For my Ellie.

And for myself.

CHAPTER 23

Ellie

No matter which direction I looked, it all looked the same. The same set of trees. The same bursts of light. As if nothing would change the fact that I was lost in the woods, somewhere in Sage City. I knew, technically, that I was in the uncharted territory behind the Adlers' house, but it wasn't as simple as that. I felt truly alone for the first time in months, maybe even years. It was always my family, then just Julie and me, then Dr. Bates. Then it was just Wil. I thought of Billy and Jane, and the other women that had been found here. Like me. I thought of the moment I first looked up into Axe's eyes: *For my brother*, he had said. *He'll take care of you.*

Had Wil taken care of me?

I pressed my palm into the bark of a tree, waiting for it to imprint my skin, as if that could demonstrate what Wil had done to me. Wil had been brutal at first, but another side had come out when he saw how much trouble I was in. He treated me like an object to be fondled and played with, but he also cared about me. Had a need to give me safety. A need to make my headaches stop. A desire to end Bates's voice, so that I could listen to myself for once. My own voice.

And what did that inner voice say? What did it want?

Through the brown branches, a flicker of red hair caught my eye. I went towards it like an insect drawn to a flame. The woman backed away, her eyes glancing over me. Then she started running. I ran too, jumping over the loose branches, my feet disappearing into the ivy covering the ground.

"Hey!" I yelled. "Wait! Stop! I just want to talk to you!"

And suddenly, she stilled. I knew it wasn't from my words, but from him; Bates's voice was telling her to stop. I walked slower as I came towards her, her back bumpy and pink, like the surface of candle wax that had been destroyed by prying fingers. A body like my own. The woman faced me, a scar on her jaw, a cut that had healed on the surface, but was still red, still burning beneath.

Her eyes traced me, going back and forth across my face, trying to read what was there. Her bare shoulders were scratched with the same lines dashed across her breasts. She moved her lips, but no words came out. I recognized her. Had we seen each other at the Skyline Shift? Or was it before that, at Women's Elite?

"What do you need?" I asked, a question Wil had asked me so often before. Strength surged inside of me then. If he could help me, then I could help her.

No. That was wrong. I could have helped her all along; Wil just showed me how.

"I want to help you," I said.

Her eyes were bloodshot, her lips trembling. "Who are you?" she asked, her voice accusatory.

"My name is Ellie," I said, my tone confident.

She closed her eyes, searching within, fighting the control taking over her mind.

"Cassandra," she said.

There was so much in Cassandra that was close to me, and so much of her that she likely couldn't access. She was probably a shell of her former self, just like I had been.

"Do you hear a voice?" I asked. Her eyes widened, but she didn't move. Didn't tell me what she heard. "I heard it too," I said. Until Wil found me. Until he introduced me to Dr. Mercia. Until I realized that the voice couldn't control me forever. "But I fought it," I said. "And you can fight it too."

Cassandra held her forehead, pinching the bridge of her nose. One wrong move and I knew she would fight me. Maybe even try to end my life. But I needed to do this. For her. For myself. For the Adlers. For Wil. To make sure that she knew what was going on.

"That voice," I said. "It's Dr. Bates. He ran the Skyline Shift." A subtle shudder ran through her. So she knew, then. The memories were coming back. "But whatever he said about finding your sister, mom, or daughter," I shook my head. "It's all a lie. They aren't out there."

Her lips quivered, but she didn't speak.

"My sister was dead by the time he released me for my final task," I said.

"So they killed her," she said.

She must have meant the Adlers, but I didn't dare say their name.

"I'm not sure who killed her," I said, "but it wasn't who I thought it was."

"It was them."

Them. The brothers who had spared my life. The man who had given me shelter and protection when I had nothing but a stranger's voice in my head.

I pulled a shirt, jeans, and an extra pair of shoes out of my bag, then handed them to her.

"Not sure about your size," I said, my shoulders lifting, "but it's better than nothing."

She gazed at me, her mouth open. But after a moment, she took the clothing and put them on. They hung loosely on her body, but it was better than running naked.

"Who are you?" Cassandra asked, her eyes blinking rapidly. "Why are you doing this?"

It was such a familiar question, and yet I couldn't explain. I had been just like her. And yet now? Now, I was someone else. I had always been this same Ellie, but I had survived what could have been described as a mind control program. And I had then been abducted, gifted to a criminal who wanted me. Who let me out of my captivity. A man I trusted. A man who I wanted, even now.

"I'm just trying to help you," I said. I held her arm. "I was you, once."

"I'm fine," she said, shivering out of my touch. "Leave me alone."

And that was familiar too. I hadn't wanted anyone's help, nor did I trust anyone, but in the end, I had to open up. I watched her walk through the trees, her gait staggering as if she was constantly afraid of an enemy jumping out from behind the trees. I didn't blame her.

The sky gave a little light, and most of the area was covered in shadows from the treetops. With each step, the ivy swallowed my feet, but I kept walking through the trees, taking a turn whenever I felt like it. As if I could walk through the woods and find my sister's unmarked grave, even if she was miles away. When I came upon a tree turned on its side, I sat on it, pulling out the water bottle from my bag, grateful that Wil made sure I had a drink.

"Hey," a squeaky voice said. I turned around quickly, finding Julie leaning against a tree. Her hair was golden in the light, as if the sun had found a way to shine on her, and her alone, her golden hair wispy and light on her shoulders. Her lips were pink and bare, just like the days we went to the Rubble River. And her body was completely whole.

"Julie," I said, breathless. I flipped around on the log, about to reach for her. "You're alive?"

She put up a hand to stop me from moving. I stilled to a halt.

"Nah," she said, a smile still on her face. "Dead. Just like you buried me."

"Then this?" I motioned at the space between us.

"A delusion."

I looked at the ground. It was still covered in ivy. It all seemed real, but maybe it wasn't.

"I'm going crazy, then," I muttered.

"Come on," she laughed. "If it were me, you'd say that this was a perfectly reasonable reaction. Probably something adult-like, nurturing and whatnot, about how a delusion was likely a way to process guilt and loss."

Maybe it was the fact that out here, without Dr. Bates's voice, without Wil, I had no one. I was truly alone. I could make a decision for myself for once.

But that didn't mean that being alone felt right.

"I'm sorry," I said, tears streaming from my eyes. My hands were clammy and wet. I rubbed them over my face, wiping it all away. "I shouldn't have let you go."

"Actually, sis. Let's be real," she said, crossing her arms playfully. "I needed to get the hell out of our place. You weren't going to stop me."

It was absolutely clear then that this was just me processing my emotions. But it didn't matter. If it made it less painful, then who was I to judge my own delusional mind?

"You were going to go to the program one way or another?" I asked.

"Yep." She shrugged. "You weren't going to stop me."

I furrowed my brow, trying to think carefully. What did it mean for us, if she had wanted to go, and hadn't told me?

"Why did you go?" I asked.

"A hot guy told me about it. Why else would I go?" She winked.

I smiled then, even though it was hard. "You shouldn't trust every hot guy you meet."

"I know."

"You shouldn't trust anyone. Especially someone who wants you to sign up for beatings and torture."

"Hah! Now that's a good one," Julie laughed. She rolled her eyes. "Come on, sis. You're one to talk."

Maybe she was right. Maybe Wil *was* a hot guy who wanted to beat and torture me, but there was more to him. Even when he wanted to banish me, he still made sure I had water. Made sure I had enough clothes to survive, to figure it all out.

But I didn't want to talk about that right now, not when I didn't know how much time we had left.

"What will I do with you?" I said, similar to a phrase I had often said to her while we were growing up. It was hard to shift from being a teenager to a parent, but I had done it. And those phrases that I had heard our mom say repeatedly made it seem less difficult: *What would*

I do without you? But the hardest part was realizing that I couldn't say it like that anymore. It wasn't a possibility. It was our situation. I didn't have Julie.

"I don't know what to do," I said in a quiet voice, my chest shaking. "I'm so lost."

"You're not lost," Julie said. "For the first time in your life, you're on your own. No sister to worry about. No Skyline Shift principles to learn. No sexy man to obey." She giggled. "You can do your own thing. No one is stopping you."

But what was I supposed to do? No matter how hard I tried, I couldn't figure that out. And now, I was hallucinating a vision of my dead sister. That couldn't have been a good sign.

But maybe it *was* just a way to cope. I had been so busy taking care of Julie after our parents died, I had never really dealt with their deaths either.

Their deaths had been an accident. But hers? I knew it wasn't.

I focused my gaze on her. "Who killed you?" I asked.

"Bates," she said.

Relief flooded through me in a hot wave. "I thought for sure you were going to say I killed you," I muttered.

"I wouldn't have let you." She smiled then, as if it were a little story of the past. "I failed a test. As part of training, one of the other students fought me, then cut me up. Bates's orders."

Which made sense, especially why she would have been in the trees right off of the campus.

"Listen," she said, breaking through my thoughts. "You're out here because Wil thought it was best for you, right? He wants to make amends to you by giving you your freedom."

"Sure, but that doesn't mean he's a good guy," I said. "I thought you wouldn't like him."

"But he helped you find me."

I scoffed. "I would think finding you dead in the bushes hardly counts."

"But still, you found me." She shrugged. "He helped you bury me too, right? Even gave me one last joy ride on the way there." She winked.

"Yeah, because driving so fast your bones fly to the floor of the car, that's a real joy ride."

She laughed. "What I'm saying is," she leaned forward, "He cares more about you than he lets on. He might even love you."

I thought about Wil, how once he knew something was going on in the woods, he decided to keep me even closer to him than before. Sure, that might have been to make sure that I wasn't a suspect, but I knew, deep down, that he wanted to protect me too. How when I attacked him, he restrained me, but he didn't punish me for doing what I was trained to do. In fact, he had brought Dr. Mercia to me. Insisted that the other women were safe at the Dahlia District. Let me go, even when he knew I had been programmed to kill his family.

"They're going to have to take down the Skyline Shift," Julie said, looking at her nails. Then she straightened and tossed her hair behind her shoulders. "Bates keeps sending more and more of us, and at some point, he's going to unleash the entire army. So either the Adlers go in blind, and maybe, if they're lucky, they burn it to the ground. Or," she shook her head, "what's more likely, they die trying." She paused, then tapped on her chin. "Or you help them."

"Why should I help them?" I asked, though this time, there was no anger in my voice. I was truly asking. "I can't just go around following the strange voices and hallucinations in my head." I shrugged. "After all, you're dead." My chest ached at those words, but they were true. "For all I know, you're just Bates in disguise."

"You should help them because you want to," she said, smiling. "Remember, you're not listening to your sister's voice. This is *you* speaking to yourself. And I know you. I am you."

I didn't know if she meant that we shared blood or that she was a figment of my imagination. I reached forward to squeeze her hand, but I was too far away. My eyes flicked down to the tree trunk, finding a sapless spot to push myself off of the bark, but when I looked up, she was gone. I was on my own again.

The Skyline Shift was a long way away. I needed to find the road. I didn't have a car, but I knew what Julie would do. If I had found out that she was hitching a ride, I would have panicked and lectured her until we both fell asleep. I would have killed to give her one of those lectures again. And maybe I couldn't kill to bring her back, but I could kill to prevent deaths like hers from ever happening again.

I had to find Cassandra and make sure that I could help her. I would see if the women at the Dahlia District were okay, and find Dr. Mercia. We could all end this together at the Skyline Shift.

Finding a purpose—whether it was protecting my sister, trying to find her, or helping Wil and his brothers take down the Skyline Shift—wasn't an issue anymore. I knew what I had to do. And I was doing it because I wanted to. I owed it to myself.

CHAPTER 24

Wil

A long line of cars trailed mine, our men armed and ready to fight. My brothers too. Even Ethan was keeping an eye on Muro's headquarters. Still, I stared out of the windshield, clenching the steering wheel with my fists. We were about to infiltrate a training base for undercover soldiers, women who had been manipulated into thinking that we had killed their loved ones. It was a death trap. But the main object was to take down Bates, then destroy the camp. With the women freed, Muro wouldn't be able to fight us like he wanted. Eventually, we'd be able to fight this, man to man.

In the end, we had gone without Gerard's permission, lying to our men in hopes that they realized that what we were doing was right for the family. War was brewing.

I had to make this right for Ellie.

We pulled around the corner, then drove off a distance, the cars staggered to avoid detection. Finally, we parked in the trees, then trekked through the woods towards the camp. Then Derek, Axe, and I stared down at the Skyline Shift, scanning the perimeter.

I sucked in a breath of fresh air, but it didn't comfort me. I coiled my fists, then uncurled my fingers one by one. Nothing seemed to ease the tension.

"It's bigger than I thought," Derek said.

A stream of women, half of them dressed in white uniforms and the other half-naked, marched between the buildings. A shorter man with a whip in his hand stood off to the side, nodding at the women, his sneer angry. A few others, like the man with the bullwhip, were dressed in white, scattered throughout, watching the women, making sure they stayed in line. It was as if the women were cattle.

Derek called one of our men over, a slender but tall and reliable man. He wasn't a man of muscle, but someone we sent for intel. Still, he was armed and could fight. Derek handed him a lab coat and a clipboard. The man pulled the coat over his white clothes, adjusting the fake badge.

"He's over there," I said, pointing to Bates. His curly brown and white hair shook in the wind, making it look as if his brain were growing even bigger.

"Get him over here," Derek instructed our decoy. "We'll take care of the rest."

"Yes, sir," the man said. I clenched my fists. I wanted to do it myself and rip Bates's fucking throat out, but we agreed that it was better if one of our men lured him out. Bates knew our faces. And we didn't want to make a scene, because the less of the rest of the camp was involved, the better.

Axe was checking his guns, making sure they were all loaded, when he stopped. He scanned the area, then narrowed his eyes.

"Something is off," Axe said. "I don't trust it."

"We're invading a camp full of soldiers that have been trained to kill Muro's competition," Derek said. "We shouldn't trust anything."

"We need more men." Axe shook his head. "Find his other enemies. Work together to take him down."

"We don't have time," I said. "We need to end this now."

"Before one of them kills us," Derek added, his hand rubbing his broken ribs.

Axe gave a subtle nod, then turned back. Bates moved to the side of one of the nearby buildings, reading his tablet. I waved a hand forward, and our decoy, dressed in his lab coat, went to Bates's side.

"Dr. Bates," the decoy said, his tone stiff. "There's a situation I want to inform you of. It's best if it's seen in person." The decoy held up his clipboard, then gestured ahead. "One of the students is lost in the woods."

Dr. Bates spoke, his words inaudible, and waved a dismissive hand at our decoy. The decoy leaned forward, his expression stretched as he whispered into Bates's ear. He put a hand on Bates's arm. Bates nodded, his eyes still staring at his tablet, but then he pulled out a different device, jamming his fingers onto it to type. Our decoy pulled Bates forward, closer to the trees.

"Here, Dr. Bates. Just ahead of you—"

"Yes. All right. Now—"

Dr. Bates looked up, and the three of us stood, our guns pointed at him. His eyes widened, then relaxed, recognizing our faces. He cleared his throat. Then the rest of our men showed themselves, letting him know that he was surrounded. And that brought a smile to Bates's face.

That fucker smiled. I could have shot him right then.

"Oh," he said. "It looks like we do have an issue here."

The decoy jabbed his pistol into Bates's back. "You're coming with us," he said.

"With you?" Dr. Bates asked. He lifted a hand, and a shot came from the woods, going through his hair, leaving a hole behind it. The campus echoed with the crack of the bullet. Who the hell had fired that closely, and still missed? But the women kept marching forward. Only the guards turned towards us, stepping forward, each of them focused on the woods.

"Huh. That is unfortunate," Bates said.

"You're coming with us, Bates," Derek shouted. "And you're going to end this torture camp."

"And I suppose once I'm done here, you'll set me free so that I'm not tied to Muro either?" he sneered. "Not a chance."

"Don't fuck with us, Bates," I warned.

"Ladies!" Bates called, his voice loud over the commotion. All of the women froze in place, then turned their heads towards Dr. Bates in unison.

Fuck.

"Don't do it, Bates," I called.

"These are our guests," Bates said to the women. Hundreds of eyes turned and locked on us. "We must be polite, correct?"

The women stepped forward, their eyes wide and glowing like gems at the bottom of a lake. They moved methodically, their hips swaying together like a murmur of crows. But none of them lifted a hand. Not yet.

"Damn it," I whispered. I glanced at Derek but kept my gun trained on Bates. "What's the plan?"

"We've got to kill them," Axe said.

"We've got to make a decision quick," I said.

"I don't think we have much choice," Derek said.

"We're not going to have a choice if we wait any longer," Axe said.

Fuck it. I pulled back the hammer, fixing the focus on Bates's head. If it was suicide, I might as well take him with me. For Ellie.

"I'd be careful with that," Bates said, eyeing me. "You don't know what I have planned, do you?" A smirk gleamed on his mouth. "Or you would have come with a better plan."

"It's over, Bates," I said. "Let the women go. The game is over."

"Game?" he laughed. "It's funny that you should use that word. That's the marvelous part of our program. All of these women," he grinned, gesturing at them, "They've been trained to be alluring. Exactly what the targets want. For instance, you—" he pointed at me, "Your name is Wilhelm, right? We programmed one of our star students into being both feisty and submissive, your dream combination. It is quite the game, isn't it?" Bates smiled. "Especially when she stabs a knife into your jaw, right as you're about to come."

Every muscle in my body tightened. But it didn't matter. None of it mattered. Despite what Dr. Bates said, Ellie had fought against her training and had still been mine. She had chosen that path for herself. I bared my teeth.

"I will end you," I barked.

"Or, you'll bow down to Muro," he smiled. "Take your pick."

I adjusted my aim, ready to pull the trigger.

"Dr. Bates," a smooth, female voice said, interrupting us. A light brown-haired woman stepped out from behind the building, wearing the same uniform as the others. Her voice sounded different, more confident. Seductive, even.

Ellie.

I flinched, and Bates noticed the movement, glancing at me, then turning back to Ellie.

"What a pleasant surprise," Dr. Bates said. "Excellent work, Ms. Jordan, bringing the targets back to the camp." Bates squeezed her shoulder. "Your sister would be very proud."

Ellie's plastered smile flickered, but she nodded anyway. "I knew the most efficient way to eliminate them would be to make sure that they were all here. Annihilate them in one exercise." She winked at Bates, stroking his arm. "Target practice."

"You are a true marvel," Bates said. "We'll have to promote you. Muro is going to need more help in the headquarters soon."

Ellie beamed at him, a smug expression on her face, and I muttered under my breath. Derek twitched, his eyes scanning towards me, but I shook my head. This wasn't right. Ellie might have been trained to kill us, but she had broken through her training.

Hadn't she?

The man with the bullwhip had his eyes on Ellie, staring at her ass, even if her figure was non-existent in that bulky white uniform. I wanted to rip his eyes out and shove them down his throat. I knew, instinctively, that he was the one that had raped her. I would kill him too.

"I've always admired you," Ellie said. She put a hand around Dr. Bates's neck. "If it weren't for your teachings, I might not have completed the task. I wouldn't have been able to avenge my sister."

"You owe it to yourself," Dr. Bates said. "You are at the top of your class."

"I have one question though," Ellie said. She pulled her body close to his, her hands teasing his arms with a gentle touch. Her voice was like milk, dripping over the edges of a bowl, marked with streaks of honey. "Did you kill my sister?"

"It was part of her training," Bates said in a husky voice. "She needed to resign." He stared into her, his eyelids lowered, overcome with lust. "I set her up for one final fight so that you would become stronger, Ellie. I did it to make you stronger. It was what you needed to become our secret weapon."

Ellie smiled, her lips parting. "And I am the strongest of them all," she said. She pulled him in for a kiss.

Everything went silent.

If I shot right then with the way they were angled, it would have killed them both with one bullet. I would put her in the ground with her sister. Because she was mine, and she knew how I felt about another man touching her.

But as strong as the jealousy was, I held back. Ellie's hand twitched in her pocket, gripping an object, pulling it out. Without leaving his lips, she jammed her hand forward, stabbing Bates in the stomach with a knife in a quick succession of jabs. *My knife.* He crumpled against her, his eyes blinking rapidly.

A few seconds passed.

"Now?" Derek asked.

No one moved. All of us waited to see if Bates was dead.

But energy renewed inside of him. He took a deep breath and kept his eyes on Ellie.

I ran forward, my gun raised.

Dr. Bates screamed, "Ladies!" Every single head turned toward him at the same time. "These are the *Adlers*. Show them a nice, warm—"

Ellie pulled him up by the hair and pressed the knife to his throat. "Not another word," she hissed.

"—*welcome.*"

The women ran toward us. A few had sticks in their hands, others knives, some barehanded, their wrists swinging, their feet moving faster than I could process. The guards came too.

I rushed through an open space, finding cover by a building, then peeked around the corner. A woman raised her sticks, about to strike me, but I immediately rammed the back of my gun into her forehead.

She fell down. I knew it was unavoidable, but I silently hoped she was okay. I checked for Ellie; she was dragging Bates off to another building, but none of the women noticed. In the end, it wasn't about protecting Bates. It was about avenging their loved ones by eliminating the targets.

Doing what I could, I knocked out some of the women, sometimes swooping out their legs, then putting them in a chokehold until they passed out, or knocking them out with the back of my gun. I looked around; one of our men was supposed to have rope to tie up the women, but I didn't see him anywhere. There was no time to search; I had to trust him to do his job. So I moved on. Two guards approached me from the sides, their bullets whizzing past me, but I shot them in the head. As I took down another guard, I glanced around at the others. Derek kept pulling tranquilizers out of his pockets, stabbing the women with them. They fell, but more always came forward. Axe had been knocking them out like I had, a blow to the head, saving his bullets for the guards. My eyes landed on that slimy sonofabitch, who had his eyes on Ellie, even now, in the midst of the chaos. She was hacking apart Bates's corpse with a cleaver, tearing him limb from limb, just like they had done to her sister. But that guard had another thing on his mind, his eyes glued to her. I ran towards him.

"You made a big fucking mistake," I growled. "Ellie is mine."

"Your whore, huh? That's funny. I had her first," the man sneered, barely glancing at me. "She's working for me, fucker."

I pulled the trigger, hitting him straight in the neck. His body shook to the floor, then he gurgled, blood pooling out of his mouth. I leaned down, staring into his blinking red eyes. He only had seconds left.

"I should have made it harder for you," I said. "But it's your lucky day. Have fun getting raped in hell."

Ellie looked up at me, but her eyes flickered, catching something behind me. Her mouth opened to warn me. I turned, finding a woman with her knives ready. The woman lunged forward, stabbing my dominant hand, the one that had finally healed and was holding my gun. I dropped my weapon. I couldn't move my fingers.

I grabbed it off of the floor, but my other hand was weak. I held it up, biting back the pain. Adrenaline surged through me, and I turned towards the woman. Shaking, steadying myself.

The woman stared at me. "You killed her," she said. "You killed my sister."

And I was back there, in my bedroom again, when Ellie had first cut me. But I saw her true intentions now. She needed her sister to be okay. She needed it more than anything in the world.

And I couldn't give that to Ellie, but I could end this, and I could do it the right way. For her.

I rammed my elbow into the woman's head, but she avoided the blow, and as I lurched forward, she stabbed my thigh, energy shooting through my body. I howled, then turned to try to hit her again, but a tranquilizer dart hit her neck. She paused, touching the feathered end, then her eyes closed. She fell forward, crashing into me with a thud. My whole body tensed, holding her up. Suddenly the agony from my hand and thigh skyrocketed, and as gently as I could, I let her down on the floor. But the tension in my body swelled, trying to fight off the pain. I fell to my knees.

I looked up, expecting to see Derek, but it was Billy, her short hair ruffling in the wind. Iris stood behind her.

"Figured I have to use my training for something," Billy said loudly, more to Ellie than to me.

"Nice shot," Ellie shouted. "Get the rest of us."

Iris lugged a huge black bag to the side of her. She kneeled down beside the woman who had stabbed me, then removed a pair of handcuffs from her bag, clicking them closed around the women's wrists.

"Who knew that *this* would be what I did with my day off," she muttered. "Helping the Adlers. What the hell?"

Ellie rushed over to me. "You're hurt," she said.

"Sure," I said. "But Bates, he—"

"A pile of flesh and bones," she said. "We need to get you to a hospital. Dr. Mercia—"

"Not a medical doctor," I said.

"We've got another doctor too. Iris had a connection from the club."

I didn't understand how Ellie had thought of everything, but I didn't question it. I was glad, relieved, even, that she was there. Another guard came toward us, and she reached over quickly and grabbed my gun off of the floor, shooting the man three times in the chest.

She turned to me. Her blue eyes flashed, and she held me tight, pulling me closer to her.

"You did it," I said. My body shook, trying to fight against the pain, but it was hard. The world grew quiet, and I wondered if any of the women had died in the fight. If we had managed to keep our promise. "You got him, Ellie. You avenged your sister."

"We did it," she said.

CHAPTER 25

Ellie

The doctor paced towards us, keeping his head lowered, afraid of getting caught in the crossfire. We used the cover from the building to keep out of the way and gave him space to work. He unfolded his pack, going through his equipment. He adjusted the collar of his shirt, the bulletproof vest poking through the opening.

"We'll have to work quickly," he said, his hands shaking. "I'm not used to these—" he gestured around, "—conditions."

"Just do your best," Wil muttered.

While the doctor cleaned and treated Wil's wounds, I held Wil close, a protective arm around him, but kept my eyes focused on everything surrounding us, a grip on his gun, holding it up, ready to kill anyone trying to mess with us. But the echoes of the fights were dissipating. Axe ran through the middle of the campus, his chest bleeding, but still running fast, scanning to make sure the guards were all dead. Derek was helping move the women over to Iris and another man, who were working quickly to bind them before they woke up. Several of the Adlers' men shot their tranquilizer darts from behind the buildings and trees. One sniper hidden at the top of a tree took out every new guard and scientist that stepped out of cover. Billy and Jane searched the domed buildings, getting rid of the rest of Muro's men. The campus was littered with bodies: white uniforms splashed with red, some naked and unconscious, and a few dressed in colorful clothing, their bodies dashed with red too.

Luckily, when we explained what was happening, every entertainer in the Dahlia District had given up their stash of restraints. It was temporary, anyway, just until Mercia could help them. And it had taken begging their security to get in front of Gerard. Luckily, he overheard me from the hallway and wanted to listen as soon as I mentioned his sons. Gerard gave up his restraints too, the ones that his sons hadn't taken yet, then went to the Midnight Miles headquarters to see if Muro was there, maybe to end this sooner.

Tell my boys that they're reckless, he had said before I left, *But that I'm proud of them. Especially Wil. For doing what's right for the family.*

By the strained look in Gerard's eye, I knew he was leaving something out, as if he knew he had let his sons down in the process, but I didn't know Gerard or their family enough to make a guess. And though it had been for the family, I knew Wil had protected the other survivors of the Skyline Shift, not for his dad, mother, or brothers, but for me.

Mercia appeared at the edge of the woods, her jaw dropping to the ground. She struggled forward. Our eyes met, and I gave her a silent nod before she turned back to the rest of the campus. The plan was to have Mercia do a group therapy session on steroids. At least—in theory, that's what she wanted to do. But from the look in her eye, she clearly hadn't expected this.

"And I'm supposed to treat *all* of them," she said, turning to me, "right now?"

I nodded. "Right now."

"All right," she said, shrugging. "Let's get this party started."

She went forward, approaching the first woman, who stirred, then got up on her feet quickly, ready to attack Mercia. But Mercia asked a few questions, and the woman stared at her for a second, cautious, but listening. That was a good sign. I turned back to Wil.

"That's it," the doctor said. He patted Wil's shoulder. "Stay out of trouble for a while." He nodded at his thigh. "And come to me when you're all done here. I'll take another look. Make sure it's healing properly." He shrugged. "You'll need stitches. But this should hold up until then."

"And you're in Sage City?" Wil asked. The doctor nodded. "Thanks."

"Anything for one of my goddess's friends," the doctor said, glancing at Iris.

The doctor ambled to the next patient, and with some help, Wil got to his feet, straightened his stance, but then he clenched his jaw. It must have been hard to be comfortable. I put an arm around him, making him lean into me.

"It's okay," I pretended to whisper. "You can use me as a crutch. No one will know."

He chuckled, but his body stiffened, and I glanced around. The two brothers came forward, meeting us at the border of the campus. A thought hit me; even with all of the gunshots, the police hadn't come yet. Based on what I knew, I had assumed law enforcement would be on Muro's side. But were they taking their time protecting him? Were they questioning their allegiance with his corporation?

How many friends, and how many enemies, did Muro have?

"Everyone's been locked down?" Wil asked.

"Tranquilized or knocked unconscious. Iris has been binding them," Derek said. He turned to me, giving me a curt nod. "Thank you. Bringing Iris and Mercia. All of that."

"You're welcome," I said, though the words sounded funny coming out of my mouth. "I take it, we're even?" I asked, turning to Axe. He had saved my life as a gift to Wil, and I had helped save them from total destruction.

Correction: *we*, Billy, Jane, Cassandra, Iris, Mercia, and the others, had helped save their asses.

"Consider us your allies," Axe said.

Wil beamed and tightened his grip around me. "And our men?"

"Toby and Josh are gone. And Markus might not make it," Derek said.

"But the doctor is with him?" Wil asked.

Derek nodded. "Working on him now."

The three of them stood silently for a moment, perhaps processing what it meant to lose more men to the Midnight Miles Corporation.

But considering what had happened, they were lucky that it was just those two, maybe three men.

We were lucky.

"We need to call Muro," Derek said. He gestured at the road beyond the campus. "Make sure that he knows that we know."

"No silence?" Axe asked. "Why not leave him guessing which enemy?"

"We can't look weak," Derek said. "He sent a message, and now, it's our turn. He started a war, and we'll fucking end it."

I wasn't sure what was right, but it didn't matter what I thought. This was the Adlers' battle; to an extent, I had finished mine. But I did want to know what Wil wanted.

"No matter what," Wil said, his voice strained, "Muro needs to be taken down."

"Agreed," Axe said. "Gerard will—"

"Gerard knows," I interrupted. "I spoke to him before coming here."

The three of them shifted, and for half of a second, Wil loosened his grip on my side, but then he held me even tighter than before.

"He's at Muro's headquarters now," I explained. "On the lookout."

"With Ethan then," Derek nodded. "We can take out the rest of his army out quietly." Derek nodded to Axe. "Your way."

Axe nodded, though his jaw was tight. He looked up at the sky, then shook his head. "More work for me," he muttered.

"Hey," Derek said, turning after his brother. Axe went ahead, going to speak with one of the other men. Derek followed closely behind. "Axe, I—"

We watched them argue as they walked into the woods. I turned to Wil. "What's their problem?"

Wil shrugged. "Axe would prefer to take out Muro's men quietly. But with this?" Wil motioned at the campus. "It'll be hard to be covert. We can't do it his way."

I stared at Axe. The scar on his lip. The blood splattered on his shirt. How many people had died by his hands, on this day alone?

"And Muro?" I asked. "Are you going to kill him?"

"Soon," Wil said. He took his phone out of his pocket.

He dialed Muro's number, then put the phone on speaker, holding it up so that we could both hear it. It rang once, then Muro picked up, his voice thin.

"I hear your father and brother have been scouting my place for the last few hours. Some of my men say it's been days," Muro said. "So tell me, Little Adler. What's the fucking deal?"

I raised a brow at the nickname, and Wil gave me a look that said, *Not now.* There were more important things to deal with than a condescending name. We walked towards one of the buildings, where Bates's remains lay, his eyes blank, looking up to the sky, his skin smooth and creamy, splashed with crimson. But soon, his skin would be blotchy too, his eyes yellow. Just like Julie.

"We found the Skyline Shift," Wil said confidently, hiding the physical pain he felt. "And it's been dismantled. Burned to the ground." That was a lie; as he spoke, the walls were still standing, and the Adlers' men were raiding the buildings for files and materials. But it was close enough. "Your men are dead, including the doctors. Bates too."

Wil kicked Bates's fleshy remains, getting blood on his shoe. The urge to stomp on his face swelled in me, but I buried it down. I wanted his corpse to experience what Julie had. Because if he could kill her, for the sole purpose of training *me*, making it so that it was *my* fault that she died, then he needed to die just like her.

Because it wasn't my fault. Bates was the murderer, not the women who had been coerced into the camp. I wouldn't let him give me or them the blame for her death. It was his alone.

"I see," Muro said. "I guess that leaves us with one option."

"It's a war," Wil said.

"Tell your brothers to be ready for me," Muro said. "And you too, Little Adler. I'll be getting rid of your family personally."

Wil sneered. "We'll be waiting."

Wil clicked off the line and sighed, the sound deep and mournful. Exhaustion was heavy on his chest, and his shoulders sunk, his weight leaning into me.

"Who would have thought that a mafia family from a coastal city would be battling one of the up and coming criminal corporations," he muttered. "This is a shit show."

There was no doubt about that. It was hard to tell how much they had to deal with now. If Muro had the power to create a camp of conditioned soldiers, what else did he have planned?

But there was only one way I could make this right.

"I want to help," I said.

Wil turned toward me, his face wincing in pain. "You know you're free, right?" he asked. "You can do anything you want. Travel. Start a family. Go to the Rubble River and visit your sister." He shrugged, then grit his teeth. "You don't have to be tied to me anymore."

I wanted to pinch his cheeks until he slapped me in the face, to pull the knife out of my pocket and make him shove it against my throat. I didn't care that we were in the middle of the campus full of dead bodies. For once in my life, I knew what I wanted. For myself alone.

"I *want* to help," I said again, narrowing my eyes. "Did you not hear me clearly?"

"Ellie," he shook his head, "I—"

"You're forgetting the most important part of this," I lightly shoved his shoulder. "I'm yours," I glared at him, daring him to tell me I was wrong. I pushed a hard finger into his sternum. "And you're mine. Don't you ever fucking forget that, Wil Adler."

He smiled, pleased that I would use his own words against him. "I hate that you kissed him."

I raised a brow. "Jealous?" I asked. He grunted. "Are you going to punish me for it?"

"You best fucking believe it," he said, putting a finger in his belt loop. Then he leaned down and pulled me in close, his weight crushing into me, our lips meeting. I pushed against him too, giving him just as much as he gave. His cock throbbed on my side, and I pushed in tighter, daring him to continue. Suddenly, he broke apart, glaring down at me.

"I'm serious, Ellie. This life—" he gestured around at the bodies on the floor, the flustered doctor running from patient to patient. The women in cuffs. Dr. Mercia speaking calmly, her fingers twitching at her side. "This war is only going to get worse. I wouldn't blame you if you wanted out."

"Take a second and listen to me," I said. I stepped back, making sure that we weren't touching at all. He leaned on his good leg, and I waited for a second, waiting for Dr. Bates's voice to fill my head, for my sister's spirit to appear, for anything to fill in the void inside of me and tell me what to do.

But nothing happened. It was just me now. And I had to do what I knew was right. For me. For *us*.

"I could have walked away and never come back," I started. "But I did come back. And I brought help with me." I shook my head. "I *am* doing what I want. And I want to help take down the asshole that inadvertently killed my sister." I shrugged my shoulders, then shimmied into him, enjoying his warmth once again. "Besides, I have a new family now."

"Is that so?" he smiled. I nodded. "I better tell my brothers."

I beamed. "I think they already know."

"There go all my good cuffs," Iris said loudly, interrupting us. "You know how hard it is to get rid of bloodstains?" Then she crossed her arms. "I do not have the room for all of them at the club."

"We've got a few vans coming," Wil said. That was good; I had forgotten about that part. "Dr. Mercia will make sure they're treated before we release them, and we've got a connection with a hotel. They can crash there."

She raised her brows, then tilted her head. "That works."

We walked through the campus, and it felt like a dream. I had been through so much in the walls of those buildings. It had been hard to let go—to accept my fate as a student of the Skyline Shift, sent to kill the Adlers, or to die trying—then to change it all and come back here, to fix what I had started.

But it was worth it.

Once the campus was cleared—the equipment taken, the files removed, the only things left being the shells of the buildings, the guards, and Bates himself—we took gasoline and drenched the place as best as we could. Then Wil took a matchbook out of his pocket, *Jimmy's* written in cursive on the top, and ripped off one for me.

"The honors, princess," he said. He smiled. The doctor had given him a painkiller, and it must have kicked in, making Wil a little loopy.

"Gladly," I said. I took the match, striking it against the matchbook, then watched as I dropped it, the flame flickering to the ground, then lighting up the campus in a flash of blue and red light. It spread quickly, the heat licking our faces. Smoke rose toward the sky.

Wil watched the clouds darken, then looked down at me, the fire shimmering in his eyes. I knew then, that his love for me was real. He wanted me, *only me*, and he would kill anyone and everything that stood in his way, anyone who tried to hurt me. The world could be burning down around us, and we would still fight for each other.

"You know I love you, right?" he asked.

I grabbed the collar of his shirt and pulled him into me. "I know," I said.

We kissed hard and deep, not caring about the destruction behind us because it was our moment. Our victory. Our love.

Then Derek whistled for everyone to get moving, and we broke apart.

"I love you too, you know," I said. A smirk gleamed on Wil's face, and my pussy clenched. I couldn't wait to get him alone. In the condition he was in, he wouldn't be able to do much, so I would worship him, like the god he was. And then he would worship me.

We walked out to the cars, and though it must have been only a few minutes, the walk back to the cars seemed like hours that stretched on, as if the world was moving faster around us.

I opened the car door, sliding into the driver's seat.

"Your dad says he's proud of you, by the way," I said.

"Does he?" Wil asked, his voice distracted. "You talked to him about that?"

"Yep." I leaned over and squeezed his hip.

"Without killing him?"

"Mmhmm."

I started the engine, and then I opened the window, letting the wind blow in my hair. A siren rang in the distance, but by the time it came, we would be gone. All that would be left was a memory.

But I had Wil, and Wil had me.

EPILOGUE

a few months later

Wil

The river shimmered with blue light, making the setting seem angelic. My brothers were with me, each in their own suits, and Axe even had a lady with them. No, scratch that. I didn't understand what his deal was with Demi, and she didn't seem happy to be there. She crossed her arms, leaning against the picnic bench. Axe, though usually stoic, kept eyeing Demi, as if he was making sure that she didn't do anything stupid. Derek had gone stag. Gerard and Clara were there too, happy for me, though my mom kept saying she wished she could have gotten to know Ellie better first.

But that was the funny part of all of this. This wedding wasn't about anyone else. It was about what *we* wanted, together. And hell fucking yes, I was going to put a ring on her finger.

Maddie came rushing out of the trees.

"All right. We're ready," she said.

Dr. Mercia, our fringe doctor turned wedding officiant, straightened her stance. And out of the trees, escorted by Maddie (the makeshift father and bonafide best friend), came my future wife. Ellie wore a white dress that flowed out at the hips, accentuating her curves, and ending at her knees, showing off her strong, thick calves. A sheer material covered her arms, making her shine with light. Her bright blue eyes met mine, and my body surged with warmth.

My wife. Ellie.

Mine.

We held each other's hands. As Mercia went over the introduction to the ceremony, my mind went blank. I couldn't pay attention. Ellie was gorgeous. She glanced down to the side of us where Julie was buried, and smiled at her sister. I wish Julie could've been here, but this was the best we could do.

"Wilhelm, your vows," Dr. Mercia said.

"I promise to be the man you deserve," I said. "To give you the freedom you need, and the chains to keep you safe, to keep you mine." It was grim, I admit that. But it was us. "Because I love you, Ellie. You're mine."

Ellie kept her eyes on me, then started, "I promise to be the wife you deserve." She squeezed my hand. "To remind you when you need to think and not act, and to always claim you as much as you claim me. Because I am yours, Wil. Heart and soul. And you're mine."

Dr. Mercia nodded, a smile on her face. "Do you, Wil Adler, take Elena Jordan to be your lawfully wedded wife, to have and to hold, from this day forward, for better, for worse, for richer, for poorer, in sickness and in health, until death do you part?"

My body tingled. Those traditional vows made the whole ceremony feel real, but it was my surname that made me stop. It was funny how something as simple as a name could have caused so much damage, and now, it had no effect on Ellie. She was even taking it as her own.

"Until death do us part," I said, my eyes never leaving Ellie's.

"And do you, Elena Jordan, take Wil Adler to be your lawfully wedded husband, to have and to hold, from this day forward, for better, for worse, for richer, for poorer, in sickness and in health, until death do you part?"

"Until death do us part," she repeated, a gentle nod settled on her chin.

"Well, Wil Adler," Dr. Mercia smirked, "You may kiss the bride."

I pulled Ellie into a deep kiss, arching her back, dipping her down to the ground. Maddie cheered obnoxiously, and after a few seconds, Derek joined in too. Axe and Demi clapped, and My mom wiped a tear from her eye. I was the youngest and the first to get married. That must have been a shocker.

We enjoyed the celebration, sitting on the ground a short distance from the water, eating Clara's famous picnic sandwiches, laughing together. Axe and Demi disappeared, and Mercia had left shortly after the ceremony, but Gerard and Clara were taking a walk through the woods, and Maddie and Derek swam around in the river. Ellie and I watched them.

"I wish she could have been here," Ellie whispered. She leaned her head on my shoulder, then rubbed the ground beside her, smiling as the dirt got on her fingers. "She would have been shocked that I was marrying someone like you."

I raised a brow, then grabbed her wrist, holding it tight in my hand. "Someone like me, huh?" I smirked. "Would she have been shocked to know what I'm going to do to you later?"

"Yes," Ellie breathed, her voice mellowed.

Later, as we packed up the cars, Clara stopped by us.

"Off to the airport?" she asked. She stayed out of the family business as much as possible and had wanted us to go on a honeymoon, but there wasn't any time to waste. Axe had asked for our help taking out a certain subsection of Muro's men, and until the Midnight Miles Corporation was taken down, it was up to us, the family, to deal with them. Ellie insisted that she wanted to help and wouldn't take no for an answer, and I knew better than to say no to her when it came to that. I made the decisions, but this? There was no doubt that Ellie was a great fighter. She was a valuable asset to the family.

And I was proud, so damn proud, that she was my wife.

"Just heading back to the penthouse," I lied, but my mom didn't need the details. "Sunday breakfast?" I asked.

Clara nodded, then leaned over and kissed my cheek. "Sunday breakfast," she repeated. "It was good to see you, Ellie," she said. "You look gorgeous, as ever."

"Thank you," Ellie said. They kissed each other's cheeks, then Ellie slid into the passenger seat. I saluted Derek, who then backed out of the parking space next to us. I expected him to call soon. He was helping Axe as well.

"You ready?" I asked. Ellie nodded, patting her knife in her pocket, then her gun holster on her waist.

"Ready or not," she said, her eyes narrowed ahead of her, as if looking straight at Muro.

I started the engine and grinned.

Ready or not, Muro, here we come.

ALSO BY AUDREY RUSH

Dark Romance

The Adler Brothers Series
Dangerous Silence (March 2021)
Dangerous Command (April 2021)

The Dahlia District Series
Ruined
Shattered
Crushed
Ravaged
Devoured

The Afterglow Series
His Toy
His Pet
His Pain

The Dreams of Glass Trilogy
Yield to Me
Surrender to Me
Love Me

—

Romantic Comedy

Standalone
The Last One Standing
Bunking Up: A Fake Marriage Romance

ACKNOWLEDGMENTS

Thank you to my husband, Kai, for being an amazing graphic designer and brainstormer, and for giving hugs so powerful that they drag me out of the hole. Thank you to my amazing alpha reading duo, Michelle and Rhonda. I said it before, and I will say it again; you two are brilliant! Thank you to my dad and Nicole for your critical feedback on the blurb. Thank you to my ARC readers for your honest reviews; you are the best supporters an indie author could ask for. (Shout out to Natalie for catching my typos.) And thank you to my daughter, Emma, for taking long, productive naps and tolerating my writing sprints.

But most of all, thank you to my readers. You are the reason I love to turn my kinky daydreams into stories. I would love to hear from you! Feel free to leave a review online or to email me directly at audreyrushbooks@gmail.com with your feedback.

ABOUT THE AUTHOR

Audrey Rush writes dark romance featuring redeemable antiheroes and the badass heroines who love to challenge them. She grew up on the West Coast, but currently lives in the South, where she raises her daughter and snuggles her husband. She writes during naptime.

Website: audreyrush.com
Amazon: amazon.com/author/audreyrush
Reader Group: bit.ly/rushreaders
Email: audreyrushbooks@gmail.com
Newsletter: bit.ly/audreysletters
Facebook: fb.me/audreyrushbooks
Twitter: @audreyrushbooks
Instagram: audreyrushbooks

Printed in Great Britain
by Amazon